AGAINST THE STREAM

Liam H 81.

AGAINST
THE STREAM

by

JAMES HANLEY

HORIZON PRESS
NEW YORK

FIRST PUBLISHED IN ENGLAND
AS *THE HOUSE IN THE VALLEY*

FOR BEN AND PEARL
with love

I

'So he didn't cut his nails, didn't he, well well! That's an odd father. Here's your cake,' Thomas said. The bright yellow seed cake reminded him of boyhood days at Llanganoch.

'Thank you very much,' said Robert, and began to eat the cake.

He sat opposite Thomas. The carriage was empty. He had never seen anybody like Thomas before, not even in Paddington, and over the seed cake he stared hard at the person on the opposite seat. He saw a middle-aged man, broad-shouldered, with a bluish-red face, small brown eyes under beetling brows, an almost shaven head; he had put his bowler hat on the rack for safety. He saw heavy thighs, short legs, hairy legs; the socks had slipped down; the utterly idle hands rested in the lap. He looked at the immaculate white linen collar, the bright blue tie. Thomas caught his roving eye.

'Like your cake? Best I could find,' he said. He looked closely at the boy. 'And how did you know he was dead?' he asked. He took a cigarette from his pocket and lighted it. The train ran into a tunnel, roaring north; they couldn't see each other.

'He was cold,' Robert said, 'I tried to wake him up and he never answered.'

'And were you frightened?' Thomas asked. His voice seemed to come from the depths; it had a soft yell in it; it amused the boy, it was a velvet yell.

'At first I was,' the boy said, speaking more clearly now; the seed-cake had vanished.

'Were you in the same room then?'

7

'Yes. I was in daddy's bed. We always slept together, dad and me.'

'Did you now. . . .'

The train rushed into light again, and the boy was crying. It moved Thomas, who had never been moved before.

'Aw! There now, but I wouldn't cry, poor daddy, but I shouldn't cry, I suppose you haven't any mother, either, dear, dear.' The teeth clicked in his mouth. 'A bright little chap indeed,' he thought, 'too bright for Greys.' 'But why did you have to sleep together like that? A big boy like you.'

Robert looked him straight in the eye. 'There wasn't any other bed.'

'Oh! . . . I see.'

It had been a queer business, the boy crying in the empty room, up five flights of stairs, Rupert Street, at Paddington. What a strange place that was, Paddington. He had heard of it, but never seen it till now. The small, fireless room, and the boy there, waiting, the policeman: 'You *are* Mr. Thomas?' 'I am,' Thomas said, giving the policeman a most authoritative look, nothing surer than that.

'You are taking this child to Helton, to a Mr. Mortimer at Greys?' asked the policeman, studying Thomas, the Welshness, gracelessness, all corners and points, the sharp brown eyes under the bowler hat. 'Been very tough for the little chap, alone here for two nights with that body in the bed. . . .'

'Dear, dear,' Thomas said, 'and there's who I am.' To make it plain he had taken a letter from his pocket and handed it to the officer: 'Mrs. Mortimer said the police had rung her up last night. . . .'

'Quite correct.'

'Sooner we get away from here the better,' thought

Thomas, and then the officer said, 'Well, sooner this child gets away the better. . . .'

'I see. What about the funeral?' asked Thomas. He loved funerals.

'There won't be any, not for him,' the policeman pointed to the boy.

'Oh!'

It was a shock to Thomas. 'It's his father, you know.'

'You had better be going,' the officer said.

So he had left, the crying child holding on to his hand, the crying child who had to be torn away from the bed, the figure under the blanket. With the luggage under his other arm they had moved out towards the station, out of Paddington for ever.

'What a queer thing.'

'There now,' Thomas said. He offered the boy his big blue handkerchief covered with little white stars, 'there now,' and he crossed over and sat by the boy. He made himself comfortable, he put up his feet on the opposite seat, he stared at a picture of 'Whistling Sands', and then said in a low voice, 'So your mother wasn't there then, where had she gone to, Bobby, can I call you Bobby?'

'If you like,' the boy said. He looked out of the window, at hurtling telegraph poles, swaying trees, flying cows, smoke from the engine; he had quite forgotten Thomas's question.

'So I said where had your mother gone?'

'Away.'

'Where to?'

'Abroad,' Robert said, and then he looked towards Thomas.

'Dear, dear, that *is* a dirty face, Bobby, that's crying for you.' He put the handkerchief to his mouth and vetted it, then proceeded to wipe the boy's face. He saw tiredness, he saw fear, he thought for a moment that he had seen a great white word painted on the boy's forehead: 'LOST'.

'Poor little lad,' he said, and put an arm around his shoulder.

'Don't do that,' Robert promptly said, 'don't do that.'

It angered Thomas, and he said quickly, 'Very well, be lonely, be lost, be afraid.' He listened to the boy crying and did not move. He took out his watch and looked at the time. A quarter past four. Out of the corner of his eye he could see the boy's head beginning to nod. 'Tired, dead beat,' he thought.

'So your mother went off abroad, did she? Well! Well! By herself, I suppose.'

'She *didn't* go by herself,' the boy said; the lively protest astonished Thomas.

'I thought you were asleep, Master Bobby.'

'Well I wasn't, and my name isn't Bobby, it's Robert.'

'Fancy,' continued Thomas. He crossed his legs lazily. 'Then I suppose it was with the lady next door. . . .'

'You're silly. She went with Christopher, it's a long time ago.'

'How long?'

'Don't do that, please,' the boy said, and for the second time moved clear of the charitable, encircling arm.

'You are a fancy one.'

'I'm not fancy.'

'All right, little fellow, you're not then. So you lived by yourself with your daddy in Paddington. Did you like your daddy as much as your mother?'

But the boy had fallen quietly, easily asleep.

'Very queer, very queer indeed. Mr. Mortimer's only daughter, too. Left her husband and run off with a man named Christopher.'

He could see the photograph again, standing in a frame on the cheap card table, in the bedroom, five floors up. He glanced at the sleeping child. 'Somehow I can't think he's one of them.' His mind made a swift journey to Greys, and returned to the body in the bed, unshaven, the matted hair, the hard, calloused hands on the grey blanket. 'Not one of them and never was with them hands, I shouldn't think. Poor Mr. Mortimer, he'll hardly like it; never saw a kid in that house all the years I been there; he wouldn't know a kid if he saw one, none of them wouldn't.'

He looked down at the boy. It made him think of freshness, a summer morning, the sparkling sea.

'Fancy him dying like that, and the kid with him, and *so* untidy that room was, those fish and chips gone cold, and that kid's eyes, like moons, frightened. . . .'

'Cold,' he said, 'he was cold a long time. I thought he was asleep, and then he wouldn't wake up when I called him. . . .'

'And fancy him never cutting his nails, fancy that.'

Very quietly Thomas got up and opened the door and went into the corridor; a draught rushed in. When he returned he sat back on the other seat, and Robert was quietly watching him. But to Mr. Mortimer's man, Bobby was still asleep. The boy lowered his eyes; he sat as quietly as a mouse, and he watched Mr. Thomas's boots; he had never seen anything like them before, and the suspenderless socks were still hanging untidily down over the uppers. If Mr. Thomas knew he would bend down and pull them up. He wondered. Should he tell him? He used to tell daddy many a time.

'Mr. Thomas.

The tiny, flute-like voice gave Thomas a shock. 'Oh, so you've woke up.'

'I've been awake a long time,' Robert said. He looked straight into Mr. Thomas's eye. 'I've been awake a long time, I watched you go out before. . . .'

'You did, did you? . . .' 'There's sly for you,' he thought, and thinking this could only remember the cold room in Paddington, five floors up, 'Queer place.' 'Well, Bobby. . . .'

'Your socks are undone, they're hanging down,' the boy said, and the man sensed a sudden boldness in the voice.

He was so surprised he could not speak for a moment. Then he looked down at the socks, the hairy calves. 'What a clever little chap you are,' he said, and hated him as he said it. So *this* was the erring one's child. Mr. Mortimer's grandson! But where on earth is his mother now? Abroad. But *where?*

'So your mother went abroad,' Thomas said. He deliberately crossed his legs; the view was utter untidiness, a greater expanse of white skin and black hair – he didn't care, damn the socks – the cheek of it, a bit of a thing like that. 'Where did she go to then? You never said.' He leaned forward, he smiled at the boy, and was pleased when the smile was returned; his whole attitude was suddenly warm, confiding; 'It was terrible, whichever way you looked at it.' He remembered the strong smell of the cold fish and chips.

'Over the water somewhere,' the boy said, 'I know it was over the water, I heard them say, a long way away, with Christopher. . . .'

'A *long* way. How d'you know it's a *long* way?'

'I just know,' Robert said.

'Have you been at school?'

'Sometimes. . . .'

'Where's that?'

'Paddington elementary, St. Judes. . . .'

'Oh!' He lighted another cigarette. 'Where did your father work then? How did he do? I mean. . . .'

'He didn't work, but he used to,' Robert said. He sat up, feeling more comfortable now; he had forgotten the socks, and he was a long way from Rupert Street. He remembered the long, rambling streets, full of people, of bustle.

'Oh! Let me just wipe your eyes, there!' He suddenly looked at the boy's suit; he knew at once it was the wrong sort of suit; he supposed the boy's father had bought it. He saw the face again, the constable drawing the sheet over it, a hard, strong, unshaven face, an aggressive face. 'No need for you to stay, take the child away.'

'Now that was odd,' he thought, 'not having a proper funeral. Perhaps the man's people claimed him, perhaps Mr. Mortimer knew it all and didn't let on, perhaps they tried to find the mother and couldn't.' It was a crossword puzzle to Thomas, who had had the surprise of his life when Mrs. Mortimer asked him to get ready to go to London and collect the boy.

'When he was working what did he work at?'

The boy did not reply. He was watching the man's hand. It fished about in a coat pocket, and eventually appeared holding a bar of chocolate. 'Here,' Thomas said.

'Thank you very much.'

'So when your father was working. . . .'

'He drove lorries,' Robert replied, then confined all his attention to the chocolate.

'And when he wasn't working?'

'I don't know that,' replied the boy.

'What did you do?' asked Thomas.

'We went to the pictures.'

'Is that all?'

'Sometimes we went to the park.'

'And then?'

'I won't tell you any more,' Robert said. He turned his head away and looked through the window, the fleeting fields, another tunnel.

'How long shall we be on this train?'

'Another hour, Bobby,' said Thomas, the gun-metal watch in his hand again.

'I don't like Bobby.'

'All right, Robert, then, perfect little gentleman.'

Lighting another cigarette Thomas puffed clouds of smoke about the compartment.

'Very comfortable,' he thought, threw up his legs and stretched out.

'Very comfortable,' he said.

'What's that?'

But he did not look at the boy, and he did not answer him. He was beginning to feel a little uncomfortable; it seemed to him entirely wrong that this boy should be almost on his own level – adult; it didn't seem right at all. And how soon he had stopped crying, how soon he had forgotten his father.

'It's not what you hide, it's what you forget to hide,' he thought. He made smoke rings. 'You'd have thought a gentleman like Mr. Mortimer would have sent up one of the family. Anybody but me. Now look what I've found out. Never knew it before. So her name was Elizabeth. Ran away and got married to a lorry driver who ate fish and chips and never cut his finger-nails. But you'd hardly think that was the result. Well, you couldn't call *him* pretty, so I suppose *she* was. Then she's got fed up with this lorry driver and run away with somebody else. Perhaps she couldn't stand Paddington, or those nails.'

'What did you say your name was?' he asked.

'Robert.'

'But Robert what?' demanded Thomas. 'You must have another name.'

'I have, but I won't tell you.'

He didn't like Mr. Thomas; his smile had not the slightest effect on him. He wasn't thinking of Mr. Thomas, but of Paddington at half past six in the morning; fog coming in through the open window, the whine of a bus, a dog's bark, and the hour of shaking and pulling at daddy, and feeling him cold all over, and shivering and crying as he went on shaking, and crying, 'Daddy, daddy,' and finally in terror pulling the clothes right over his head, to keep the cold out, his father's cold, and he remembered looking at his father and shouting, 'Mummy, mummy.'

'There! You're crying again,' said Thomas, 'there now, be a good lad. I'm very sorry indeed about your father, very sorry, but it won't be long now and we'll soon be home.'

'*Are* you Mr. Thomas?' cried Robert through his tears.

'Of course I am,' and in a moment he was sitting beside the boy, and this time he put his arm round his shoulder and it was not removed. 'There, there. It's been bad for you, sonny, and a great, great pity your mother wasn't there. She should have been there, Bobby, instead of being at Paris. . . .'

'It wasn't Paris, it's Rome,' Robert cried, correcting him.

'There,' Thomas told himself, 'I've got it now. If I hadn't said Paris he wouldn't have mentioned Rome.' He could work on from there, very slowly, in his own

15

good time. A matter of curiosity. The Indian Army officer, traced through the army lists, came to his mind; so he could trace an erring daughter who married a lorry driver, and then went off to Rome with a man named Christopher.

'Did you like this man named Christopher?' asked Thomas, and Robert supplied no clue.

'He gave me a big box of chocolates,' Robert said.

'Did he now? That was very kind of him. And did he give you the chocolates because your daddy didn't give you any?'

He waited for the answer which never came.

'Where am I going?'

'To your grandfather,' said Thomas. 'He sent me all the way to London to bring you back with me, and I think we'll soon be there, it's nearly six o'clock.'

'Is it really? And will there be anybody else? Where is it where grandfather lives?'

'In the country, a little place named Helton, the name of the house is Greys. You'll like it. When the nice weather comes I'll show you how to put two fingers under a trout's belly and tickle him out.'

He was immensely pleased when Robert laughed, as though the tension, the tight cord of memory had snapped and the child was free of the room, the Paddington air.

'Will you?'

'Of course I will.'

There was a momentary silence, then Thomas added, his hand tapping the boy's knee, 'I like you.'

'Do you like me?' cried the boy, he jumped to his feet, he shouted, 'Hurrah.' Thomas grasped his hands and shouted, 'Hurrah, hurrah, hurrah.'

'I'll remember that terrible room as long as I live,' Thomas thought.

'Who else is there?' asked Robert, as he stood by the window watching the world fly past, a new world; he had never seen the country; he viewed it with wonder, and a hidden terror, which he never once revealed to Thomas.

'There's your granddad and your grandmother, and there's Miss Agatha and Miss Isobel – they'll be some sort of aunts I suppose – and there's Geoffrey and there's Arthur, and they'll be some kind of uncles, too. And there's Joan and there's me.'

'Who's Joan?'

'She works in the kitchen,' replied Thomas. 'One day I may marry her, but I'm not sure. . . .'

'Aren't you sure?'

'No, Master Robert, I'm not.'

'Why aren't you sure?' inquired the boy. He leaned down, looking confidingly at Mr. Thomas.

Laughing, ruffling the curls with his long fingers, Thomas said, 'Don't know,' and Robert turned away. He watched the green deserts float by, the new world.

'Now the question is, how did they live when he wasn't working, the two of them? He couldn't have had much money, a lorry driver isn't a millionaire. Now I wonder if his mother gave her husband money; she'd have money, you can't go to Rome without money. Perhaps she did. Just to be free of him. I'm sure she'd hate fish and chips for supper. And that tin jerry in the corner – awful. Wonder how it all came about. Ah, but I wonder how they're going to take him; never had children there, not in my time, and Mr. Arthur never liked them much, so I gather. That's fair reckoning. They'll have to get him to school, I expect. Jawch! but he didn't half want a wash either when I found him; I had to wander all over that mad house before I could find a bathroom, and no towels. Good job I brought two handkerchiefs with me. But I think he'll look quite pretty when he's dressed up. A nice little lad, a bit cute I think – "don't come too far over on my doorstep and I won't come too far over on yours. . . ." '

'There's a station coming, I can see it,' Robert shouted, and Thomas flung himself at the window. 'But keep your head on, little boy, if you still like your little curls,' and he put his arms round the boy, and he said to himself how he liked that child from Paddington, that little lost child.

'It's only Marle,' he said, 'there's three more stations and then we're there.'

'And then,' demanded Robert – he leaned against Thomas, bent back his head and looked up at him – 'who'll be there?'

'Nobody 'cept us.'

'Won't grandfather be . . . ?'

'No. Not beyond the gate. He never will. You'll have to join our little procession one evening when I go down to the gate. He always will come down with me when I'm locking the gates. "That's right, Thomas," he'll say, "shut the world out," and I shut it out, then we go back up the drive and I see him to his room. I help him dress for dinner. . . .'

'He must be very old,' said Robert.

'Not old really, but likes being if you know what I mean.'

'And what do you have for dinner, Mr. Thomas?'

'Not fish and chips,' Thomas said, and grinned at the boy. 'I don't think your grandfather would like the smell of them.'

'Another station coming,' shouted Robert, and Thomas held him tight, and holding him he could tell how free his boy was, how far travelled from that

Paddington room, five floors up on a cold February morning. 'Only two more now,' he said. He could feel the boy's soft hair rubbing against his chin. Then he went back to his seat. He reached for his bowler hat and balanced it carefully on his knee, holding it gently between finger and thumb; it had come from its hiding place after years of care, a lost hat, but here it was again, all black and shining.

'That's a funny hat.'

'Jawch! Isn't it funny,' said Thomas.

Periodically he had Welsh urges; the smell of the slate was strong, the rain, the white cottage under the hill – exciting moments drew it out of its anchorage, the Welsh yell, 'Jawch! isn't it a funny old hat. I've had it ten years, Master Robert.' He saw the boy's mouth open wide with astonishment.

'Ooh . . . ten years?'

'What was his name?' asked Thomas suddenly. 'It wasn't Corleston, was it?' A wild guess.

'Whose?'

'Christopher's. The man who ran away with your mammy,' replied Thomas slowly.

'No! It wasn't that name,' said Robert, and seriously, very slowly. 'No, it wasn't Corleston.'

Thomas's finger ran round and round the rim of the hat. 'Um! Won't give it. Staunch little devil he is. He was going to tell me something else in that room this morning; he said it was one night after his mother went away.'

'I was in bed, and dad was in bed. I heard a noise and I woke up, and when I opened my eyes the light was on, and there was a woman with no clothes on at the door, and she said, "Come on. . . . " '

'To do a thing like that,' Thomas thought, 'the kid there. Who was she? You can guess of course. One of them sort. But in that awful room! I'll bet that kid's head is full of fancy pictures, bet he saw things. Expect what happened was that the chap was two days dead, before somehow or other the police found out . . . ', and he saw the shivering, frightened child, wanting to turn away from his cold father and afraid to go, and crying because he was cold and miserable, and that jerry full of water and those chips on the floor. 'Expect there's a lot more and it'll never come.'

He stared at the boy for a long time but did not speak.

'It's all country here, all the way along,' cried Robert.

'All the way, every little bit of the long way, green and green and green. I expect you'll wake up one fine morning, and there'll be your mother at the end of your bed, with a blue dress on, and flowers in her hand, come through the night all the way home from Rome. And downstairs a big box of chocolates from that Mr. Christopher.'

Robert looked up at Thomas, but he said nothing; he wondered what else the man would talk about if he didn't speak.

'And she'll give you such a big hug, Master Robert. *What* a hug. Did you love your mummy very very much . . . ?'

'Not like daddy,' Robert said, 'not after mummy went away; I liked daddy more then.'

'Fancy that now,' Thomas replied.

He stood up and put on his bowler hat; he looked into the mirror, and set it on dead straight.

'There! Now we're ready and we're nearly home.' Then his expression changed; he heard the boy laughing and swung round. 'What are you laughing at, little man?'

'You look funny,' the boy cried, and he went on laughing; he flung himself back on the seat and shouted, 'You do look funny, Mr. Thomas,' and Thomas said to himself that this child was as far away from Paddington as anybody could ever get, and just as far from his daddy as he had always been. 'He loves his mother,' he thought, 'he never loved anybody else.'

'How long now, Mr. Thomas?'

'You tidy yourself together now, there's a good little boy, and put on your cap. Do you want to go outside a minute?' He looked searchingly at the boy, who said, 'No, nothing,' knowing exactly what Mr. Thomas meant, and then the train roared into the quiet station of Helton, and Mr. Thomas altered at once. He pushed away the Mr. Thomas who had climbed the Paddington stairs, and put on the greenish tail coat of Mr. Mortimer's man, who solemnly wheeled his master down the drive to shut the world out at six o'clock in the evening.

'Steady now,' he warned, and there were ten years of ministering inside the hand that fell on Robert's shoulder and held him tight until the train pulled up with a screech.

'Is this it?' asked Robert, his head out of the window, his eyes ransacking everything. 'Helton,' he spelled out, 'Helton', his eye on the station master, the porters, the two old ladies with umbrellas in their hands, looking so anxiously up at the station clock, and he forgot Thomas. He saw the taximan down the platform waving his hand, a porter hurrying up to them, 'Here you are then, Thomas,' he said.

'Gently does it,' Thomas said, pulling Robert's hand away from the door knob. He opened the door, called 'Wait!' and descended to the platform. 'Just you don't be in too much of a hurry, little man,' as he helped the boy down.

The taximan stared hard at the boy, 'No luggage then,' he said to Thomas.

'Just this fragment and himself,' he said. He took the boy's hand and they walked slowly down towards the door to the street, the boy a little in front, as though he were pulling Thomas along to the big house, and he thought of himself entering and his grandfather standing a long way off, waiting. The rhythm of the wheels still sang in his head: the journey from Paddington had been a dream journey.

'If that journey hadn't ended I might have asked him some questions I oughtn't to have asked,' mused Thomas as he passed through the door and handed in his tickets.

'I'm glad I'm back,' he thought, 'and I still can't understand why they sent me up there. Four of them there doing nothing.' He helped the boy into the taxi, 'We'll soon be home.'

Robert stood all the way. He had shouted excitedly, 'We're off, Mr. Thomas.'

The dignity of a very superior servant had slowly returned to Thomas. 'Sit down, and don't make all that noise, Master Robert.'

'There's a funny house. . . .'

'Sit quiet, don't shout like that. . . .'

'I expect they had a reason for sending me, but it's strange they couldn't have gone themselves. Now look what I've found out.'

He pulled the boy back on to the seat, 'I said sit down, little boy.'

Robert sat down; he caught the strap as the taxi took a sharp bend.

'You're home,' announced Thomas, as the taxi passed in through the gates.

II

A T Greys the sun refused to come out. Mist from the river still hung about the place, great folds of it enveloped the house, and looking from his bedroom window that morning Mr. Mortimer was distrustful; he hated this sort of morning, with its bogus daylight. But he had bathed, dressed in the usual way and gone down to breakfast. Now the meal was over. It had had the air of a committee meeting, the conference over, the directors leaving the room in a dignified manner. Consols were still at par, nothing to lose and nothing to expect. No change. Gabriel looked down the wilderness of table and caught his wife's eye. He then watched the others get up and go out, one after the other, in silence. It was easy to follow them, he could see them separating, going their varied ways. Agatha to her room, Isobel to the morn ing room to read *The Times*, to hope that that aun in Brisbane had not forgotten her, to search diligently in the Obituaries. Geoffrey would go to the spinney to see what had turned up in the night, and Arthur would return to his little cell to begin another day of brooding. The door closed at last, and there was a momentary silence. Gabriel looked down the table again, 'Well, dear?'

'There's some news for you,' Mrs. Mortimer said, as they rose simultaneously, Gabriel to sit in the leather chair in front of the fire, whilst his wife preferred to stand and lean against the mantelshelf. Gabriel thought, 'How small she really is.'

'Yes, what is it?' he asked. He seemed irritable, he

wanted to go, he said, 'I've things to do, Celia, things to do.'

'Nonsense. That's your trouble, dear, you've nothing whatever to do. Sit down.'

He had half risen from his chair, he wondered what the news might be.

'That man is dead,' Mrs. Mortimer said.

'Dead! What man?' Gabriel asked; it had given him quite a shock, and she had spoken in the most casual way.

'Elizabeth's husband,' replied Celia, her elbow on the mantelpiece; she had to reach up a little to maintain her hold.

'*Can't* you sit down, dear,' he said, 'you look rather ridiculous standing there like that.'

'I'm going directly. I have the kitchen arrangements to make which never wait, and Joan will be in here at any moment to turn us out,' she indicated the breakfast things with a wave of her hand.

'Then don't beat about the bush, just say what you have to say and don't be so mysterious about it. I wondered what on earth was coming, those signals to me, rather frantic I thought, just as Geoffrey was going out, he's certain to think we wanted to talk about him, suspicious devil, that's his natural weakness . . . ,' but Mrs. Mortimer wasn't listening and wasn't thinking of anything except Thomas speeding towards London on the eight five express to Paddington.

'What you mean I imagine is that Elizabeth's husband has died,' said Gabriel, he spoke slowly, with calm. 'You know I often think that you should have gone on the stage, some natural impediments apart, you have a real flair for the dramatic. Please finish what you are saying and let me go. I've my letters to look to.'

Celia, ignoring what she called 'this air', said, 'He is dead and the boy is coming here. The police rang up last night, very late.'

'How disgusting – what boy is coming here? Do be precise.'

'I couldn't be more so,' she replied. 'I've told you her child is coming down here, to us, do you understand that? Your mind is so woolly in the mornings and around this time of the year you fall into a general moodiness, a sort of self-pity. I wish you wouldn't, dear, it helps nobody, not even yourself. He should be here around dinner-time. Thomas went up on the early train to collect him.'

'Thomas! No wonder he didn't put in an appearance. It's extraordinary at what a loose end I feel if he isn't about. That man, why I could tell, I could almost feel he had left the house. But this child. What on earth are we to do with him? It's very serious, really. We've never had any children here, and besides, we're getting on, all of us, it doesn't seem right. And where is Elizabeth now anyway? She never writes me at all.'

'But you know very well where she is, and you don't bother to write her much yourself, now do you, dear?' And at once Gabriel shook his head and said no, he didn't. He was afraid he had neglected her lately, but it was her duty to write to him first. 'And this man?' he asked.

'They lived in Paddington, father and son, it was only through finding some letters that we were traced. Apparently the man had some relatives in a place called Deptford. Do you know where Deptford is? But the poor child was alone in that house for two whole days, Rupert Street I think they said.'

'How horrible. I've passed through Paddington

once or twice in a car,' said Gabriel, 'but that was years ago. Places change. It may be different now.'

'But don't wander away, dear, your grandson will be here at seven o'clock.'

'Good Lord! And you never told me a thing, it's too much, dear. After all I am the head of this house. I should have been told at once. This is very serious. There are the others to think of. They may not like it, besides I've never even seen the child . . . how old is it?'

'I believe *he* is seven. I'm not sure, but he's not eight, I do know that, perhaps a little younger. . . .'

'Seven – eight – heavens,' thought Gabriel, 'is it all that time since my girl ran away with that horrible bounder. And now their son is actually coming here, to *this* house.' He wished he had had more information, and earlier than this, 'to this house.'

'What are you going to do then,' he asked. Getting up he went across to her, he put a hand on her arm. 'As the only practically-minded member of this family, what are we going to do?'

'We are going to have the boy, at least for the present. There may be other complications. . . .'

'It's disgraceful,' protested Gabriel, 'just fancy that girl running off with that bounder to Rome – Rome of all places, the next thing we'll hear is that she's been converted to Catholicism, the things people do, it's astounding. The poor child. I wonder what he's like . . .' and following a pause, 'but the others, they'll have to be told. . . .'

'I'll tell them. Before dinner if the train's late, otherwise at dinner.'

'I'll enjoy seeing their faces when you do. Arthur'll be against it, I feel sure, can't stand children of any kind, never could.'

26

'It's a matter for you entirely, not your brother,' said Mrs. Mortimer. 'I think I can hear that girl coming to clear the table, we had better 'go,' taking his arm. 'I shouldn't worry too much about this matter, dear, you are given to worrying over trifles.' She could feel the pull on her arm, the disinclination to go, the news had been too much for him. The rhythm of his day broken, he had lost his way a little. He was so hopeless in a crisis.

'Come along, dear,' as the door opened and Joan came in carrying a large empty tray.

'Morning, m'm.'

'Good morning,' Mrs. Mortimer said, 'we've held you up, I'm afraid, I'll see you in the kitchen directly.'

'Very well, m'm.'

'Good morning,' Gabriel said as he passed out of the room, moved towards the stairs, his study, the letters to be opened, the pencils to be sharpened, the little private worries about Thomas. They stood for a moment at the bottom of the stairs.

'You know, Celia, this is quite a shock, it's so sudden, I'll have to think carefully about it, very carefully, I must find out where Elizabeth really is. I wonder if they've told her?'

'Who?'

'Who do you think, the police of course.'

'I doubt it, Rome is a long way away.'

'And this man, is he buried?' he felt a squeeze on his arm, and Celia said, 'Ssh!' in his ear. 'I'll come up and talk with you later about that matter. You go and be quiet in your room, dear. You look worried even now. Go along. It's going to upset things, I agree with you there, but it cannot be helped. I'll talk with the others about it. You needn't worry one bit. I do hope he's a nice little boy, and the words followed

Mr. Mortimer up the stairs, with dread, it made the whole thing so terribly true.

Before that it was news, it might have been a colourful story from the morning paper, but, 'I hope he's a nice little boy' telescoped everything. He saw the boy, he saw many boys, he could hear them shouting all over the house, upsetting Arthur. He was the one to think about. 'Poor Arthur,' he thought, turned suddenly and said, 'Yes, dear, you had better come up and discuss this more fully after you have finished with the kitchen.' Half way up the stairs he stopped, 'Extraordinary,' he said, then went on up.

He fumbled at the knob of his study door, and hoped Thomas hadn't forgotten about the fire; he might on a morning like this. What a surprise for him. Being rushed off to London like that, so early in the morning. For a moment he saw his wife leaning against the mantelpiece in the dining-room, 'What a practical little woman she is,' (he could hear Agatha in one of her bitter moods), 'a dwarf amongst the giants.' But a very practical little dwarf, he thought, a smile playing about his lips. He opened the door and went in.

Thomas, who forgot nothing and remembered the slightest detail, had been in; there was the fire lighted, his letters laid out, even a new pencil to be sharpened, another pencil to put in the cedar box at the back of his desk; he didn't know how many the box held, quite a lot he supposed, but Thomas would know. The cushion on the chair, the coal in the bin, the wood on the hearth, the morning papers on the table; what would one do without Thomas?

He sat down and looked through the letters. Then he raised his eyes and glanced out of the window. The mist was still there, the sun hidden behind heavy, low-lying cloud, a soundless morning, the vision of wet grass, the dripping leaves in the spinney, the machinery of February creaking towards March. He imagined he saw a figure at the end of the lawn, under the cedar, but it wasn't. It might have been Elizabeth. Poor Elizabeth, just imagine that, her child seven years old.

'How it makes you feel you're travelling backwards, behind the horrible wall' – that high, dark wall, going back inevitably, no matter how hard you clutched. 'Poor child,' he said, 'poor child,' and, opening the first of his letters, he began to read.

'We would again remind you that your subscription to the *Bee Keeper* is now nine months overdue.' He dropped the letter as though he had been stung. How on earth had Geoffrey's letter got mixed up with his own? A circular about the efficiency of the Dropmore Cistern, a reminder about rates, the *Missionary Annual*, that would go to Arthur's library. He opened a long letter from a friend in Brazil, 'I suppose you are still tucked safely away at Greys, and simply waiting for the undertaker. Since I've been out here I've been able to realize the complete hollowness of Europe, the façade is crumbling, it's finished,' and on and on and on.

Gabriel put down the letter. It reminded him of something, Thomas's uncle in Brazil, Thomas's burning passion for Brazil when he was a young man. 'Poor Thomas,' he thought, 'but he never gives me the impression of a frustrated man, quite the contrary.' And then the uncomfortable thought, 'Thomas should never have gone. It was wrong of Celia to have packed him off like that, without a word to anybody. I would rather have gone myself. That's one stupid thing Celia has done. That kind of thing is so terribly private, so seriously our affair, God knows what he has seen and heard by this time. Coming back with that boy, a long train journey, he won't just sit mum and be a good servant, no discipline, heaven alone knew what would pass between them.'

'I'll just dig that thing out before Celia comes up, she never liked her I'm afraid.' He crossed to his desk and began fumbling under a pile of papers in its bottom drawer, and then out it came. He stood it on the desk, sat down and stared at it. Elizabeth at seventeen. What a pretty child she was. 'I hope the boy is like her, I hope very much so.'

From the back of his mind, out through the dust and distance of time, he saw the wording of the last letter she had ever written to him, a month after she had gone. 'You are living in the backwaters and nothing ever happens, you don't understand.'

It made him smile, it made him remember. He saw the clear pattern of Greys, the life there; those others, the feeling of being safe, of being left alone, they were safest there, that was the place to be. 'Backwaters,' he thought, 'why, I rather like it.' The ebullience and ignorance of youth! Here we are, still together, we disagree, we argue, we sometimes get so angry with each other that we don't speak for days on end. Nevertheless we are still together, firm. He had held Greys together against the onslaughts, the torrents, the pressure from outside. He realized how they held close by virtue of a shared inner resolve, a quite instinctive thing, the strong link. One tiny disruptive note and the whole thing might fall apart, crumble.

'We are not with the stream, and we are not against it, our time is autumnal, we've had our sun.'

'I suppose I dislike Arthur's moral nature as much

as anybody, and I know I can't stand Isobel's intolerance, and sometimes Geoffrey's hypocrisy sticks out a mile, but deep down we are all together. A splendid thing, and we are left alone. That is what is important.'

The girl in the photograph stared back at him; she might have been listening. He was struck by her expression, he could only think of a ruthless honesty, a startling frankness, 'such a pretty child, but she never fitted in here, especially after I brought Celia along.' It had disappointed him deeply. It had been such a triumph, working Celia into the Mortimer pattern, conquering her, it had been a battle with all of them. And suddenly Elizabeth had gone.

'Poor girl, I expect she's learned a lot since she ran away. Only thing is she may have learned too much. One can.'

He thought he heard steps on the stairs and hurried the photograph back to its hiding-place. Yes, somebody was coming upstairs and he knew at once who it was. He knew the owner of every footfall, and didn't wait for her to knock, but said, 'That you, dear, come in,' and there she was, her head round the door, saying: 'It's me, I must see you,' and at once Gabriel, remembering Thomas, replied. 'And I must see you, too. Close the door.'

'Sit down, Celia, there's something I wish to say.'

He left his desk, he stood over her. 'Why did Thomas have to go to Paddington?'

'Who else would have gone, Joan? She's only a child, never been out of the village yet to my knowledge.'

'I could, I *would* have gone. I'm angry with you that you never mentioned the matter to me at once. Thomas had no right to go at all. This is very private business of our own. He is only a servant here, and you must know the man by this time. God knows what he has dragged out of the child by now. I wouldn't mind if it wasn't for the background. . . .'

'And what do *you* know about background?' Celia demanded. She hadn't quite expected this. Had her practical mind let her down again?

'I don't know,' said Gabriel. 'I don't have to know, I can imagine it all too well. I'd rather anybody had gone but him. However, it's done now and there's the end of it. I've said what I wanted to say. Let's forget about it, shall we? You did what you thought was best, but I regret it. Leave it at that. Now what did you want to say, dear?'

He bent down, he put a thin white hand on her hair. 'My dear, my dear.'

She lowered her eyes, she would not look at him.

'I am not to blame for your imagination,' she replied, her voice was cold, she folded her arms on her lap.

'No, dear, you're not,' said Gabriel. He drew a cane chair alongside her own and sat down; he held her hand.

'You have always been so very good, Celia, and most sensible in all things. The coming of this child is a problem. If there were another child here. . . .'

'The hall clock has stopped again, did you know?' asked Celia, and drew her hand away from him. 'I do wish you would see about it.'

'Certainly, dear.'

'And Joan says that the drains are blocked again.'

'Oh dear. Those awful drains again,' he said.

'Well, you *will* live here. . . .'

'Not that again, please, I couldn't stand it. I think I'll go out for a walk, is Geoffrey anywhere about?'

'I don't know. Please stay where you are. I haven't told the others yet, and they will have to know.'

'Naturally.'

'Will you tell them, Gabriel?'

'Well, yes, of course, but I thought you were going to tell them at dinner.'

'It's only a child. You don't like telling them, it might upset them, you wish me to do it.'

'You do these sort of things so much better than I do. I'm hopeless in practical matters, you know that, dear. . . .'

'It's still only a child, Gabriel, a rather desperate lonely little boy.'

'I *am* a coward, my dear, we all are, I admit it, I admit for all of us.'

'Very well.'

It had pleased her to hear him say it; she had wanted this, and she had got it. She was prepared, in the circumstances, to break the news. She got up.

'This matter of sending Thomas,' she said, 'you're entirely wrong, I have that man's confidence and he has mine. I know his limitations and you don't. I know how far he'll go. Please don't worry your head about it.'

'You say the train arrives at six fifty-five?'

'Around that time, I wouldn't be sure.'

'A school will have to be found for the boy. What is his name again, I forget it.'

'Robert, dear.'

'As soon as that boy arrives he must come direct to my room,' said Gabriel, the clock and the drains were tucked securely away in a niche in his mind.

'Naturally, he's *your* grandson, not mine,' replied Celia.

He seemed barely aware of it but she was out of the

chair and out of the room, she might have floated away.

'Expect she's right, always is, though I hate admitting it. Damn those drains. Why don't people do things? I must go down and see to that clock. The others never think of anything. I'm glad Celia is to do the explaining, I know in my bones they'll protest, we're a selfish opinionated lot, we really are.'

He looked almost regretfully at the pencil that wouldn't be sharpened this morning, and picked up the reminder from the *Bee Keeper*. 'Must give it that fellow. Always thought the chap a prompt payer in these matters of subs.' He shut the door and went downstairs.

The house was silent, save that far off in the kitchen region he could hear his wife talking to the girl, Joan stuttering her replies. He hadn't been inside that kitchen for three years, it didn't seem to matter any more.

'Expect I'll have to go down and see the builder's man again. I can't stand the fellow . . . still . . .' he glanced up at the clock.

'The years that old thing has gone, such a good old clock,' he opened the door and put a finger on the hands. He gave the pendulum a swing, 'there'. He stood looking at it, undetermined in mind; he ought to go back to his room and run through those newspapers, but now he couldn't settle, he couldn't get Thomas out of his mind. He could not understand his wife.

'On the most private business, it's unbelievable, and what a poor excuse to make, that they, he, the others, couldn't have been bothered.' It upset him. 'I think I'll go into the garden,' but he did not move, it required Thomas behind him to give him a push. 'I wonder what the fellow's doing in that spinney every morning. I could go and give him his letter, anyhow.'

There was nobody in sight, he wouldn't see the others yet, not for an hour, and Arthur wouldn't appear at all until lunch-time.

'An extraordinary thing when you come to think of it, an unfrocked priest in the house, sitting up in that room battling with his conscience for two years and never a move in any direction.'

He went out into the garden. The air was damp, everything dripped, the sun was stubborn. He walked down the lawn, he shivered a little, 'To the bottom of the garden and back,' he thought.

'Pity Celia spends so much of her time in that kitchen. Often wonder what she pays that girl, she hardly does a thing. Still one daren't think of her going, and she can certainly make beds, and she doesn't grumble. I wish that man were back. A stupid thing to have sent him up.'

He stood listening. 'Spends all his time in that place, horribly damp.' He turned suddenly, his wife was calling him, 'the boy can't have arrived already,' hurrying back, excited, and she, from the other end of the lawn, was watching him, seeing the tell-tale signs, the halting, fragile step, and when he reached her, the puffing, the appearance of utter exhaustion.

'Only sixty-three,' thought Celia. 'I think he really likes being old.'

'There you are! Did you find Geoffrey, I gather you wanted him?'

'No. Just took a turn on the lawn, how neglected it looks now. Arthur used to be so good at keeping it up.'

'Of course. When his present mood is over he

35

might get on to it again. But let him have his mood,' Celia said, 'he enjoys having them.'

'What is it?' he asked, a little gruffly, staring hard at his wife. 'How extraordinary,' he thought, 'she's my junior by only two years and yet how astonishingly young she looks, so different from the rest of us, we all of us look so haggard, so . . . I don't know . . . I suppose the answer is buoyancy of spirit, Celia's full of it,' he was seized by sudden dread, 'if anything ever happened to Celia,' but Celia was very much alive, and she was saying hurriedly, and as though it were most important, with not a minute to spare, 'I've just seen Agatha and told her.'

'Indeed. What did she say?'

'She seemed rather pleased. But you mustn't stand about like this, dear, you'll catch your death of cold,' taking his arm, moving off. 'Thomas put a fire in your study and I find you standing here like the silly old man you are. . . .'

'Celia,' exclaimed Gabriel.

'Well, aren't you?' and she laughed up at him, and he was glad of that, he liked to hear Celia laughing.

'Agatha will tell the others, I'm going to see them all in a minute,' she went on. 'You needn't bother about anything, come along, we'll go up to your room. I've finished with Joan now,' and Gabriel nodded his head, and said, 'Yes, I'd better go in. It is very damp this morning.'

'And terribly dull,' said Celia, and nothing seemed more definite than that.

'Isn't it. A horrible sort of morning.'

'We're going into Helton on Friday,' she announced, 'Thomas has managed some petrol. I've arranged it. Agatha and Isobel are coming in, too.'

'I ought to see that man Griffiths,' said Gabriel, and

36

immediately Celia said, 'I'll see him.' He hesitated on the stairs, 'I'll see,' he said.

'That's all you ever say, dear, you'll see, then nothing happens, one of these days something *will* happen and then where will you be. I hope you're not having a wintry mood, too.'

She opened the door and gave him a gentle push. 'Go and sit quiet, dear, and don't worry about anything. You'll be able to watch the reactions at lunch instead of dinner,' and she closed the door and went on to her own room.

He was relieved that Celia would see the builder, 'I can't stand the fellow at all, so impudent,' how good she was at those sort of things. He felt so pleased with the shifting of responsibility that he took up the cigar Geoffrey had left him and lit it, and sat back smoking contentedly. His mind sang praise of Celia. How good she was, how sensible, and how patient with them all, he had never thought she would harness in, but she had, and it pleased him to think that after Monica had died he had had the courage to ask her to marry him. How delicately she had sailed through the critical seas, how quietly trampled over the snobbery, the heads in air, 'But of course Elizabeth wouldn't like her, and didn't like her from the start. That couldn't be helped. Five against one. Anybody could see the result.'

He had never forgotten the wonderful loyalty of Agatha. She had smoothed many paths. Life on the whole had been calm, and full of contentment.

'Poor Elizabeth, if only she had triumphed,' he thought, 'over her narrowness of mind.' In the end it was Celia who stood out. 'The dwarf amongst the giants.'

'I wish we could trace her. That poor child. There

must have been something in the father after all. It must have been a strange life for them both. Curious. I never liked that fellow Christopher.' He went across to his desk and picked up the pencil, took a pen-knife from his pocket and started to pare it.

'If we could trace Elizabeth and get her back here – things would be different, Celia could never raise any objection now, the boy would be the link between them. I do wish I knew where in Rome she was staying, if she's still there. But I remember that fellow very well. Such a wanderer, such a wastrel in his way, how I could wish they'd never met. Odd name the man had, Dolphin or something like that.'

He took out the photograph again and sat down with it, looking at it, thinking of the child, and suddenly realizing that a growing excitement was stirring in him, 'I do hope he looks like her. I wonder what he'll think of us, I wonder.'

III

'WHERE'S Arthur?' inquired Geoffrey as soon as he came in.

He smelt strongly of earth, ferret, rabbit, an enormous man, he filled the chair. He turned and looked at his sister, 'Isn't Isobel down yet? My God, the hours she spends in that bathroom, you'd imagine she was young and pretty,' he stretched his long legs.

'You know what it's about,' answered Agatha.

If she stood up she was her brother's height, all of six foot. The Mortimers were all tall, and graceful in their carriage, as Gabriel was wont to boast. She looked across at her brother. She saw a broad-shouldered man, in his middle fifties, with thinning sandy hair, a pencil line of moustache of the same colour, small, vivid blue eyes. In everything he was on the heavy side. Large hands, big features, a heavy sensual chin, big teeth, yet not out of proportion to his height and weight. A buccaneer from Malaya, retired. Interested in things earthy, in his stomach, his indigestion, his clothes, new ideas about trapping, ready to mount anything from donkey to elephant. Intensely active, generating energy. A reader of *The Times*, *Horse and Hound*, the complete works of Surtees, an old Blue, living on a small pension, a tiny investment in rubber.

'I wish she'd hurry. Where's Gabriel?'

'Where would you expect to find him at this hour of the morning?' asked Agatha.

She was quite grey, with thin, ashen-like features. Her soft grey eyes had a sparkle to them, she was enjoying this, it wasn't so often that the Mortimers got together, and her response to Celia's news would have surprised her brother had he seen it. 'You'd think Gabriel would have come down,' she remarked, but there was no comment on that observation.

A widow, her husband having died in India, she had returned to her home and settled there, determined that her travelling days were over. Like Geoffrey she had a small pension, something in tin. In the summer time she looked after the flowers, helped Thomas in the vegetable garden. Of the Mortimers, she and her sister Isobel were the only members to attend church. She believed with great earnestness, she was sincere in her duties. Her brother's fall from grace had been a bitter blow to her, and she had never forgiven him.

This morning when he came in, banging the door behind him, he wore an old sports coat and a dirty pair of flannels; he was unshaven, without a collar, the ones he had disgraced were carefully wrapped up in brown paper and lay at the bottom of his chest of drawers. He looked different from the others, and certainly he did not look like a clergyman; he might have been a struggling tenant farmer. He crossed the room and flung himself on the couch. The room rang out with, 'Who's dead?' It might have been an ultimatum.

'Nobody's dead, old chap,' replied Geoffrey, 'so far as I know.' He puffed away at a pipe filled with shag.

'Sounds mysterious. Isobel came to my room and told me just this minute.'

'Trust Isobel to make the most of anything,' said Agatha, she turned round and looked hopefully through the window, 'I actually believe it's getting lighter, I hope it clears, I hate being kept in, I love being out,' but the steady drip, drip of leaves came to her ears.

'What a hope,' said Geoffrey, 'everything's sodden.'

'February can be the most horrible month some-times,' ventured Arthur.

Geoffrey stared up at the ceiling, sent clouds of smoke flying everywhere. Arthur sat quiet now and waited. Morning at Greys was not the best time for making conversation, the breakfast atmosphere was still about, as though the committee were in secret conference. Then the door opened and Mrs. Mortimer came in. They all looked in her direction, what she might say did not for the moment matter, they concentrated on her person, her look, her walk. It had always astonished Arthur that this small, plump, middle-aged woman could have so moved his brother to a physical passion; it was the unsolved mystery of the Mortimer family. They watched her come down the room with the air of spectators at a mannequin show. She caught Arthur's eye, and he looked glumly at her; he was prepared for the worst. She sat next to Agatha folded her hands in her lap and then looked at them one by one. Where was Isobel? Not still in that bathroom?

Out of the depths of his throat Arthur grumbled, 'Dressing, I believe,' he did not look up, but kept his eyes fixed on the pattern in the carpet.

'How she loves dressing and undressing, if she'd ever married she would have driven her husband mad,' remarked Geoffrey as he drew up his long legs and laid his pipe on the table nearby.

'Well,' began Mrs. Mortimer, she glanced at Agatha, 'you already know. . . .'

'The last time I came into this room,' said Arthur, 'was when Jackson read out Tommy's pathetic little will. Who now?'

Ignoring this Celia said, 'We are having a new guest

41

here, possibly this evening. Although you all of you suffer from shortness of memory, you will remember your niece. Her boy is coming down here today, his father, that man Dolphin, is dead.'

Geoffrey sat up at once.

'No, he isn't really. What a queer bloke that was. So the little beggar's coming down here. For how long?'

'For always perhaps,' replied Celia. 'I got quite a shock last night, you probably heard the telephone ringing late. It was the police from Helton.'

'The police. How dramatic,' Geoffrey said, and knocked out his pipe and pocketed it.

Agatha sat watching him, rather amused.

Arthur looked up. They were astonished at the pained expression on his face, and he said, 'Coming down here, to this house?'

'Yes, of course. Why not. Where else should he go?' Celia replied.

'I don't know,' Arthur said, but he couldn't disguise the shock it had given him.

'Does Gabriel know?' asked Geoffrey, on the point of rising.

'Naturally, he would be the first to know of it. He has left everything to me.' She kept turning her head towards the door. 'Where on earth can Isobel be?'

'Oh,' exclaimed Arthur, the word fell as cold as a stone, he immediately got up and went out.

Geoffrey, too, got up and left the room.

Agatha was at once relieved, she would have hated Geoffrey's indulgence in his brother's weakness. It had shocked her when he had referred to his brother as 'that great runner for Christ'.

'I often wonder what Isobel does all the time in the bathroom,' said Agatha, reclining comfortably in her chair, 'you'd think one bath a day was enough for anybody, and all the trouble there is to keep the hot water system functioning in a normal way.'

'Nothing except lie in the bath, she loves her body far too much. She requires a bathroom lined with mirrors.'

'Here she is.'

'There you are at last,' Celia said, 'what on earth do you do in that bathroom all these hours, Isobel?'

'Hours!' replied Isobel. She seemed quite offended by the remark.

Isobel sat down, but not comfortably. She could never sit down comfortably in anything. Although she adored her body it outraged her sometimes; she could never quite control the mercurial movements of the weights and measures chart. Nothing fitted properly after a month. She suffered from afflictions of the flesh born virgins are heir to. Isobel by nature and design was pure virgin. She had never married, she would never marry, she liked her independence. She had never left home, she would never leave home. She had few interests. She was forty-six, without ambition, indifferent to hope. She had a slight interest in landscape gardening, water-colours, crotchet work. She was a dutiful, muscular Christian, lacking Agatha's deep belief and unflagging sincerity. She irritated Gabriel and annoyed Geoffrey by her bad habits, her general air of untidiness, complete indifference to time. She sat bolt upright and studied everybody. Her round red face made one think of cherries, her black hair sat untidily on her head, she wore spectacles. She had the build of a wrestler, a formidable physicalness.

'Well,' she inquired, 'and what's all this fuss about?'

Celia smiled. 'He'll be here in time for dinner.'

43

'Did you say he comes from Paddington? I know somebody very well in that district, he has a little property there. I've never been of course, and shouldn't think of going.'

'Well we must make welcome this little guest,' Agatha said, 'I'll quite enjoy going for walks with him.'

'Arthur isn't impressed at all,' said Isobel, she fidgeted with her spectacles.

'That won't effect anything in the least,' replied Celia, 'after a while we shall arrange about a school for him, for Robert I mean.'

'Robert, is that his name?'

'Yes.'

'Wasn't his father the Dolphin Elizabeth ran away with,' said Isobel, and at once Agatha said, 'You know quite well it was.'

Isobel knew, but she would like to make sure, and she'd like her sister-in-law to do the explaining.

'It's curious,' Agatha remarked, 'when our kind breaks away like that, they inevitably return to base in the long run. I wonder what he's like?'

'Fancy Thomas going up for him. He *will* enjoy himself. Welsh people seem to go quite mad when they get to London,' said Isobel.

'News to me, I didn't know they went mad,' said Agatha.

'Well there it is,' Celia said, she got up from her chair, 'I had meant to spring it on you all at dinner. I do hope the train won't be late.'

Isobel got up. 'Not with Thomas on it, it won't,' she said, she flounced through the door. Agatha followed her out.

'Did you find my needle, dear?' asked Isobel.

'Yes, come up to my room and you can have it.'

Celia was standing waiting for them.

'I do hope you'll welcome this child and try to make him feel at home, he's had such an awful time, poor little boy.'

Isobel and Agatha went upstairs. 'It's mysterious, isn't it?' Isobel said.

'I've been wondering ever since if Elizabeth got to know, or if anybody is going to get in contact with her. Arthur knows where she is, I think, and so does Gabriel. It's surprising news anyway,' concluded Agatha.

They went into her room.

Isobel was silent. She sat down whilst her sister searched for the needle in her work-box.

'Here you are,' Agatha said, handing her the needle.

'Thank you, dear. Actually I think you've got the nicest room in this house.'

'It is a nice room, isn't it? It is the best in the house, I admit.'

She looked out through the window. From it she had a clear view of the drive, right down to the gates. One could see everything from this window, and what Agatha called, 'the world moving up and down'. Agatha liked to sit here and watch the traffic coming up and down the long drive, so badly in need of repair. She could watch the Rector on his motorcycle, the butcher's van, the postman, the children with their missionary cards, collecting, the doctor in his green car.

'I haven't seen sight of Gabriel since breakfast. Lately he's got as bad as Arthur, hiding himself away. I wonder which room Celia will give the boy.'

'I don't like the look of Gabriel of late,' Agatha replied, busily sorting out things from her basket, 'he doesn't look well at all, perhaps something is worrying him. But he's so secretive, and so quiet about things. Somehow he hardly lives *with* you. I wouldn't doubt but this has come as a bit of a shock to him, constitutionally he's not built for them.'

'Fancy Celia sending that man up to town. And not even mentioning the matter to us. I would have loved to have gone and collected him.'

'Would you really?' Agatha smiled. 'I believe she really would,' she thought. 'Celia might have let us know, I agree with you. Geoffrey would have gone, but Arthur would have refused. Only an earthquake could get him out of the house.'

'Geoffrey would never have gone. Ever since he has had to change his subscriptions to country instead of town he won't go near either of his clubs. He can't afford it, and I think he feels humiliated. I'm certain he wouldn't go near town at present.'

'Gabriel is so fond of praising Celia's good sense, but to have sent that man to Paddington was unwise, and I'm surprised at her. *Thomas.*'

'I would never have let him go. After all he's only the servant here. I wouldn't expect anything from Thomas except good manners and his feet securely behind the line chalked out for him. I admit Gabriel is allowing himself to be run by this man, he's become a sort of aide-de-camp, it's an intolerable position, it can lead anywhere.'

'Just look at the time, half-past four.' Isobel got up. 'I think that's Celia coming up now with Arthur's tray.'

He refused to sit out tea in the afternoon, he hated what was served up, the fresh soggy scones, the sticky, sugary toast, the China tea. Arthur had a more robust appetite and no palate at all.

'Gabriel's never been the same since Elizabeth ran away,' said Isobel.

'It's strange,' said Agatha, 'I could never understand Elizabeth not falling for that Rodney Trears, such a nice boy, and he had some money, I believe. Doing well at the bar now. Christopher was the last person to occur to me. I *never* liked him. Gabriel *and* Celia share my dislike of him. And no matter how bad, or how common that Dolphin man was, there was the question of honour,' Agatha concluded.

'A man like Dolphin probably wouldn't see it that way,' said Isobel, and she added quickly, 'but he's dead now. Expect we shall hear *all* about it at dinner.'

'From Thomas you mean,' said Agatha.

'From the child himself. Gabriel wouldn't have Thomas narrating at dinner, there is a limit to everything.'

Isobel opened the door. Agatha looked at the strong, masculine hand gripping the knob. She seemed to personify iron resolution.

'I wouldn't remain in the room,' she said, 'what an idea, Agatha.'

'You're quite wrong about limits, dear, there aren't any these days.'

'And there's the bell,' said Isobel, 'and I'm going,' banging the door behind her.

Agatha took up her work-basket, and returned it to its place on the window table.

'I'd better go down, too. What a fuss there seems to be about that man going to town. Rather ridiculous. The man's all right when he's kept in his place, and that's Gabriel's duty. She has a suspicious nature, she always had. But he's no menace, and even if he became one I shouldn't be in the least worried by it.'

She went down to the drawing-room. There was only Geoffrey and Isobel there; they were having tea, and as usual they were sitting as far as possible from each other, divided by the immense length of table. Geoffrey studied the racing column in *The Times*, Isobel pretended to read her fortune in the teacup. They did not look up and they did not speak when Agatha came into the room. Remembering at the last moment, Geoffrey let fall the paper and rushed violently forward to pour out tea for his sister, upsetting his own in the process.

Upstairs in Gabriel's bedroom Gabriel and his wife took tea quietly by the window.

'You know, Gabriel, if you could rid yourself of this awful weakness, it's a habit and nothing else, this habit of turning every little thing into a big problem, you wouldn't have to abase yourself so often. It's sweet of you to be so thankful, but to tell the others was nothing really. Nothing can upset the calmness of this house, you know that. But I do wish you wouldn't go about with that puzzled-looking expression on your face. Life is no long complication, not here at least, it may be outside, but we are not interested in the outside, none of us are, I think of Greys as the little island. I've done nothing out of the ordinary.'

'But that's just what you have done, you've saved me making a lot of explanations, and you are always doing it. It makes me feel so helpless sometimes, not being able to face such ordinary things as the drains, this child arriving, the ordinary little everyday things. You're so good and patient in everything, and I must say my thanks, and I must be allowed to say it in my own silly way, without you waving your hands in the air and saying I fuss. I knew from the first that Arthur wouldn't like it. Did you notice?'

'Arthur will have to like it,' Mrs. Mortimer said,

'I can't stand the man, I wonder why you have him on here like you do, in some ways he's insufferable. . . .'

Gabriel smiled. 'He's rather a pathetic creature, dear, if you only knew. You don't know him like I do. By the way, I'm glad you're going to see that man Griffith. Nobody can handle him better than you.'

But Celia had had an afternoon of it, and now she thought, 'That's the limit,' and she held her tongue and refused to speak, and refused to be drawn. There was such a thing as being nice, and being gracious, but one could get too much of it.

'More tea?' she said, her voice was firm, even cold.

'Please,' Gabriel said, and 'thank you,' and that was the end of that. They had said enough. He knew it. To add another word either way would be fatal. He drank tea, he stared at the picture on the wall. Celia got up. 'Joan will collect the tray,' she said, and then went out.

'Yes, dear.' He smiled the most agreeable smile.

'Already,' he thought, 'she has planned everything. Robert to go in Elizabeth's room, Robert to have the piebald, Robert to be introduced to Mr. Rivers, Robert to have his own table at meals. Everything arranged. They'd simply be lost without Celia. Pity Arthur's so hostile, the others took it very well. There's plenty of time for changes though. Things may look very different by morning,' and finally, before he got up, before he went off to his study for a final glimpse at the paper, a vision of Robert, seven, or was it eight years old, black haired, like his mother . . . 'They say Dolphin was a red-haired fellow, extraordinary how strongly red runs with those kind of people.'

In the study her photograph came out again, the portrait that his wife could not bear, the gay, laughing girl, lost somewhere in Rome – what a place to have gone to, might even have turned Catholic, people sometimes did. But how sad for that child. 'I hope I'm not going to be upset by this. . . .'

Thought stopped at the sound of a gunshot, Geoffrey's gun: rabbit for lunch tomorrow, he had an idea that it had been rabbit for lunch today.

'Strange times we live in. People like us are being slowly bled out, I expect we'll all rot in the end.'

Well, he would rot here, and rot he hoped with sufficient dignity. But how menacing everything was, even a fine strong chap like Geoffrey could feel it, something in the air. 'It's as though we were all quietly asleep in our beds, and then the noise of the battering ram in the middle of the night.'

He went to the window and looked out. He had a quick vision of a man named Dolphin, wearing a grey peaked cap, and he was leading the boy across the lawn, moving quickly towards the front door.

'How odd. For a moment I almost thought I recognized the fellow, though I've never set eyes on him in my life before, and if he had not been dead would never want to see him.'

Suddenly he espied Geoffrey coming down the lawn, a gun at the trail, a rabbit hanging in his other hand. He could not prevent himself from calling down, 'Not another one, surely there is a limit.'

Geoffrey held high the rabbit, Gabriel saw his big strong teeth parted in a grin. 'Best you can put up on a day like this, unless you like cat.'

'I don't think that's at all funny.' Gabriel snapped down the window.

Geoffrey shouted up. 'But I do,' and swung the rabbit about, and laughed.

Gabriel could still see him standing there; he thought he looked quite idiotic. He opened the window to say: 'My God, can't you go away with that thing,' and then he heard Arthur's voice from the next room. He could see his brother quite clearly, he was seated in his winged armchair, the Bible on his knee, 'Probably plodding through Job,' he thought. 'Said the other day he had had a fierce battle with Saul, always relates his battles to me, never thinks of going to anybody else with them. Poor devil. It was tragic really. There he is buried in his own little cell and hardly ever comes out.' He thought of the teaching job at Cambridge, the choir, the boy named Francis, a bad business. 'I don't suppose anything will ever happen to Arthur now, except possibly death. Only forty-eight and finished.' It seemed so terribly unfair when you thought about it. 'He's become so morose lately, and those letters, oh dear, those dreadful letters, all of no avail. But Bishops are Bishops and live on their high and holy dignity.'

He felt he could voice that thought, he was barely Christian himself, a hanger-on at the fringe. The breaking of Arthur had set the seal upon this final and inevitable attitude. He could not believe that Arthur had been given a fair hearing. And there was the ugly side, the pathetic, blind fleshiness of it; the inadequacy of human beings had never seemed clearer.

'But sometimes I have to think of him lying in his own wound and rather enjoying it.'

He could hear his brother shouting through the window at Geoffrey. 'Perhaps that's hardly the thing to say, I'll go in to him. He hardly ever barks at me.'

He went out and knocked on the door of the adjoining room.

'It's only me,' he called and went inside.

Not often did he enter Arthur's room, and his first thought was of chaos, a terrible untidiness, as though discipline and order were wrecked the moment they crossed the threshold. 'And the books,' he said to himself, 'the books,' everywhere, piled high, and the fireless grate, 'a silly sort of penance,' he thought. The hearth was littered with matches, cigarette ends, torn papers. The bed was tumbled, as though he slept on top of it and never beneath the sheets. The stale air – Gabriel glanced almost desperately towards the window he would like to open but dared not. There was his brother slouched down in his chair. What should he say to him?

'Well, old chap,' he began, unable to think of another opening, 'just had tea?' a silly question, nothing was more obvious, there was the tray beside his chair. He sat down gingerly on the nearest chair. 'Well, Arthur,' he said.

Arthur suddenly looked up from his book. 'I'm going away,' he said. Gabriel was startled by his appearance, he looked ravaged, and what was worse, thought Gabriel, he hadn't even shaved today. 'Yes,' said Arthur. 'I can't stay here.'

Was this a joke? Gabriel laughed.

'Going away where, my dear fellow?'

'I don't know, just away,' replied Arthur. He extracted a cigarette from his pocket and lit it; it gave out a strong, pungent smell.

Gabriel got up. He stood over his brother, he patted his shoulder. 'Nonsense, old chap,' he said. 'Where could you go. You know right well there's no place you could go.'

Arthur remained silent. Gabriel continued. 'I hope it's not on account of the boy coming down, a poor innocent child, who, if all that I hear is correct, has had a pretty rough time of it. I hope you weren't thinking of temptation, Arthur, that's just silly. You remain here. You have your room, you have everything you want. . . .'

Arthur stared up at him. 'That's all you ever think of, that's all you ever wanted, and now you've got everything you ever wanted and a damned lot of good it's ever done you. . . .'

'I daresay that if I had my time all over again I would follow the same pattern, mere contentment is not a form of cowardice as you appear to think, on the contrary, it's a form of courage, but why go on . . . I have never been able to understand you, Arthur, never. If you had had any sense at all you would have gone to that post abroad and given the church a wide berth. Life has done me no harm, and also, it's not always been as pleasant, and as easy-going as you would like to make out,' Gabriel went on. 'I have had my own troubles. But to say to me now that you are going away, when you have no place to go – I'm not rubbing it in, old man, it's just stating a fact, clearing out is just stupid. Remain where you are and try to conquer yourself. Don't be afraid of a little child coming here.'

'Nothing to do with him coming here, nothing whatever,' snapped Arthur.

'Of course I know that – well, we had better not discuss the matter any more.' He bent down again, looked into his brother's eyes. 'You be sensible,' he said. 'That's all that is required of you. See you at dinner.'

Arthur heard the door of his brother's study close. Perhaps Gabriel was right. Nothing to do except sit tight. He was nothing now, and he had nothing.

IV

ROBERT sat as far away from Mr. Thomas as he
possibly could after his rebuff; he did not speak,
and stared resolutely through the taxi window
until the car finally pulled up outside the front door of
Greys, where Mrs. Mortimer was already standing
waiting to receive them. Above, in Agatha's room,
Isobel, Geoffrey and she crowded the window, alive
with curiosity, trembling with excitement. Nothing
like this had ever happened before. It was as though
an unseen finger had suddenly touched their lives,
separately and together; as though from this moment
there would be a change.

As he sat quietly in the corner Robert was determined not to look at Mr. Thomas, and not to answer
any more questions. He was excited, he was afraid,
and he knew he did not like Thomas any more.
Thomas was disappointed. Once or twice during the
drive he perked up, began describing the country
they were passing through, familiar landmarks, he
described the village in detail, but the boy was un-
responsive, and then Thomas knew that something had
happened to him. Their relationship of the long
journey was over, camaraderie was finished, this
was new territory and the boy's silence said, 'Keep
out.'

He thought of his father again, he felt lonely, he
wanted to cry. Only the sight of the man in the bowler
hat prevented it. He refused to show Thomas anything more. And Thomas had laughed at him on the
train. He remembered that, laughed at him twice.
He heard Thomas speaking, 'Here we are, Master

Robert.' He sat up suddenly, looked out on his side of the taxi. He saw a long, tree-lined drive, and through the trees he caught a glimpse of a stone wall, which as they drew nearer, proved to be the great stone pile of Greys itself. And suddenly the car was at the door, the engine had stopped, the driver was getting out, Thomas getting out, whilst he sat on, peering through the window, still feeling lonely, afraid, very bewildered. The moment Mrs. Mortimer caught sight of him she gave a little smile, and she thought he looked the most tired child in the world. Thomas opened the door and Robert stepped out. Celia came forward, Robert intently watching her, and dutifully behind stood Thomas.

'Well, little man,' she said, and the boy gave her a smile.

'Hello,' he said, and at once Mrs. Mortimer swept him up in her arms.

'You poor darling,' she said, and kissed him; then quietly to Thomas, 'That will do, Thomas. Thank you.' She glanced across at Shane, the driver of the taxi. 'On the Mortimer account.'

'Very good, madam,' he said, and got into his taxi at once and drove away.

A sea of faces crushed against Agatha's bedroom window, but Robert did not see them.

'A pretty little boy,' announced Agatha, she turned to her sister, 'don't you think so?'

'I thought he might have red hair,' she replied. 'I feel quite relieved.'

Geoffrey leaned over her shoulder, 'I say, did you ever see anything so menacing as Thomas standing there with his bowler hat on,' and they all laughed at that, they had suddenly remembered Thomas. Agatha drew away from the window.

'And now, dears, perhaps you'll crowd out. I must tidy my room.'

'Silly Arthur never even as much as showed his nose. Ass. He can't dodge him at dinner, anyhow,' remarked Geoffrey. He bounded forward and opened the door for Isobel. 'Ought we to go down?'

'I don't think so. I shouldn't be surprised if Celia isn't already putting him to bed. He did look tired, poor little chap. She may keep him there. It'll seem strange hearing a boy's voice about the house. Makes you wonder how Elizabeth is getting on, I wonder just where she is at this very moment.'

Geoffrey slipped out, Isobel paused. Agatha was adjusting the curtains.

'Agatha.'

'Yes, dear.'

'What do you really think?' asked Isobel.

'What, about what?'

'About Elizabeth's child of course.'

'It's too early to think anything, but I quite expect to see him at dinner. Gabriel will want to show him off, and I'll bet that's where he is now, at this moment, closeted in his room. He wanted to see the child alone.'

'Oh!'

Isobel then went out. She stood listening on the landing.

'Of course, I can hear Gabriel talking to him. How strange, never been a child here before.'

She tried hard to remember, down the years, but the echo of a child's voice never reached her.

In a way it was exciting. They were bound to hear news of his mother, his father. Suddenly there was Celia.

'We decided not to come down,' Isobel said, and

Mrs. Mortimer said, 'I think that was very sensible of you all.'

'He's with his grandfather now,' she went on, 'poor little boy, he looked so tired, so lost.'

'Thomas didn't half make a picture,' said Isobel, 'it's not often that he can make us laugh,' but Celia did not see the joke.

'As usual I must get along and chase after that girl in the kitchen.'

Isobel went down into the garden. She always walked round the garden before she went up to change for dinner. She could hear Geoffrey talking somewhere about, she looked up and caught his eye. He was standing at the open window, his hands in his pockets. Arthur's voice came clear. It was obvious that Geoffrey was getting after him again. How those two wrangled.

'Poor Arthur, he gets so little peace. Still, servo him right, it was quite horrid of him to do what he did. Sometimes I wish that something could happen to him for his own sake. I wish Geoffrey would try and get him away for a few days.'

She walked to the end of the garden, and finding the wooden seat under the ash to be wholly dry, she sat down. She looked up the valley. It had been a horrible day, never a bit of daylight, and now it was growing dusk already.

'Arthur's scared really. Of course he hasn't a cent either. Living on poor old Gabriel. I often feel quite sorry for Gabriel, he's so good and patient, rarely complains, his pride wouldn't let him do that. Wonderful how he's managed to hold this place together for so long, and us, for that matter. But it must be a burden to him. I like that pride. He's quite right, there is something in standing together. Pity Arthur ever returned,' and the moment she thought of it, she was sensing the softness of her brother's heart. She thought of Geoffrey's jibes. She thought of Celia's attitude towards Gabriel. 'She thinks him silly, ineffective, but he's not really. I can't understand Celia when she talks of his being unimaginative, and even without feeling.' Clouds swept thickly over the hills. She thought of this child as the ripple on the calm lake.

'It may do Gabriel no end of good, it may force him out of himself. He will certainly liven things up.'

She could hear Arthur saying how he could not stay now.

'It may be the making of him if he went away,' she thought.

Raindrops were suddenly falling on her hair. She got up and returned to the house. As she climbed the stairs to her room she was suddenly aware of the silence. It was as though the whole place were sleeping. The hall clock was striking seven as she went in. She hurried to her room to change. Queer, animal-like noises were coming from the bathroom and she realized that Geoffrey had got there before her. Nobody could make noises like him; the water splashed, things clattered to the floor, bottles rattled. Quite often he sang in his bath, in a rude bass voice, snatches of popular ballads, never quite in key. He was tone-deaf, with no ear at all for music. With the exception of Gabriel and Agatha they all suffered from this disability, but were never conscious of what Agatha called, 'their poor affliction'. When she reached her room she could still hear her brother singing, a few bars of 'Thora', a snatch of 'Deep River'.

'And here *is* your grandson,' announced Mrs.

Mortimer; she came in holding Robert by the hand, 'and a very nice little boy he is. Don't keep him too long, dear, he's very tired. I think I'll put him to bed.'

Mr. Mortimer turned round in his chair and saw the boy. He got up and went to him.

'Hello, little man,' he said, 'how are you, Robert?'

At that moment Celia slipped out, the door closed quietly behind her.

Gabriel took one look at the boy and was pleased. This was Elizabeth, this was a Mortimer, not a Dolphin in sight.

'Come and sit down, darling,' he said, 'I hope you'll be happy here.'

He led the boy to a chair, then he sat down beside him.

Robert said, 'Yes, sir,' and 'thank you, sir,' and Gabriel thought, 'How strange to hear a boy's voice in this very room.'

He put a hand lightly on Robert's head, pushed back his head a little, and remarked, 'You're so like your mother, dear, so like your mother.'

He was suddenly holding him tight in his arms. 'Poor little chap, you've had a rough time of it. Never mind. Everything'll be all right now, Robert.' The grave face turned to his own made him say quickly, 'Can you smile, little boy, let me see your smile,' and he smiled himself.

Robert smiled and stared back at the grey-haired man with the soft voice, and remembered Paddington and Mrs. Mores, and his father. He wanted to cry, but he saw that the grey-haired man was quietly, intently watching him. 'I won't cry here, I won't cry in this room.'

'You're a very tired little boy, Robert, but in a minute or two your grandmother will be attending

59

to you. Your hair is so thick and so black, just like your mother's hair. Do you remember your mother, dear?' He was searching in his mind for the time, the date, how long ago was it since she – since she had cleared off with that bounder Christopher, and then he got his answer.

'The lady,' the boy said.

'Your mother,' said Gabriel.

'The lady,' Robert said, 'she went away. A very big man came to our house when my daddy was away on the North Road. . . .'

'But she *was* your mother, darling, she was your mother.' The boy's words had astonished him, 'the lady'.

'Yes, sir.'

'You loved your mother, Robert, didn't you. Didn't you love your mother, dear?'

'And my daddy,' replied Robert, in a high chirpy voice, 'I liked him better than mummy. He used to take me to the pictures. Once he took me for a ride on his lorry to Camden Town. We used to go to a pull-up, we used to buy fish and chips and tea and eat them on the lorry. . . .'

Gabriel stared. He was in a foreign country, he was listening to a new language, he could not understand this, he went on staring at his grandson. 'We must have a long chat about that some time,' Gabriel said, 'you can tell me all about it.'

The boy's whole demeanour suddenly changed, the direct, inquisitive stare softened to a smile and it lifted Gabriel's heart.

'Thomas knows,' cried the boy, 'I told him.'

Mr. Mortimer leaned over the boy, his mouth close to his ear, he felt like a conspirator. 'What did you tell him?'

'About daddy,' Robert replied.

Gabriel stood up. 'How high he is,' thought the boy, 'how high he is, higher than daddy.'

'But not about the lady,' said Gabriel, the shock was still with him, extraordinary thing for a child to be calling his mother the lady.

'How old are you?' he asked.

'I'm seven . . . nearly, I think I'll be seven in October,' he paused and put his finger to his mouth, appeared contemplative, 'in seven months and two days.'

'What would you like for your birthday?'

Robert shouted. 'A dog, I'd like a dog.'

'A *dog*?'

'Yes, sir.'

'But what kind of dog, dear?'

'The kind daddy liked, they chase rabbits at the dogs,' the boy replied.

'They what?' and suddenly Robert shouted. 'A whippet.'

'You're an odd child. Tell me, did Thomas ask you questions?'

Robert burst into tears.

'My little boy,' said Gabriel, lifting the boy in his arms.

'Let me go. Let me go. I want to go back where daddy is,' cried Robert, he struggled frantically in the old man's arms.

'This child,' thought Gabriel, 'this child' – he walked across the room and pressed the bell push. 'He's like somebody, he's . . . oh dear, dear.'

Thomas appeared as though by magic.

'Tell Mrs. Mortimer to come here at once,' Gabriel said.

'Yes, sir.'

'That's Thomas,' cried Robert, '*that's* Thomas.'

'Yes, little man, that's Thomas,' holding him tight, calming him, saying softly, 'There! there!'

Celia came in. 'I was just coming up,' she said.

Gabriel put the boy down. 'Now go along with your grandmother, like a good boy,' he said quickly, and then the boy said, 'Yes, sir,' and Gabriel took out his handkerchief and dried the boy's eyes.

'That's right, dear,' Celia said, 'come along now. We're going to have something very nice for dinner, aren't we, grandfather.'

'That's right,' Gabriel said, 'something really nice for dinner.'

'Can I have fish and chips, I love fish and chips.' He looked shyly into Mrs. Mortimer's face.

Mr. .Mortimer stood watching them as they disappeared through the door, he could hear his wife asking, 'What is that, dear,' and the boy crying back into the quiet corridor 'They're nice and hot, daddy always bought me fish and chips for supper.'

Mr. Mortimer sat down. So Thomas had been asking questions. 'I must talk to him. I wish to God Celia hadn't been so mad and sent him off like that. Nobody in their right senses would ever have done such a thing. He knows too much already.'

Arthur suddenly shot into his mind. He hated him for his mock show of nobility, there seemed something wholly bogus about his self-sacrifice. 'He depends on me, and I depend on the other one. I never thought I should ever have reached such a level. I'm rather selfish, I expect, I've tried to hold all this together. It's been difficult sometimes. But I could wish that man had never gone. Each time I think of it the less able I am to understand Celia, it's such a fall from good sense, really, but then she doesn't know everything, and I hope never will. But one must simply resign oneself to the situation and do the best one can.' He sat there, deep in reflection, until the gong warned him it was time to get moving.

'Wish I could be like that fellow, Geoffrey, carefree, he just doesn't give a damn about anything, or like Isobel who is so hearty, a bit wearing at times, Celia thinks I'm just an old plod along, but she doesn't understand everything.'

'Gabriel,' Celia called, putting her head in through the door, 'you'll be late.' She hated unpunctuality. 'Where is Robert?'

'Thomas has done just what I expected he would do,' said Gabriel, 'probing the child, asking all sorts of questions, I simply can't understand your doing such a thing, dear, it's not like you, any of us would have gone. . . .'

'Rubbish. You're all of you unreliable,' snapped Celia, and dashed off to her room.

The final gong went. 'Oh well,' he thought, 'suppose I'd better go down.' His wife joined him at once.

'That child seems to like only one kind of food,' she said. Her quite unexpected laugh cheered Gabriel up.

He paused on the stairs, 'Where is the boy?'

'You'll see. Come along now.'

When they entered the dining-room the boy was already there. He sat at the top of the table; when he saw them come in, he shouted, 'Hello.'

Mrs. Mortimer was pleased with him; Joan had certainly worked wonders. The bright, shining face still seemed out of place. Listening to him talking in the bathroom, she had suggested bed.

'How funny,' Robert said, 'why it's only seven o'clock. Sometimes my daddy and me had supper at eleven o'clock at night. Once we went to Fred's.'

'Where is Fred's, darling?'

'Deptford,' said Robert. He splashed some water from his glass and laughed.

'Do be careful.'

Mr. and Mrs. Mortimer took their places.

'So there you are,' Gabriel said, not expecting this, and not liking it. He glanced at the clock, a quarter to eight.

'Are the others coming?' he asked.

Agatha arrived. Her eyes found the boy at once and she gave him a smile. Isobel appeared a moment later, followed by Geoffrey, and at last, Arthur. It pleased Gabriel to see Arthur come. He made a point of going up to him, 'Good man,' he patted him on the shoulder, 'now we're all here.'

'Stand up, Robert,' said Celia.

'This way,' she said, beckoning, and the boy left his place and walked down the room. He stopped, he looked up at them; how tall these people were, he thought.

'Not like Paddington.' He thought these people were giants.

'This is your Aunt Agatha.'

'How do you do, Robert,' asked Agatha, she bent gracefully forward, offered him her thin white hand.

'Your Aunt Isobel.'

'Hello, sonny, how are you?'

'Very well, thank you, lady.'

'How charming,' Agatha muttered to Geoffrey.

'*Auntie*, dear,' Mrs. Mortimer corrected.

'Very well, auntie, thank you.'

Isobel's hand stuck out rigid, like a stick.

'Your Uncle Geoffrey.'

'Well, little man, we must go and catch a rabbit tomorrow, shall we?'

The tiny hand was lost in the big paw.

'Yes, sir,' and Geoffrey, touched by such gravity, laughed and said, 'Goodo.'

'Your Uncle Arthur,' said Celia.

Everyone looked at Arthur, he reddened a little. 'How do you do, boy.'

Robert looked squarely at Arthur and replied, 'You're like my daddy.'

The hand fell, Arthur turned his back on the boy, and Celia cried suddenly, in a high sing-song voice, 'Come along, everybody,' and there was an immediate scrambling back to chairs, and adjusting of napkins.

Mrs. Mortimer kept looking at Robert, seated between his grandfather and his Uncle Geoffrey. The door opened and Thomas came in. Dinner was served. Thomas circled the table, then withdrew and stood by the door. Robert never took his eyes off him. Where was the bowler hat?

'Hello, Mr. Thomas,' the boy shouted, and waved his hand.

Thomas lowered his eyes, remained motionless.

'You haven't got your funny hat on,' cried the boy, and Mr. Mortimer whispered, 'Ssh! Manners, dear,' then glaring across at Thomas, 'Leave the room, Thomas, we'll ring when we want you,' and Thomas bowed and went out.

'You mustn't speak to Thomas like that,' said Mrs. Mortimer, she looked at Geoffrey, 'must he, Uncle Geoffrey?'

'Certainly not, not to him.'

'You *never* speak to Thomas unless you are told to,' said Gabriel.

'Eat up, little man,' said Agatha, endeavouring to lighten the atmosphere. It was the general signal to get on with one's dinner.

Robert lowered his head. He did not like all these

people staring at him. He ate quickly, nervously, he spilt his soup, his knife fell with a clatter. Quietly, Agatha bent down and picked it up. She gave him a reassuring smile.

'How's the battle going, Arthur?' asked Geoffrey, looking at his brother, 'bridge still holding?'

He pushed half a potato into his mouth, watched Arthur glower down at him.

'Are we going in on Friday?' inquired Isobel.

Nobody appeared to have noticed her. Now all looked in her direction. She had finished her soup long since, and was patiently waiting for Thomas to come in again.

'I'm going in,' Celia said, she glanced at her husband, 'are you?'

'Of course I'm coming in.'

'No, my day for villaging,' said Geoffrey.

'I'd like to come if there's room,' remarked Agatha, and Isobel said, 'Yes, do come, dear.'

They had not noticed it but Robert was nodding over his empty soup plate, they had suddenly forgotten he was there. The extra chair did not help. But when the plate crashed to the floor everybody looked at him.

'The poor child,' cried Isobel, she leapt out of her chair and went to him.

Without a word, and quite easily, Robert had fallen asleep.

'He's been crying,' said Agatha, 'extraordinary, I never noticed, did you, dear.'

'Never heard a sound,' Geoffrey replied.

Gabriel looked up, 'What's that?' he asked.

'Robert's fallen asleep,' said Isobel, 'and he's been crying, fancy your not noticing it, Gabriel.'

'I was thinking of something else,' stuttered Gabriel, 'sorry, I didn't see.'

'The drains I expect,' said Arthur. 'You did say you were going to see the builder chap about them, I believe, they're in a horrid mess.'

'Of course,' Gabriel replied gruffly. 'Do ring for Thomas, dear,' he said.

'*I* am seeing Griffiths,' Celia said, 'may we now leave the drains in their proper place, if you don't mind, Arthur,' her voice carried an acid note.

They stared at Isobel. She had Robert in her arms. 'Poor little boy.'

'Kid's dead beat if you ask me,' Geoffrey said, 'want any help, Issy?'

'Which is his room?' Isobel walked slowly to the door. It opened, Thomas came in carrying the large tray.

'Can I help, m'm?' he asked, he put down the tray and went to Isobel.

'No you can't,' snapped Arthur, 'get out.'

'Yes, sir.'

'I say, old chap, that's a bit stiff isn't it,' Geoffrey's voice was full of protest. 'What the devil's got you?'

'One moment, *please*,' Mrs. Mortimer was on her feet, she could not conceal her anger. 'How disgraceful. . . .'

'Which room?' inquired Isobel, she was beginning to feel the weight of the boy, heavily asleep in her arms.

'I'll come with you,' Celia said, she pushed back her chair, she called back, 'Don't wait,' and then left the room with Isobel.

'Poor little blighter.'

'He should never have been brought down,' Agatha said, 'ridiculous.'

'But he *did* want to come,' replied Gabriel, 'he did want to come,' his tone of voice was almost apologetic.

'Daddy,' shouted Robert, 'Daddy.'

They sat motionless, listening.

They heard Isobel say, 'There, he's awake now.'

'Daddy.'

Gabriel felt as though a piece of ice had fallen down his neck.

'I want him,' he was crying again, 'Mr. Thomas knows.'

Thomas left the room.

'How distressing,' exclaimed Agatha. She looked at Geoffrey, but he appeared not to have heard; he sat back, head in air, and seemed to be sniffing. He glanced at Agatha and exclaimed under his breath, 'My God! Veal again.'

'You must not,' said Gabriel, the frown he wore caught their attention at once, 'you must *not* act in that way, Arthur. Thomas is only the servant here I know, but he has his rights as well as his duties. You should never put a servant in an embarrassing position like that. I wondered what had come over you, and I'm surprised. You should *not* have ordered him out like that.'

A dead silence came over the room, all eyes were turned towards Arthur.

Only Geoffrey seemed aware of the tray that was lying on the sideboard, and that whatever lay under those dishes was getting cold.

'Whilst I am in this house I will have things done properly and I won't put up with outbursts like that. And from *you*,' continued Gabriel, '*you*. Why I felt quite sorry for Thomas.'

Geoffrey got up, walked to the end of the table and pressed the little button underneath.

'I quite agree with you there,' he said, 'but I think he ought to return and serve. This food is getting cold.'

'Very well,' replied Gabriel, the grudge still pregnant, his eyes never left Arthur, who, staring back at his brother, looking rather stupid, and carrying too high a colour.

Celia and Isobel returned and walked quietly to their places.

'I've rung,' Geoffrey said.

'Thank you,' said Mrs. Mortimer. She sat very erect in her chair. She often found this somewhat tiring, but she hated her disadvantage in height. She thought Nature had been very unfair, and she was conscious of it now; heads towered above her own.

Thomas returned.

'You may serve,' she said.

They remained stonily silent whilst Thomas went round the table. By a flick of her finger she dismissed him. They ate. Nobody spoke. The clock chimed half-past eight; the tones struck into the silent room. They did not look at each other, and they ate leisurely.

'Must we always have calves?' asked Geoffrey. It broke the silence.

'We left Robert fast asleep,' Mrs. Mortimer said, in her quietest tones. 'I had been so hoping that he would forget, but perhaps it's too soon, I'm afraid.'

'There must have been something decent about Dolphin,' remarked Geoffrey. He pushed his plate away, slightly disgusted. 'Only natural for the boy. Loved him of course. Why shouldn't a boy love his father? Had to. Nobody else to love. Elizabeth wasn't there, was she? Fanning herself at Mentone probably. And what about it if he did like fish and chips. As a matter of fact I'd eat some myself if they came along, we had veal Saturday, we had veal Monday. Jug a hare some day. They're about. Get you one tomorrow.'

'You love nothing except your stomach,' Isobel commented.

'And why shouldn't I?'

'Please, dears,' begged Celia, 'it's time for Thomas. We won't have this sort of thing. . . .'

'No, but I feel dashed sorry for that poor little beggar,' continued Geoffrey. 'And we haven't heard the last of it, I'll be bound. I have a feeling . . .' he stopped suddenly as the door opened.

'He'll settle down,' ventured Agatha, 'in a few days he'll have forgotten all that background. He's just a very distressed tired little boy at present. A dreadful shock for one so young and that long journey on the train.'

'Quite right, dear,' Gabriel patted her hand.

Silence again. Thomas had departed. Isobel said, 'Excuse me,' got up and left the room. Geoffrey took the decanter from Gabriel, 'Thanks.' He filled his glass, shot the decanter along to his brother, 'Here, old boy.'

'Thanks.'

Gabriel waited. He said, 'Celia?' and Celia said, 'No thank you, I'll take some coffee later.'

'Agatha?'

'Half a glass please,' and Arthur poured it out.

'Bet that youngster's rousing the house down early in the morning,' said Geoffrey, then, tired of waiting, 'May I?' he looked nervously at Gabriel. Nobody seemed to hear him. He said, 'Pass it along, old boy.'

He took a case from his pocket, said to his brother, 'Have one of these.'

'Rather have my own,' Gabriel replied, 'I often wonder where on earth you pick those things up.'

Agatha got up. She walked down to the window, stood there looking out to black night. The curtains had not been drawn, the cold night air beat on her face.

'Agatha, dear, you'll catch your death of cold standing like that.'

She went and sat by the fire. Celia rose.

'We'll leave you to your own devices,' she said. Agatha joined her and they left.

'I say, he's gone, too, I never noticed, did you?'

Gabriel looked down the table, 'Never even heard the fellow get up.'

'Nor me.' He blew smoke rings. 'Not a bad cigar at all,' he said. Rising, he made himself comfortable in Agatha's armchair.

Gabriel got up, 'Come now,' he said, 'don't hang around here. They want to clear up. You know how they complain if we keep them waiting too long,' and Geoffrey said, 'How you dread offending them, in fact how you dread offending anybody. You'd think Thomas and that girl were the only servants in the world.'

'In these parts they are,' Gabriel said.

They went out together.

V

HE was in the dead room. It had taken a whole day to get the stale air out. The window had been dropped right down. Outside the dark mass of the tree shivered, the swaying branches tapped with wooden fingers against the glass. In the darkened room the night-light glowed like fire. Wood creaked, the curtains moved. When the owl squeaked he quickly buried his head under the bedclothes. He had never heard an owl. He had kissed the good lady good-night, he remembered her leaning over his bed, speaking to him in her soft voice. She smelt of flowers, her hair was soft, her hands soft, stroking him.

'Poor little man,' Mrs. Mortimer crooned, 'go to sleep now. You are *such* a tired little boy. Tomorrow will be a lovely new day.'

'Yes, lady,' Robert said, he looked boldly up at her, 'will I see the lake tomorrow?'

'Your grandmother, darling,' Mrs. Mortimer said, and the boy said, 'Yes, lady grandmother.'

It made her smile, she brushed his cheeks with her lips, 'Good night, dear,' she was gone.

He was alone in the big room, listening to the wind, the owl; he watched a moth fly round the flame, he sat up, listening to a creak on the stairs, the opening and closing of a door.

'What is an owl?'

The owl squeaked again, it might have heard his questioning. Quickly his head disappeared beneath the clothes. He lay motionless, frightened. It wasn't like that other room where he and daddy lived. His eyes opened wide into the tunnel his raised knees had made. How cold the sheets were. Not like the blankets at Rupert Street, daddy and he warm beneath their greyness. Where had daddy gone? What was dead? Those people had never asked him about his daddy, not once. He supposed they didn't like him, those high people, even the doors they passed through were high. They all looked down at him and called him little man. Through the darkness of the tunnel he could see the railway lines all the way back to Paddington, right up the stairs in Rupert Street, right into the room. The policeman was sitting there, he was talking to Mr. Thomas.

'He'll never know, and he wouldn't remember,' the policeman said.

'Who's he?'

Robert spoke into the tunnel in a hushed whisper.

'Daddy,' he said, 'daddy,' and cried quietly in the darkness, and each time the owl squeaked he clutched hard at the cold sheets.

'They don't like my daddy, they don't like him. The cedar quivered under a fresh gust, the wooden fingers tapped at the glass.

'If they ask me about my daddy, I won't tell them, he let his knees sink lower, the tunnel grew longer, narrower, 'I won't tell them, I don't like *here*, I won't stay.'

Suddenly he was asleep. The night-light burned down, waves of wind circled the room. He dreamed. He was running along the tunnel, along the railway lines, his feet hurt, he did not stop running until he reached Rupert Street, he ran upstairs into the room, 'daddy.'

'You've woke him up, are you satisfied?' Dolphin said.

He shut the bedroom door and stood by the table, looking at the remains of the morning meal, still lying

73

there, remembering the mad rush of the morning. 'I hope you're satisfied.'

He stood there, angry, helpless, covered with the dust of the Great North Road. His thick red hair was tousled, the weather-beaten face had the shine of wet leather, the hands resting on the table edge seemed no part of him, but separate from his body. 'You saw him again today.'

Silence.

'You saw him again today.'

He looked across at the woman standing just inside the door; she was dressed, ready to go out. He looked at her with bitter longing. 'You heard.' He loathed her, hated her. 'One day it'll stop for good.'

'It was your loud voice that woke him,' Elizabeth said, and Dolphin shouted, 'Damn you for everything you are.'

Among the Mexican blankets Robert lay listening, through them he could see the yellow of the electric bulb. He felt sick after the supper, he did not like liver like daddy did.

'There'll be an end to it. I was all right when I was in an officer's uniform,' Dolphin growled.

'You make me tired. I think you're a beast, though you don't know it, you haven't enough brains to know it. I wonder what made me do it, I must have been crazy.'

'You were, without the shadow of a doubt,' he said, 'you *are* mad.'

He sat down amongst the debris of that day; he thought, 'It's me, I'm mad.' He looked up, 'You've been out all day?'

She did not answer, he did not move.

'I'll kill that swine if I lay hands on him.'

'You're not clever enough for that.'

Suddenly she sat down, she was calm, she was in no hurry, there was plenty of time. Robert and she had had tea together. She had taken him to a café, Miles', they always had tea together when Dolphin was out; Robert liked tea in the café, she liked it, it was away from this room, which was not her room, and not his, since there was no link to make this room home. Disgust drove her out. Eight years married and he hated her.

'Oh, damn you,' he shouted. He got up and went into the bedroom. As he thought – the boy was crying. Tears, rows, where would it end? His crazy voyage had begun at the Officers Club, and moved, via Purley and Wimbledon, to so many places, always endeavouring to find something, something that would last, something like home: a long voyage, and here was the end of it. Three rooms in Rupert Street. 'What a bloody fool I am,' he said.

'Hello, son,' he said. He sat down on the edge of the bed and played with the boy's fingers.

'Has she gone out?' asked Robert.

'Who, your mother? Yes. To see her friends,' Dolphin said.

'You're on nights now, aren't you, daddy?'

The tiny fingers crawled along the big hand. 'Can I come with you, daddy?'

'Where?'

'Where you're going.'

'It's a long, long way, and dark all the way. Not good for little boys.' He held him in his arms, 'You shouldn't say lady, you should say mother, what makes you talk like that, it's silly.'

'It isn't silly.'

'I say it is.'

'Yes, daddy.'

75

'What did you do at school today?'

'Sums.'

The door of the outer room banged.

'She's gone, I'm a fool, I should have set about her,' he said to himself.

'Where's she gone?'

'I don't know. Some place. If you're a good little boy and go to sleep again I might let you come with me at twelve o'clock,' his father said. 'We'll have a feed together, I know a fine place.'

'Hurrah! Hurrah! Thank you, daddy.' He flung his arms round his father's neck.

'Where did you have tea?'

'At Miles', we had bread and butter and tea and cakes, and hot toast.'

'What time did you come home from school?'

'Same as yesterday, four o'clock.'

'Was your mother in?'

'Yes, daddy.'

'What was she doing?'

'Nothing. She was in the big bed.'

'What did you do?'

'Played with the trains.'

'Did anybody call, did a man come here today?'

'Not today, but on Monday a man came, daddy, he gave me chocolates,' Robert said.

'Go to sleep now, there's a good lad. She always wakes you up, doesn't she?'

'Sometimes, daddy, sometimes.'

'Daddy's going to sleep, too, as soon as he's had something to eat.'

'At the café?'

Dolphin jerked his thumb towards the living-room, 'In there. Go to sleep.'

He went out and banged the door after him. In the

living-room he stripped off his shirt and started to wash from a bucket. The broad shoulders shone under the light; they were browned by sun. As he gave himself a brisk rub down, his eyes slowly took in the whole room and everything in it. He did not like it – the untidiness, the unwashed things, the neglected child. It had been such a good beginning, he had been so proud of her. And now, this. The rot had begun to set in.- They no longer spoke the same language. Each day it became more and more difficult to understand her. He had worked hard for them both, he had done his best. One Saturday he had come home, tired, weary, but happy in heart, to their little house at Purley, and outside the door Robert in his pram. He had worked extra hard that week. He felt proud, he had a big pay packet, he felt on top of the world. The image of her rose clear in his mind; he loved her very much, she was so different from anything he had ever known, and so lovely to look at, it was worth all the grind of the day, just for the satisfaction of coming home to her. She had been so good at the beginning, he felt she really loved him, that it was worth while, he had been so certain of that. She was there, smiling, so clean, so fresh, the house shone, he caught her eagerly and hugged her, 'Elizabeth.'

'Don't do that,'

'Do what, darling?'

'That,' she said, 'for God's sake go and clean yourself up.'

He laughed, 'All right,' he said, and went out and washed and changed, then came back red and shining. They ate.

'Why don't you try and make yourself a little more presentable, a little more gracious, look at your hands, they're filthy really.'

'It's a funny thing, Elizabeth, but it just never occurs to me.' He smiled, the surprise was still to come; he took out the wage packet and handed it to her. 'Here you are, dear,' feeling proud, the work done, the money earned.

'I don't want your money, keep it,' she said.

'What's the matter?'

'Nothing.'

'Well then. . . .'

'Well nothing, I'm sick of you, that's all,' Elizabeth said.

It had hurt him deeply, he had never forgotten the discarded wage-packet, it had meant so much, earnestness, devotion, belief, trust. He had stared so hard at the packet before he flung it to the floor and went upstairs. He found her crying, leaning against the wall.

'Elizabeth, darling.'

'For God's sake leave me alone,' she said, she turned her back on him.

It enraged him, he felt confused, frustrated, he didn't understand it. Below the child was crying in the pram, a neighbour calling, 'Your child is crying.'

'What the hell's come over you?' he asked, flinging himself into a chair. His heart thumped, his hands trembled. 'I'm so happy, I thought you were. . . .'

And the child crying, and the neighbour calling, 'That child will have convulsions if you don't go to it.' Its screams struck his ears like blows.

He went downstairs. For a moment he looked down at the livid face in the pram, purple from screaming, while a neighbour or two looked on from behind green curtains. 'Even the kid's like her,' he thought, searching frantically for something of himself, but there was nothing, as though they had never been man and wife, had never loved.

'Poor little chap,' he said. He bent over the pram and the child stopped crying; it suddenly gurgled, looked up at him. He lifted it out of the pram.

'There's something the matter with your mother, she doesn't like me any more' – he talked to the child – 'something has happened to your mother today.'

He thought of this, lying under the blanket, he had not undressed, he couldn't make the effort.

'What a long time ago,' he thought, 'what a long time ago.'

The moment the clock struck he was up. He glanced down at the sleeping boy. 'I don't know what time she'll come in, she may not come in at all, he'll cry, he always does, he hates being alone. I wonder if it was her who taught him to call her lady, putting ideas into the kid's head, what a bitch.'

'Bobby,' he called, his mouth wet against the boy's ear, 'wake up.'

Robert opened his eyes. 'Where am I? Is that you, daddy?'

'It's me. You can get up, you can come with me if you want to. . . .'

'I want to, please let me come.'

'You'd better hurry then and rub the sleep out of your eyes. We're going that long journey in the dark,' his father said, 'and the big lights shining fine ahead of you, you'll see rabbits running across the road.'

'Rabbits, daddy?'

'Rabbits. Hurry up. You needn't go to school tomorrow,' Dolphin said.

The room smelt of stale air. Dolphin hated open windows, night airs affected his chest. The child began dressing himself.

'It'd be rather wonderful, daddy, if we saw a lion running across the road in front of your big lamps.'
He drew on his trousers.
'D'you love your mother?' he asked.
'Yes, daddy.'
'And me?'
'Yes, daddy.'
'That's all right then.' He hugged him. 'Ready?'
'Ready,' shouted Robert. 'I'm ready.'
'Not many little boys have been on a night journey down the Great North Road, so perhaps you're lucky,' Dolphin said, and suddenly the hardness was gone, the features softened under the instantaneous and gentle recollection of Elizabeth, in the first week of their marriage, themselves lost in the heat and thrill of passionate abandonment, 'the happy days'.
'The happy days,' Dolphin said. 'I wonder what happened. I wonder what made her change. . . .'
'What's that, daddy?'
'Nothing, are you ready now?'
He looked at the dirty muslin on the window, the stains on the wall, the mug half full of cold tea, the grate stuffed with newspapers, the tossed, soiled bed, secure on its vast iron legs, proud with its brass knobs.
'Come along then,' he said. The boy's hand in his hand, they went into the other room. For a moment he stood looking round.
Looking at this room he saw something about it that frightened him; the table itself was never cleared, the carpet was never lifted, the fire was never bright. Odds and ends, the chairs, the sofa. All the way from the Officers Club, all the way from Purley and all the way from Wimbledon, the black afternoon with the screaming child, the pay packet tossed to the floor. He was in the jungle, lost in the uncertainty of the

tunnel, of misunderstanding. Only his heart could reach out, as his hands had reached out for her on that radiant night, big red hands, gentle under the thought of love.

'She's sick of me, she hates me, but I was all right in an officer's uniform,' the grudge as hard as rock, he could feel it as a physical presence, 'she's clever and I'm not. But she must be mad.'

Robert stared up at his father, and waited, and thought of the light flashing, the rabbits scuttling before them, and then the lion, the lion springing. . . .

'Daddy! Daddy!' he screamed, it seemed to wake up the owl, which began to squeak again, and the wind tossed the branches of the cedar, the curtains swayed. He crouched between the sheets, he was lost in the tunnel, he flung off the clothes, he shouted into the darkness, 'Daddy, daddy,' then he stiffened with fright, a face there, a shape moving, the eyes staring back at him. He shut his own, he gripped the sheets, he shouted again, 'Daddy.'

'What's the matter, little man?' Thomas said.

He spoke very softly, he leaned low over the bed and Robert could hear him breathing.

'Tell me. What's wrong. Are you frightened?' Thomas said, and the boy suddenly shot up his hand, held it against his face as though he were expecting Thomas to strike him a blow, but it was only Thomas's teeth glittering in the darkness. The breathing came closer, on his ear, his cheek. 'You'll wake the house up, what are you frightened of?'

Robert heard him moving, he heard a match struck, he opened his eyes and watched. Thomas had put a match to the night-light, he watched him as he bent over the table, he was wearing a big nightshirt, white with blue stripes on it, his hair was covered with oil, his head shone brilliantly under the light. And when he turned Robert saw oil on Thomas's face. It wasn't like Thomas at Paddington, or Mr. Thomas on the train, his face wasn't red any more, but a kind of grey, an ashen look, and the boy thought, 'he uses oil at night to rub the red off his face.'

Thomas's hands came down and rested on either side of the pillow. He smiled. 'You've been dreaming.'

'Open your eyes, little boy,' he said. 'I'm not going to eat you, though I do know at least two little boys who were eaten once upon a time, a long time ago, but eaten just the same. But I'm not going to eat *you*.' The features broke into a grin; it frightened and puzzled the boy.

'As it happens my room is next to yours. I hear the owls squeak, too. I often hear them grinding the mice in their teeth. The wind comes down my chimney, too. I lie listening to it, little boy. Sometimes I think the wind comes right over the hills from my country, just to remind me of the granite and the slate and the rain. You've been dreaming, little man. I could hear you screaming, so then I got up and came in, and here I am,' smiling down. 'You started shouting,' he paused, and then a sudden accusation, 'you've waked up the owls, they're all squeaking now.'

Robert held his eyes shut, he would not look.

'Listen,' Thomas said.

There was something about Thomas's voice, its extreme softness of tone, that made Robert at last open his eyes and look up again.

But there was the oil, the matted hair, the night-shirt, the grin, the expanse of pearly teeth.

'I don't like you,' Robert said, 'you go away.'

'I am going,' Thomas said, 'because *I* don't like *you*,

I don't like any little boy who wakes up screaming and wakes everybody up. Cover yourself up and go to sleep. If you were a very nice little boy I could kiss you good night.'

He stood there, staring at the small, white, frightened face, then he turned away from the bed and the boy watched him walk towards the door, and he was the man with the bowler hat who had given him cake and chocolate on the train, who had sat on the bed in Rupert Street, talking to the policeman. He could see Mr. Thomas's hunched shoulders, the loose nightgown blowing about the bare feet, see the glint on the matted hair. He jumped out of bed, he ran after Thomas, he dug his nails into him. 'What did you do with my daddy?'

Thomas stopped dead. He started at the feel of the nails in his back, he swung round.

'Why, you little beast,' he cried, and gripped Robert by the shoulders. 'You've been dreadfully spoiled, that's what you have. Kicking up all this fuss, waking people up in the middle of the night who have been so kind to you.' He picked him up by his arms and carried him across to the bed, put him down, covered him up, then sat down again on its edge.

'If you really are a good little boy, and I begin to wonder if you really *are*, then say a prayer, even the tiniest little prayer and you'll go to sleep, and perhaps you'll have a lovely dream.'

'What have you done with him?' Robert shouted in a frenzy, 'what have you . . .'

Thomas put a hand on the boy's mouth, then he saw the tears begin to run.

'You be a good boy, go to sleep and dream about your daddy,' he said, and his oiled face came nearer, 'for that's the only way you'll find him now.'

At that moment the door opened. Mr. Mortimer was standing there, looking at them. He had a lighted candle in his hand, he watched.

'What are you doing here, what is the meaning of this?'

'He was having a nightmare, sir, the shouting woke me up, I came in to see if I could do anything.'

'And did you?' Gabriel came over to the bed.

'Why are you crying?' he looked down at Robert.

'I want my daddy, he took my daddy away, I hate him,' Robert shouted, and the tiny fists clenched either side of the pillow.

'I couldn't make him out, sir, I did my best. I think he's frightened here, the noises, the owls, the open window.'

'Are you frightened, little man?'

The boy did not answer, he kept looking at Thomas, and he was crying bitterly. He was far away, and he was lost, and no matter how hard he tried, and how hard he shouted, nobody came. Now he was lost and he couldn't shout any more. The high man was there, the high man who said, 'Your name is Robert Dolphin, what a pity.'

'Return to your room, Thomas. Leave him to me.'

'I did my best,' Thomas said, there was a growl in his voice, 'and I was just leaving the room when he jumped out of bed and came after me like something stark staring mad, sir,' he pulled up the sleeve of the shirt, and Mr. Mortimer saw the blood drawn on the white, hairy skin.

'Go to bed, Thomas.'

'Yes, sir.'

Gabriel put down the candle and sat on the bed.

'Why did you do that?' he asked. 'That was very, very naughty, little man.'

'He did something to my daddy. He caught hold of me, he held me all the time on the train and I wanted to go back and he wouldn't let me. He said daddy wouldn't wake up, but he could, I know he could, and they talked about me.'

'Who talked?' Gabriel suddenly realized he was shivering with cold.

'They did. Mr. Thomas and the policeman.'

'Dry your eyes, Robert,' said Gabriel, he drew a handkerchief from his pocket and wiped the boy's eyes. 'You must not call Thomas *Mr.* Thomas, d'you understand?'

'Yes, sir.'

'I'm your grandfather.'

'Yes, sir.'

'And Mrs. Mortimer is your grandmother.'

'Yes, sir.'

'And the other ladies and gentlemen are your aunts and uncles. Come along, little man, you can sleep in my room for tonight, but only for tonight mind, to-morrow I'll tell Thomas to shoot the owl as soon as ever it squeaks. What were you dreaming about, eh?' He helped the boy up, Robert climbed out of bed.

'How your little heart thumps,' exclaimed Gabriel. He held to the child pressed against him, but Robert had gone down the tunnel again; he was sitting with his father beside the big wheel, the lights were flashing down the road, the rabbits leapt across.

'I wasn't dreaming nothing, sir.'

'Anything, Robert, anything.'

'Anything, sir.'

'This way,' said Gabriel, turning away from the bed. 'Thomas said you were having a nightmare, a night-mare is a very bad dream. You were dreaming about your daddy, poor little chap.'

'I wasn't dreaming about my daddy,' cried Robert. 'I *wasn't.*'

'My bed is nice and warm, you can sleep in it just for tonight. After Thomas has shot the owl you will come back to this room.'

The door closed. They were on the landing. Mrs. Mortimer was standing there. She was dressed in white, she looked frail, she called in a high, shrill voice, 'Is he all right, dear?'

'He's all right, do go back to bed,' replied Gabriel and she went back to her room.

'Hold this candle.'

'Yes, sir,' Robert said.

'No, you'd better not,' said Gabriel, noting the flame begin to dance, the grease drops falling on the dark polished floor.

'Yes,' he thought, 'this is a really *very* frightened child, poor little boy.' The bedroom door shut silently.

They were snug and warm in the bed. Gabriel blew out the candle and lay down. He told himself that this was the most extraordinary thing that had ever happened to him, the child in his own bed, to feel the warmth of the tiny body. He had never imagined any child would lie in a bed at Greys.

'Are you awake?' he asked.

'Yes, sir.'

'You must be a brave little man and not cry any more. Perhaps some day you will tell me all about your father. Then that will be finished and nobody will ask you any more questions, ever again. And you must tell me about your mother.'

Robert lay quiet, his eyes tight shut; he was sitting beside the big wheel, his father was humming a tune between his teeth. He could not see his mother, she was hidden behind the man who had given him the chocolates.

'I won't tell,' thought Robert, 'I won't tell.'

And he said quickly, with a rising voice, 'I won't tell.'

Gabriel was struck by this reply, the ruthlessness of it surprised him.

'Go to sleep. You must be good. You must learn to understand. You must try to see that we are all doing our best to help you, dear. Tomorrow is a new day. Good night,' and he kissed the back of the soft neck, then realized that the boy had fallen asleep, his head in the crook of his arm.

'What an appalling experience for a child. Elizabeth *must* be found, until then we will just do the best we can, but we're so unused to this sort of thing, so totally unexpected. I know Celia will try her best, but even that won't be anything, it's Elizabeth who is wanted here. We must try and contact her, wherever she is.'

'Even if it means having to bring that man here,' visualizing the boy as a life lost, floating on an endless ocean, helpless, without the one anchor that would save.

'I suppose Dolphin was good in his way, poor devil, expect he did his best. There must have been *something* in the fellow. Elizabeth isn't such a fool as all that, I'm certain. Poor devil, what an end.'

He could see the picture a little more clearly now; the last flick of the film, the child crouching over the dead body, in the iron bed, frantic under the clothes, bewildered and frightened, and thinking of this he shuddered at the callousness of the child's mother, his own daughter. If anybody had come to him and forecast such a state of affairs he could only have exclaimed, 'Absurd.' He would have thought him mad.

But the living truth lay warm and palpitating beside him, and he glimpsed in that moment one of the terrors of the world, the world that lay beyond the iron gates of Greys, the gate locked at six o'clock every evening by Thomas.

'What the child needs now is kindness. Celia's got heart, and that's what we lack, really. I'm so weak and stupid myself.'

That was the truth of it, and the truth of it kept him awake, long after the boy's sleep had quickened to calmer depths. Tenderly he reached out and touched the boy's hair, his neck, he was struck by the softness, the living warmth, of the innocence that lay beside him.

'I shall speak to Thomas tomorrow, I'll always regret his having been sent up there, always. He knows too much already. He must have said something to the boy to have frightened him so,' and he could see Thomas standing there in his ridiculous nightshirt, the oiled hair and skin, 'a most repulsive habit,' and something quite new to him. Coming upon Thomas so suddenly in that big room, standing beside *her* bed, he felt he had pried open the deeps and secrets of Thomas's life, a new and ridiculous Thomas.

He thought about Arthur, he often did. Arthur was such a responsibility.

'Saying he must go, how stupid, where could Arthur go now?'

He turned over on his side, he composed himself, he tried to forget about Arthur, but he could not reach a calm area, as though this child had in some way filched sleep from him. He lay and listened to the quiet breathing of Robert.

'Greys will be his, this child's, he'll have it. Oh yes, I must find Elizabeth.'

He thought of life at Greys, floating on a calm lake, the others, their quiet lives, unchanging, and not wanting to change, fast in the unalterable rhythm.

'I'll be satisfied when I see him in her arms.'

Poor, wayward irresponsible Elizabeth. 'I can forgive her now. She was so young, too young to know.'

'Gabriel.'

He started up, exclaimed, 'Who is that?'

'Only me, dear,' Celia said. 'I couldn't rest. And something told me you couldn't rest yourself. This little boy, he's . . .'

'Ssh!' said Gabriel, 'he's fast asleep, poor little beggar. I've never seen anybody so scared, Celia, scared of what, I don't know.'

'But it doesn't matter now. In the morning he will have forgotten all about it.'

'His mother will have to be found,' said Gabriel.

'I expect so,' and he noticed the faint sigh of the voice, like a momentary regret.

'Yes, we must find Elizabeth.'

'Of course. But don't think of that now, Gabriel. You must get some sleep yourself. Leave him here. Come to my room. He won't wake till morning.'

Gabriel stole quietly from the bed, stood motionless for a moment, then whispered, 'I'm afraid if he wakes, he'll start again. He's been so used to having somebody in bed with him. I gather he and his father always slept together, after she ran away from them.'

She stood waiting for him to move, like a white sentinel.

'Come along.'

They tiptoed out.

'It must have been very unhealthy, really,' Celia whispered, as she quietly turned the door knob, 'no child should ever sleep with its parents. . . .'

'No, dear, that's quite right.'

Instantly they stopped, looked back, listened. There was no sound. Robert was out of the tunnel and the noise of the great wheels had ceased. The owls were fast asleep and the lion had sprung.

'He's all right, he's asleep.'

'Yes, dear,' Mrs. Mortimer said, 'and now we must sleep.'

The door creaked as she swung it to.

V I

'AND who *do* you like best in the house?' Uncle Geoffrey asked, and at once the boy answered, 'Aunt Agatha.'

'You *do*, do you. But you like your grandfather and grandmother, too, don't you?'

'They're never nice about my daddy, but Aunt Agatha was,' replied Robert.

He stood with his hands clasped behind his back, looking up at this very tall man, who was at that moment changing his shirt.

'What a lot of hair you have on your chest, Uncle Geoffrey,' said Robert.

Geoffrey burst out laughing, Robert laughed. 'You're an observant child.'

'A what, I'm not a child, I'm a boy,' protested Robert. 'Shall we go on the lake again today?'

'Definitely no,' Uncle Geoffrey replied, he put on a tie. Then he crossed to a chest of drawers, saying, 'You do want to see my medals?'

'Oh yes, goody,' cried Robert. He ran across the room, 'are they real gold?'

Geoffrey nodded. He glanced around the room. This was the boy's first visit to it; they were alone in the house, Thomas having driven the rest of the family into Helton. Gabriel at the last moment refused, but after much persuasion elected to go with them, but he did not want to go, he felt unhappy about it, and Celia looking at him was again disturbed by his appearance. There had been some confusion at the start, the car for some reason had refused to start, but Thomas's ingenuity eventually triumphed. Robert was keenly disappointed at not being able to go. Aunt Agatha had waved to him from the window and promised to bring him something nice from Helton. This fact was registered very securely in a corner of the boy's mind, and even his keenness to see uncle Geoffrey's youthful triumphs did not cloud it out. Geoffrey had been detailed to look after him until the party's return at five o'clock. They themselves would be going on to a neighbour's for tea.

Uncle Geoffrey felt a keen delight in the companionship of this boy, though he revealed it only at certain high moments, and one of these had been in their sail round the lake. Robert seated in the stern of the small boat had explored many seas and oceans. But one can be on a lake too long, one can row too long, and an ageing athlete knows the time to stop. He had forestalled Robert's greediness and disappointment by promising to show him his cups and medals. Here they were now, arrayed for the boy's inspection, whilst Geoffrey stood by, trying to remember how many years it was since anybody had shown such a keen interest in his youthful glories. There they were, the medals, the cups, the swords, the photographs, the groups of well-fed, confident-looking graduates, the dumb-bells, the indoor rower which he could screw to the floor, sending plaster and dust into the drawing-room below, much to the annoyance of Thomas and Joan who had to clean up the mess.

Robert admired this tall, broad-shouldered man with the hair on his chest. He sat quietly in the chair, watching his uncle moving one object after another with careful, admiring fingers. He had changed into a blue shirt and blazer. Robert could see the small bald patch at the back of his uncle's head whenever he bent down.

'Look,' Geoffrey said, and smiled as he saw the boy's open mouth.

'Ooh!' cried Robert, 'and is that *real* gold? Can I hold it in my hand?'

'Of course,' and thought, 'what a long, long time it is since I had such an admirer.'

'What did you get that for, Uncle Geoffrey?'

'Running, little man, running ten miles,' he patted the boy's head, and heard him say, 'How far is that?'

'A long, long way. Here's a cup for boxing,' and from a small cardboard box he took his favourite prize. He removed the tissue paper, he read from the inscription, 'GEOFFREY MORTIMER, LIGHT-HEAVYWEIGHT CHAMPIONSHIP, 1917.'

'Isn't it lovely, and it's bigger than the other one.'

'Here's something else,' uncle said, tremendously pleased at the child's interest. He glanced round the walls. How much there was to show him.

'There,' said Geoffrey. He took down a sword from the wall and gave it to Robert; the silver handle flashed in the tiny hand. 'And what do you think of that, eh?'

'Ooh! Are you a great man, Uncle Geoffrey? My daddy was. He used to drive a big lorry, it had eight wheels, it was bigger than this room.'

Geoffrey took away the sword. 'That's the best one of the lot,' he said.

'My daddy is like you.'

Geoffrey did not answer. He thought of Gabriel's, 'You must try not to mention his father, you must never make reference to him, discourage the boy, he'll soon forget. Nothing will go right until he does.'

'Well,' thought Geoffrey, 'I'm doing my duty. Without doubt there would come a time when the boy would forget he had ever had a father.'

'*This* one,' he said, removing the other sword from its hook, 'I won that in India.'

'Where's India?'

'A long way off. On the other side of the world, Robert.'

'Is the other side of the world like this?' asked the boy, just as the door opened and Joan put her head in.

'Yes, Joan?'

'I've laid out the tea, sir, it's just four o'clock.' She gave Geoffrey a sheepish sort of smile, she always did.

'Thank you,' replied Geoffrey. He began to hang up the swords, he wrapped the cups up in their tissue paper, he put the boxes carefully back in the bottom drawer, he carefully wrapped the medals and put them away.

'I wonder why she always smiles at me like that, the little ninny. I believe there's an invitation behind that smile every time.'

'Off we go,' he cried, 'shall we slide down the banisters like yesterday?'

Robert shrieked with delight. 'Oh yes, let's, Uncle Geoffrey,' and rushed out of the room.

Geoffrey, feeling a loosening up of muscle, at once ran after him; they slid down together and arrived in a heap at the foot of the stairs.

'Hurrah.'

'Hurrah. That was a good one, wasn't it?' Robert shouted at the top of his voice.

'Ssh! Not so loud, little man,' Geoffrey cautioned, and grasping his hand rushed off with him to the drawing-room.

'Why do you say "little man"?'

Robert sat up, looked boldly across at his uncle.

'Because you are a little man, I suppose.' Geoffrey began pouring out tea.

'Will I be as big as you one day?'

'I hope so. Look! Joan has made some nice fresh scones, do you like scones?'

'Yes,' replied Robert, and stuffed his mouth at once.

Geoffrey sat watching him. Without a doubt there was something about the boy, a winning quality. He had been so interested in those things, he was so full of life.

'You're a fine, healthy little animal,' he said.

'I'm not an animal, I'm a boy.'

'That's quite enough,' Uncle Geoffrey replied. 'Get on with your tea like a good child. And do try to behave like a little boy. Sit up straight in your chair, and don't stuff your mouth like that.'

'No, Uncle Geoffrey,' Robert mumbled, he assumed a serious expression, 'I want to be big like you, Uncle. I want to win medals and cups, and that shining silver sword. . . .'

'Then sit up and be a little man.'

'Yes, Uncle Geoffrey, could I have some more scone, please?'

'That's the boy.'

'I wonder,' Geoffrey thought, 'just how much Gabriel likes having him here. If there had been anywhere else, would he still have had him?'

'It's quite astonishing the way that boy has taken to Geoffrey,' Gabriel remarked as, his wife on his arm, they strolled together down the drive.

Mrs. Mortimer, very preoccupied, answered after a pause, 'Yes, isn't it.'

'You're miles away, dear,' he said. 'I do wish when you come out for a walk that you wouldn't go off daydreaming. You're always accusing us of doing it. What on earth are you thinking about?'

'Lots of things,' replied Celia, her head high in the air.

'You drag me out,' he protested, 'and then you wander off somewhere, one can't get hold of you at all.'

She laughed. 'It's a curious thing, but sometimes when I'm bustling about in the kitchen, helping Joan, I become suddenly conscious that right over my head is a bed of stagnation. I often wonder what you do up in that room of yours, hours on end. You ought to get about more, dear, it's not good to be stuck in like that, the others barely see you, and it's a bad thing to be so wrapped up in yourself all the time. Actually I'm hoping to see something of a change in this house, and I think it's a good thing that boy has come here. He's certainly turned Geoffrey into a new man.'

'That's Geoffrey's nature, comes natural to him, he likes gadding about, always did, and besides he's twelve years younger than me.'

'Getting you out for a bit of fresh air is like taking the crutches away from a cripple, the white stick out of the blind man's hand,' Celia said.

'Well, here we are, I've come out. Are you satisfied? You know quite well that I like to be left alone in the mornings. The rest of the day I'm willing to share, but mornings, they are my own, dear.'

'And in the afternoon when Geoffrey and the girls' — she always referred to Agatha and Isobel as 'the girls' — 'are about, you're nowhere to be seen. Why you hide yourself away heaven only knows.'

'I've come out for a walk,' Gabriel said, 'not a sermon.'

She leaned against him and pressed his arm, 'Tell me, dear, why was Thomas so long in your room this morning, and I thought you looked very worried when you came out. Is there something which only he and you can share? There's nothing wrong, I hope?'

'Nothing.'

'Is Arthur upsetting you? He has me. He infuriated me, he acted like a peasant this morning.'

'It's either God or the raging lion,' said Gabriel, 'I've never seen a man make so much out of his misfortunes. He wallows in self-pity. This morning he talked to me of going away. . . .'

'That would be the best thing he could do,' said Celia.

'Maybe. But where can he go? Can you think of any place? I'm worried about him.'

'Couldn't he go to one of the Colonies, Gabriel?'

'He hasn't a cent.'

They had reached the gate. 'We had better turn back,' she said. 'How that boy has taken to Geoffrey and Agatha, Isobel seems rather jealous.'

Gabriel laughed. 'Geoffrey and Agatha are nice people, Agatha I love very much, in fact she's my favourite.'

'Poor Arthur. What a pity he ever entered the Church,' Celia said, and Gabriel exclaimed gruffly, 'Lord, are we back on that thing again? How any man can sit in that room day after day, and week after week, doing absolutely nothing but read, and when he isn't reading commiserating with himself, I really don't know. Sometimes I wish he'd really break out and do something, even if it only meant rushing about the house smashing things up. I'd forgive him anything in the world if he showed the slightest nobility of spirit, which is what I most admire in men. But to lie with your tail between your legs, sulking and pitying yourself because of one foolish action which

cannot be erased is, to say the least of it, disgusting.
Though I hardly ever see him, I know he's there,
stuck in that room, you can feel Arthur all over the
place. Look at Agatha, look at Isobel for that matter.
Now there are two women who had cruel disappoint-
ments in their lifetimes, but do they ever show it,
no, and never will.'

They had reached the house.

'He was always different from the rest of you,' Mrs.
Mortimer said, 'always.' She was rapidly forgetting
Arthur, the Mortimers were receding into the distance,
she could only think of the kitchen, wonder what Joan
was doing, and, looking at her watch, suddenly regret
the lateness of the hour. She had better hurry away.

'I expect you'll sit and mope yourself until lunch-
time,' she said, she smiled and went off, leaving him
standing on the lawn.

'Awkward bringing Arthur up like that,' he thought,
'I do wish the fellow would do something. I doubt
very much if I can keep him any longer. And this
thing has gone so far now, it's difficult to retreat. I've
tied myself in a nice little knot. If only I could be like
Agatha, she's so calm, so unperturbed . . .' and then
he was listening to Celia again.

'He was always different from the rest of you, last
in everything. From wherever he came he arrived too
late, he doesn't somehow fit in.'

'How very true,' he thought, he felt a sudden ad-
miration for Celia, 'how very true.'

'More tea? How about one of these lovely biscuits,'
said Geoffrey. He looked at the clock, 'they'll be back
any moment now,' he thought, he wished they
wouldn't, he was enjoying himself, he had never
enjoyed himself so much. It was Robert who stole

into his bedroom at night to hear the stories told, it was Robert who woke him at the too early hour of half past seven in the morning, it might become a perfect orgy of story reading. It was Robert who disinterred the memories, revived the old glories. They roamed the house, the stables, the attics, explored the lanes, climbed the hills, spent hours in the spinney. The eels in the river had forgotten the long shadow on the water, the flash of the hook, the rabbits nibbled in peace in spinney and lawn. The crows sat high in the trees and croaked with abandon, the rooks perched in peace, Geoffrey had moved into new country.

'Why doesn't Uncle Arthur come down to tea with us?' asked Robert.

'Uncle Arthur always takes tea in his room,' began Geoffrey, when he was interrupted by, 'But he doesn't come down to lunch either, Uncle Geoffrey.'

'When he's not feeling very well he likes to have his meals in his room.'

'Is he ill?'

'I hope not,' Geoffrey replied, 'have another biscuit, Robert?'

'Thank you.'

He smiled at his uncle. 'Can I go and see Uncle Arthur?'

'Afraid you can't, little man. I don't think he likes little boys very much.'

'Why?'

'Another scone?' Uncle Geoffrey said, 'I do like these cream ones, don't you?'

'They are nice of course, but I don't want any more now, thank you, uncle.'

Geoffrey suddenly sat up. 'I thought I heard the car, did you?'

'Why doesn't he like little boys?'

'I don't know, I've never asked him.'

'Shall I ask him, Uncle Geoffrey, shall I ask him now?' Robert got up, and at once Geoffrey rose, too.

'No,' he said, 'your uncle is very busy at the moment, I know he is, he is reading. Do you read?' he asked, as he pushed the boy back into the chair; he had never read a book in his life, and the cups and medals, the heads and skins had always ruled out the possibility of a bookcase in the room.

'Daddy used to read to me,' Robert said, he sat up, his eyes shone, he was proud of his father. 'I think my daddy would like you, but he can't now because he's dead. I know he's dead, Mr. Thomas told me. . . .'

'Thomas,' said Geoffrey, correcting again.

'Every night he used to read to me in bed, sometimes I dream about my daddy.'

'Do you indeed? And mummy, too, I expect you do.'

He pushed back his chair and got up. 'Suppose we go down the drive and watch for the car coming back, shall we?'

'Oh yes,' Robert shouted. 'We'll sit on the gate and wait for it to come up. Shall we run down the drive, like you used to run when you won all those medals. . . .'

Geoffrey groaned inwardly at the very thought.

'I rather think not. Come along, Joan is waiting to clear away. This way.'

They went through the window on to the lawn.

'Do let's run,' cried Robert, and Geoffrey said, 'You run and I'll catch you.'

He was breathless before he had reached the top of the drive. The boy seemed to move on wings, he floated into the drive, it made him feel uncomfortable.

'I *am* in a shocking state, by heck. I *must* do something about this, what a kid, I'm so glad he came. I like to hear him shouting and running all over the place. By God, it may be the making of this place, clear out the cobwebs. It makes you realize what a mouldy lot we really are.'

He puffed his way down the drive, he cried, 'Wait,' but the boy did not hear, Geoffrey stopped dead and roared into the distance, 'Stop.'

'I'm right out of condition,' he thought.

The boy's interest had gladdened him, and had also made him sad. The slack muscles, the paunch, the flabby flesh filled him with memories of bygone triumphs, 'Awful thing age, awful.'

The boy was sitting on top of the gate waiting, watching him come slowly down.

'There's six o'clock striking,' Uncle Geoffrey said, 'they'll be here any minute now.'

'I know it's six o'clock, daddy taught me the clock.'

'You're a smart boy.'

'Am I, Uncle Geoffrey?'

'Yes, you are very smart,' he replied as he climbed up the gate and sat beside him. He looked at Robert's ruffled hair, the bright eye, the nose. 'It's her all right, without a doubt. Wonder what he looked like? Queer sort of fish, I believe, though you can't believe everything you hear. Poor devil. What an end. She could be as hard as nails, yet I'll swear she never got it from us, we're the other way, too soft. But you can't alter the frame-work.'

It was too late, twelve o'clock had struck, and the sun had gone in.

'We all had our chances, we *like* this sort of thing, we can't change. Too far down the river.'

'I can hear a car,' Robert shouted, all attention. He jumped down and started to pull back the gate.

'Half a minute,' said Geoffrey, his fifteen stone

balancing precariously at the top, and he got down very carefully and helped the boy to push it back. He could see the old Bentley coming up the drive, panting as usual. 'Astonishing how that car has lasted all these years.'

As it drew nearer he could hear something grinding in its rear. Then he glimpsed Agatha's face, Agatha's hand waving to the boy from the window. The boy's sudden yell as he ran towards it pierced Mr. Mortimer's ears, he had come to dread these wild shouts, the Red Indian whoops of delight or dismay, they woke him in the morning, they confused him, the alien sound eating into the pattern work of Greys.

'Hello, darling,' cried Agatha, as the car came slowly through the gate, 'I hope you've been a good boy.'

'I have, haven't I, Uncle Geoffrey?' as the car passed them and went on up the drive.

'You've been very good, little man,' replied Geoffrey, they walked slowly back towards the house, Geoffrey's hand on the boy's shoulder. The car vanished under the trees.

Robert was suddenly withdrawn and silent. He could hear his uncle talking to him, but he did not answer him, his gay spirits had deserted him. The protecting arm on his shoulder was only the next step to 'time for supper', which meant bed. He dreaded the big room, the desert, he could not get used to it, after the warmth of daddy under the Mexican blankets. In an hour he would be alone again, lost in the desert.

'You're very quiet, Robert,' said Geoffrey as they went into the house.

But the boy was now too far away to hear him; he

allowed himself to be led towards the small room behind the drawing-room which Mrs. Mortimer had turned into a sort of private dining-room for him. Here the boy had his supper alone. Here he waited for the dread knock on the door and the chill of Joan's voice saying, 'Ready, Master Robert.'

And he was always ready to be led off. They took it in turns to shepherd him to bed, sometimes Agatha, sometimes Geoffrey, once, Aunt Isobel. He did not like Aunt Isobel, but he did not really know why. Promptly at a quarter to seven Joan came in and took him along to the bathroom. She had forgotten the horror of the first bath, and was proud of her accomplishment. Robert cleaned his teeth, he combed his hair, he trimmed his nails, but he hardly spoke a word to the girl in the bathroom. Like Aunt Isobel she was too authoritative, her keen and direct way of handling him was so different from Uncle Geoffrey and Aunt Agatha. Joan would stand no nonsense, she knew how children ought to behave and on that first evening had put Robert securely in his place, indifferent to tears.

'So far as I'm concerned you're just a little animal, and nothing else.'

'I'm not an animal,' and the boy had splashed water over her.

She had pressed him forcibly under the water. 'Oh, yes you are, Master Robert,' and had scrubbed thoroughly. Robert came out shining and fresh, but very subdued. When the tall people had seen him they all smiled, and seemed pleased at the sight.

He was back again now, his napkin round his neck, he hated this, he sat waiting for his supper. Geoffrey said, 'Have a nice supper.'

'Do stay, Uncle Geoffrey?' and then the girl came in with the tray.

'I'm afraid not, little man,' replied Uncle Goeffrey, 'time for you to be off to bed,' he bent down and kissed the boy good night.

'Good night,' Robert said, sad, pleading, but Geoffrey shook his head, this really was the end of the day.

Later when a knock came to the door Robert knew it wasn't Joan. Joan never knocked on his door, but walked straight in and gave orders in a loud voice, 'Hurry up now and remember I'll be back soon.' And then he saw Aunt Isobel's head peeping round the door.

'Hello, Robert,' she said, and came in.

She sat watching him eat. Robert said 'Hello,' then pushed away his plate. He immediately got up. He came round to Aunt Isobel, 'Aunt Isobel.'

'Yes, dear?'

'Can't I stay up, just for once,' pleaded Robert. 'Daddy used to let me stay up often.'

'I'm afraid you can't, dear, grandfather likes you to be in bed early, he wants you to have plenty of sleep and to grow up a big man like him. Besides you're up too early in the morning, Robert. Go and finish your milk.'

'Would you like to come for a walk with me tomorrow,' asked Isobel.

Robert bent over his plate, he looked at her under his eyes.

Isobel felt slightly jealous of her sister, and resented her brother Geoffrey's monopolizing of the boy. 'Finished,' she asked, 'that's quick.'

He came round to her, he leaned against her and smiled. Suddenly she caught him in her arms, 'You are a nice child, really, I'm so glad you came here.'

'I'll go with you for a walk tomorrow,' said Robert, slowly seating himself in Isobel's lap, he paused, 'if you will let me stay up, I will.'

'What a cute child,' she thought, 'bargaining already.'

'No, Robert I'm afraid you can't. Your grandfather won't allow it.'

'Grandfather didn't like me today,' Robert said, 'and I know it was because I asked him if I could sleep with him tonight.'

Isobel smiled.

'Grandfather was quite right, little boys sleep in beds of their own.'

'Not all of them, I didn't, and I know others, too.'

'Come along now,' Isobel said, with the firm authority of a hospital matron, 'come along, dear,' and led him towards the door.

She felt displeased that a child should have made such an ordinary thing as a walk into an excuse for disobeying her brother's strict rule. She shut the door with a loud bang and said, 'Run along now,' and followed him up the stairs.

Half way up he stopped and turned round to her.

'I'm cold,' he said.

'What nonsense,' she said.

They reached the bedroom. She told him to undress, she told him that this was his mother's room, that was her bed, there was her little table, here her books, 'See,' opening the wardrobe door, 'there are mummy's clothes. Mummy used to sleep in this very bed,' concluded Aunt Isobel.

She sat on the bed and watched him undress.

'She's not my mummy now because she's gone away,' Robert said, and Aunt Isobel was struck by the hardness in the childish voice, a kind of resentment.

He put on his pyjamas. He looked at the big embroidered curtains that would soon be drawn, the night-light that would be lit, the piled darkness beyond the window. He looked at the stout, grey-haired woman sitting on his bed, 'It's so cold here, Auntie.'

'Get into bed like a good boy. If you are very good and go to sleep and don't make noises, I'll read you a lovely story tomorrow. Come along, in you get.'

He did not look at her, he did not answer, Aunt Isobel was like Joan. He did not like her.

'I'm afraid,' the boy said.

'Tut, tut,' said Isobel, 'say your prayers now, come along, kneel up.'

He knelt, he repeated the words after her, she bent down and kissed him.

'Nighty-night, darling.'

He did not reply. He put his head beneath the clothes. He drew up his knees, he made the tunnel. He didn't like this place, he would run away from here, far away. He didn't like anybody really, except Uncle Geoffrey. Grandfather hardly noticed him now. Slowly his head appeared from under the sheets. He looked at the curtains, the waiting dragons, he would climb on a dragon's back; there was the ship on the wall, he would sail in that. He lay listening, he heard a downstairs door banged and he knew Aunt Isobel had gone. The room was silent, and on the table that seemed so far away the night-light glowed. He got out of bed and went to the window. His hands trembled on the sash, he felt terribly afraid of the blackness outside, he remembered the story his father had told him of the wolves in the forest, and he dreaded the blackness. The branches of the cedar moved, the tree sighed, he drew back, gripping the sash firmly in his hands. He shut his eyes and pressed hard. The window slammed down with a loud bang. Then he crept back into bed.

'At first they used to ask me about my daddy, and now they don't ask any more.' The head vanished under the bedclothes. He felt angry, why had they stopped asking him questions about his daddy? Perhaps they didn't care about him any more.

'I wish my daddy were here,' the boy broke into loud sobs, he shut tight his eyes, he gripped the sheets, 'Daddy, oh, daddy, I wish you were here.'

The sights and sounds of the day, packed tight in his mind, slowly tumbled out. He followed himself about, he could see Uncle Geoffrey rowing the boat, he recited the names of the five oceans and the seven seas about which Uncle Geoffrey had talked so much. He could hear Uncle Geoffrey laughing when a small wave overlapped, came into their boat. He saw Aunt Agatha's soft white hand waving to him from the window of the car, he heard Aunt Isobel say to his grandfather, 'I hope you saw that man Griffiths about the drains.' What were drains? Who was Mr. Griffiths?

He suddenly stiffened himself in the bed. He heard movements in the next room. He knew Mr. Thomas was there. Only once since he had come from Paddington had he caught sight of Thomas, but, lying awake, early in the morning he had heard his plodding steps in the yard, going towards the garage, the door opening with loud creaks, which reminded him of the owl. He wanted to see Thomas in the garage, but why, each time he sneaked past the kitchen door, did Joan pop out of the kitchen, as though she were hiding behind the door, waiting for him, why did she push him along and say, 'You mustn't come in this part of the house, Master Robert, you mustn't come.'

The question moved round and round in Robert's mind. And why did Uncle Arthur not like little boys?

Uncle Arthur sat at the dinner table, but he wasn't shaved and clean like the others, he didn't wear a collar and tie like grandfather and Uncle Geoffrey.

The fiery eyes of a dragon were staring at him. He didn't like this room. Why was grandfather so angry when he asked if he could sleep with him? Why did these people stay in their rooms and only come out to eat? Why, when he went towards the kitchen did Joan shriek and Thomas laugh? They were so angry when he looked in through the kitchen door.

'They don't like my daddy, I know they don't, grandfather looks angry when I speak about him.'

Robert opened his eyes. There was nothing there. Only the darkness, the tiny light, the cold feel of the sheets.

'I think I like Uncle Geoffrey best of all.'

'Tomorrow we'll have a picnic, we'll go into the spinney and I'll show you how to catch a rabbit. We'll have sandwiches and cake and a big bottle of milk. It'll be fun,' Uncle Geoffrey said, and there he was, looking at him from the other end of the tunnel, the tall man with the sandy hair, he was putting on a blue sweater.

'What a lot of medals he's got,' Robert thought. 'Real gold. And all those cups, and the swords. And he laughs and laughs, he's not like the others, I like Uncle Geoffrey best of all.'

'No,' grandfather said.

'Please don't bother me now, dear,' grandmother said.

'No,' shrieked Joan, 'you can't go that way.'

'No,' said Aunt Isobel, 'not this evening, perhaps another evening.'

'I don't think so, darling,' Aunt Agatha said, 'we'll see tomorrow.'

Robert could see them all, there they were, all lined up for judgments.

Suddenly they all shook their heads and cried, 'NO.'

But if he shut his eyes tightly and pressed his knuckles against them, they would all go away. He lay wide-eyed, staring at the ceiling, watching the shadow cast by the night-light, feeling the tree move outside his window. The owl was squeaking again, but he wasn't afraid any more. He was only frightened of forgetting daddy, the dark room in Rupert Street. He had forgotten the dark man who had come there one morning and taken his mummy away, but he remembered the big box of chocolates, the smiling woman on the blue cover, the scent of the box. Once Aunt Agatha had given him a fruit drop out of a paper bag. They weren't like other people. They did not eat chocolates or sweets. Daddy gave him sweets nearly every day. The woman next door gave him caramels, even the policeman had given him a packet of sweets the morning Mr. Thomas had taken him away.

'Stop crying,' the policeman said, 'I'm sure your daddy is very happy.'

Robert sat up in the bed. He knew now. 'Thomas knows,' he cried. 'Thomas knows. Thomas knows where daddy went.'

Tomorrow he would sneak past the kitchen door, he would find Mr. Thomas, he would say, 'Where is my daddy?'

'If they don't ask me about daddy any more I'll know . . . they don't care about him any more.'

They wouldn't let him go with them in the motor-car this afternoon, they left him with Uncle Geoffrey, and when he sneaked to the kitchen door that was

when Thomas was laughing and Joan shrieked. He
would ask Thomas in the morning, and then he would
run away from here, he didn't like them, it wasn't
like Paddington any more, 'it's so cold here.' Only
Uncle Geoffrey laughed, the others shook their heads
saying, 'NO.'

'Of course if I run away from here Uncle Geoffrey'll
cry, I know he will.' Perhaps Uncle Geoffrey would
run away, too. Perhaps he would ask him tomorrow.
He was sure Uncle Geoffrey would like a ride in
daddy's big lorry, the big wheels would screech as
the lorry rushed down the hill. Uncle Geoffrey would
see plenty of rabbits running in the light, in front of
the big wheels.

'Have you ever seen a lion, uncle?'

'Lots of them.'

'Have you really?'

'Yes, I shot half a dozen lions in my time, one
sprang at me once.'

'How exciting. Once daddy told me I'd see a lion
running across the road in front of his lorry if I wished
hard enough.'

'Indeed. Where?'

'On the North Road.'

'Just fancy that.'

As he had the night before, the boy cried himself
to sleep.

VII

I T was often Arthur's habit, on nights when he couldn't sleep, to get up and dress and go downstairs. The ghostly footsteps worried nobody. He would go into the pantry and spend perhaps five minutes replenishing himself with odd bits from the dishes. Usually, after that, the front door closed and Arthur was out. Nobody worried, nobody wondered where Arthur might go. They supposed for a walk. To a household that retired at a certain hour, and made a strict point of this, Arthur's habit, though tolerated, was looked upon as a little odd. It certainly didn't seem right for him to be roaming about the house, and, as they correctly surmised, roaming about the lanes, too. And once right through the sleeping village. The idea of Arthur bumping into Police Constable Ware on his night prowl had worried Gabriel quite a bit, but, like most of his worries, this one remained strictly private. Agatha, who often read into the early morning, being a prodigious reader of old books, could, even from her room at the end of the corridor, hear Arthur moving about in his. He had been moving around for some time; once she had heard two distinct thuds as of some object falling, but she had dismissed this and calmly continued with her reading. It was half past one in the morning. Suddenly she lay the book down, wondered *what* he might be doing, and at that precise moment the footsteps ceased. Probably, she thought, he's walking up and down the room to tire himself out, for her brother had the mariner's habit, and any room of his became, after a few days, any ship's bridge. She listened for a while longer, and then noted what seemed to her the final silence. She went on casually with her reading.

Arthur had entirely suspended movement. He lay quite motionless, with closed eyes, but very wide awake. He was intent, he was watching a film, his film. The film projected fantastically, he saw the end first. A tall, heavily built man with bent shoulders was walking away into the distance, towards an always receding horizon. This made him remember the packed suitcase at the end of the bed. Had he forgotten anything? And he went over the contents in his mind. A black suit, a grey suit, two pairs of flannels. A sports jacket, two of Geoffrey's collars, three ties, three pairs of walking shoes. His Shakespeare, his Horace, his pocket Spinoza, and lying at the bottom of the case his note case, his letters, his photographs, his pipes. Arthur had made up his mind. He was going. Where precisely he did not know, and at the moment it did not seem to matter very much. What mattered was that he had made up his mind. The suddenness of his resolution had shocked him. Slowly he opened his eyes; the tense expression softened under a knowing smile. He sat up and looked around the room.

'At last they'll be able to come in and clean it out.'

He thought of the surprise they'd get at seeing it empty, he could see them all crowding in, their ransacking eyes, looking for mysteries, secrets.

'I'll go, just like that,' he thought, then he rolled himself quietly off the bed and went to the door. A stair creaked as he went down. This time he by-passed the pantry, he wasn't hungry, he would go out by the rear entrance. The damp breath of the long stone corridor caught him roughly as he turned the corner. He opened the door and went out, he drew it quietly shut behind him. A moon was up. The night seemed coffined in a frozen silence. He walked up the back drive, passed through the open gate and found himself on the lawn in front of the house. He stood for a moment looking away towards the hills, and then he sensed the extraordinary silence. The house rose frigid under the cold light. He walked to the end of the lawn and sat down on the seat. For a long time he sat staring back at the house. He felt suddenly at peace with himself. He could not remember ever feeling like this, so calm, so resolved. So often had he hurried away from the house, as far away as possible, tramping the lanes, climbing the hill, endeavouring to tire himself out thoroughly, in order that he might go back and fall quietly asleep. The windows looked down on him like enormous eyes, he thought of the sleepers behind them, and then he noticed the light still on in Agatha's room. Had she heard him go out? Bound to have done.

'I'll push off around six o'clock, I'll walk to Marles, I'll catch that first train to London.' Here the map finished abruptly, the future was uncertain after that. But he must keep his mind fast on the main object, getting away. As far away as possible. He could go on no longer. He was simply living on his brother. Something was worrying Gabriel. He wondered what it could be. The very atmosphere of the house had changed in recent weeks. It wasn't the boy, nothing so innocent as that. He could read Gabriel's mind like a book.

'I should have got out long ago. And yet, if I'd been in Geoffrey's position, or even Agatha's, I wouldn't go. I'd stay on.'

Life had seemed to finish very abruptly that sunny

afternoon two years ago when he sat waiting in the oak panelled room for the Bishop to come in. His words had made a deep groove across Arthur's mind. 'You have drowned innocence.'

'I've been a damned fool,' he thought.

He stared up again at the lighted window, it accentuated the darkness and silence of the others. What had he done since then? Nothing. Moped in his room for two years, pitied himself, cut himself off from the rest of the family. Taken advantage of his brother's generosity, his one weakness. How they had all sympathized. He remembered the evening he had returned home. He remembered the eyes.

'Well?' Gabriel said.

'Damned bad luck, old boy,' Geoffrey speaking.

'A nice thing indeed,' exclaimed Isobel.

'Poor Arthur,' said Agatha.

Celia's silence, and Thomas's smile, 'Nice to see you back, sir,' as if it really was. Feeling suddenly cold he got up and began pacing the lawn. He supposed that, in their way, they were happy here. One had stayed, kept the ship anchored, the others had wandered far, and now returned home. And he had got as far as Cambridge and back. The world shrank. He thought of days in their lives, a winter's day. The great damp house and the dead air, the eyes at the morning windows, sensing the coming day, and down in the too hot kitchen Joan and Thomas contriving. The movement from rooms, down the big, chilly staircase, and the thought of returning before they had even reached the breakfast room. The silent meal, the fugitive glances at each other, which seemed to say, 'What on earth is it all for?' And afterwards the study for Gabriel, the spinney and the fields and the set traps for Geoffrey. The kitchen for Celia, the lukewarm morning-room for Isobel, and new obituaries in *The Times*, and knitting for Agatha. Walks in the gardens, excursions to the village, out to tea with friends, exchanging boredoms, sharing a fellow feeling for dampness. The summer mornings that sent sun streaming to the rooms, warming the chilled bone, a feeling of lightness. Chairs on the lawn, Agatha absorbed in her flowers, Geoffrey mending rods on the lawn, Isobel off for mannish walks in the hills, enjoying a mannish stride. The spring that could bring nothing new, the resignation of autumn.

'Yet they're happy, they are content. They want nothing more.' He looked away towards leaden-tipped hills, he suddenly turned and walked back by the way he had come. In his room he sat down on the bed.

'They'll think I've gone because of this boy, but they'll be wrong. It's true it gave me a shiver when I heard he was coming.'

He bent down and ran his hand over the packed suitcase. He glanced around the room. Then he got up and crossed to the mantelpiece, his fingers touched ornaments, pictures on the wall, pulled at the curtains, fondled the small clock – he had a fondness for these things, they were very close to him. If he went they would all come in to look. Then Thomas or Joan would start to clean it up. Everything would be moved, things altered. He continued to move slowly round the room, he gave every single object a warm glance, in two years they had built themselves into his little world. Lying in the grate, carefully wrapped in tissue paper, lay the collars he would not wear again. He bent down and stared at this, then he lighted a match and watched it slowly burn. He took his overcoat from the door hook, picked up the suitcase and went out of the room. He crept downstairs, went out by the back way, and was soon standing on the lawn again. The cold tang of the night air bit into him, and he drew the collar of the coat closer about his neck. 'I've done it, now I *am* going, and I'll not come back.'

For a moment he felt a slight lifting of the heart, a pride in the decision, the accomplishment of will. He gave a final glance at the house and moved on, turned quickly into the long drive. The trees flung monstrous shadows across his path, the owls hooted, rabbits scattered like chaff. Once he stood in the drive and listened. When he turned his head again he could no longer see the house.

'I'll go to London, as for the rest . . .' and thought stopped.

Ahead he could see the closed gate, remembering the ritual of its closing. How often he had walked up and down this drive, on nights such as this, the moon touching the tree's tip, light flooding everywhere, the feeling of coldness that heightened silence. Suddenly he stopped and put down the case. He leaned against the railings, he stared at the broken, neglected drive. 'What a pity,' he thought, 'if I'd not gone to that place, if Elizabeth had stayed, I wonder . . .' then he picked up the case and hurried on. When he reached the gate he stopped again, he looked through the bars, his eyes straining towards the lane, the lightning-struck elm, as bare as bone. He put out his hand to pull on the gate, but he never pulled. For beyond the lane and beyond the tree he saw the void, he saw it as a great mass of impenetrable cloud, and as he watched the pattern came clear. There was a familiarity about all this, the packed suitcase, the lightness of step down the drive, the hand on the gate, the urge to pull on it and the urge to leave it alone. He turned round and walked quickly back up the drive. He let himself in by the same door, he removed his shoes and crept quietly up the stairs, he reached his room. At once he started to unpack his case, he put everything back where it had been before, he looked at all those objects of his affection that would not now be moved, he looked at the books piled everywhere, he crossed the room and hurriedly drew the curtains. He switched on the light. From a bottle on the table near his bed he took two capsules which he swallowed in a tumbler of water. Then he began to undress. He climbed into bed, relaxed, his hand reached casually out and switched out the light. From the lawn one bright eye glared into the silent night.

Thomas had heard it all. Thomas was awake, flat on his back, reading a letter. 'Another try,' he thought, 'I expect they all heard him, really, they never let on.'

Dear Sir: I am coming down on Friday afternoon to collect my grandson, Robert Dolphin, which is more my grandson than yours, seeing as your daughter ran away that long time ago and left my poor, unfortunate son, who never should have married one like her who was no good to him and won't be to anybody else, not having ever seen her myself, but in these matters one just knows. I'm surprised that you had the cheek after all that silent indifference to send a man all that way up to take my boy's baby away, him being dead and all. He was always a happy lad till he met your daughter who was never anything but horrible to him and who only married him because he had something others hadn't got. Since she was never a mother to my little grandson he was, and so fond of him it would have killed him all over again had he ever come to know where his lovely little boy had been took. God finds out more things than you'd expect and in this case he knew where real love was and where it wasn't ever. Please have him ready. I know you're all old down there and that you don't understand anything that happens to people outside your big gate which was what my son told me, and was what she told him herself soon after they married and he went to live in Surbiton with her, at the time when she was trying to be a kind of mother to Robert but didn't understand him at all not being built that way. I shall take my grandson back to Deptford a place where he'll be happy and get all the love he wants in this world. My husband would himself come but unfortunately he's ill in bed at present and can't go beyond his own street being on sickness benefit and we have to be careful of the health visitor who might call when he was out and so his money'd be stopped. My dear son used to tell me time on time as he had it from her when she first ran away that all you have down there is coldness and you don't understand much. When I think of my little grandson left with my poor dead son like he was my heart heaves, but you wouldn't understand that as she told him long ago that none of you didn't understand and that's what love is the heart heaving all the time for somebody. I shall arrive about four o'clock please have the boy ready for me to take back to his proper home which is Deptford, Hersian Street, by the Cross. Yours respectfully,

DORA DOLPHIN

'I had a feeling all the time that this would come, and so it has.' Thomas sat up in bed, he carefully folded the letter, and put it back in the envelope he had steamed open. It would appear on Mr. Mortimer's morning tray. 'I'd like to see his face when he opens it and reads what's inside.' Was there any way of hanging back, just to see?

'Who's that?' and Thomas jumped up as the door opened.

Robert came in in his pyjamas, he ran across to the bed.

'Did you hear those noises, Thomas?'

'What noises, what are you doing here in my room, eh? Who told you you could come in here? What cheek! Who'd you think you are? I ask you,' and he reached out a long arm and clutched at the boy's neck. 'Well, I ask you.'

'Those noises woke me up.'

Thomas leaned over, 'Haven't been any noises, you've been dreaming again. If you were a proper natural little boy you'd be asleep now and not have any dreams. . . .'

'I tell you. . . .'

Thomas clutched with both hands, Robert smelt the oil, could see the plastered hair.

'Why do you oil your face like that, Thomas, and your hair's all wet with it.'

'You're nothing but a sly little devil, I haven't forgotten this morning, no, you little bastard I haven't forgot. Sneaking up on us in that kitchen, seeing what other little boys have no interest in seeing, why'd you do it?'

'I only wanted to see the kitchen . . .' protested Robert.

'You only *wanted* to see the kitchen, you were angry because your grandfather told you to run away and not to worry him, and your Uncle Geoffrey said he couldn't be bothered with you today. D'you know what, little boy, they're getting tired of you already and I'm not surprised, the likes of you coming here to live with gentry, which your father never was. . . . Here, you little . . .' and Thomas grasped the small hand that had scratched down the side of his face, 'you did that before, you're the most vicious little devil I've ever come across.'

With his finger and thumb he pressed hard on the bone of the boy's wrist, the other hand he pressed against his mouth.

'You should never have come here at all, I can see that now. You're just a little barbarian, with your fish and chips, talking about such things at table with your betters. If I had my way here I'd start in to tame you, you sly little . . . I should think you'll be happy back where you belong. Why they only pretend they like you, that's all, just pretending, all excited at first, but not now. It's different, they don't care who your daddy was or that his name's Dolphin or anything, you know they don't, why even your Aunt Isobel says you act like a savage, and no wonder seeing where you lived, London, you can't trust anybody from there, you never could.'

'And don't whimper, either,' he said, pressing harder.

'When you come to a room door you knock, understand, you K N O C K,' he cried into the boy's ear.

Robert shuddered with terror. Thomas could feel this passing up his own arms, he suddenly dropped them and the boy was free.

'Well, don't stand there, Robert Dolphin, get back to your room. In the morning I will tell what has happened to Mr. Mortimer. In fact I think I'll . . .' but now he talked into the empty air. Robert had gone, the door stood wide open behind him.

Thomas got out of bed, his hands trembled as he put the newly sealed letter between the pages of a book, on which he placed the heavy brass candlestick. He then climbed back into bed. Nothing like this had ever happened to him before. His privacy had been invaded, and he was angry. He put his head close to the wall and listened, but he could hear no sound. Perhaps the lad had fallen asleep.

'Should never have come here, they don't understand kids, never had them here before.'

Shutting his eyes he saw right back to grey morning, he could hear the noise of the turbulent river, in spate after heavy rain. He was taking up early morning teas. When he reached Mr. Mortimer's room he found the bedroom door wide open. It was eight o'clock. Then he saw the boy, standing beside his grandfather's bed, leaning forward, talking.

Thomas drew back behind the heavy curtain and listened.

'But I don't *want* to see you now, dear,' Mr. Mortimer was saying, 'run off back to bed like a good child. It's far too early in the morning to be dashing into people's bedrooms. They don't want to see you so early. We don't like little boys wandering all over the house at eight o'clock in the morning. Run along now.'

The small, pyjama-clad figure came out, passed Thomas but did not see him hidden behind the curtain.

'That boy is a nuisance in the mornings, Thomas, it's absurd, can't you think of anything?'

'Your tea, sir. Think of what, sir?'

'Oh nothing,' said Mr. Mortimer, ruffled, 'thank you,' and Thomas went out. As he shut the door he heard a loud grunting noise from the other end of the corridor, it could only be Geoffrey.

'Go *away*, little boy, see you later. Go and play in your room.'

Thomas smiled. What would Robert play with in his room? His mother's work-basket perhaps. When he took tea into Geoffrey's room he found him in deep sleep. He put the tray on the table, said softly, 'Eight o'clock, sir,' did not look at the sleeper, walked out and silently shut the door.

At Arthur's room he knocked and called out, 'Tea, sir.'

'Leave it there,' it was never anything less than a growl, it always upset Thomas.

Thomas was winding the clock in the hall, he came on the boy as he came out of the breakfast room.

'Hello, Thomas.'

'Hello.'

Thomas, concentrating all his efforts on the unpredictable clock, wound slowly; his back was bent, Robert could see Thomas's shirt rucked up at the waist. He watched. Isobel appearing from nowhere said, 'Oh, Thomas, I can't find the papers this morning,' and Thomas said, 'They went up to Mr. Arthur's room, he specially asked me last night if I'd take them up as soon as they came,' he went on winding, he did not alter his position, he did not once look at Miss Isobel. He could *feel* the boy behind him, he felt sure he was staring, being inquisitive again, 'Always watching, that kid, I expect he learned it from his old man, and his old man learned it from her.' He would have liked to have swung round on the boy and barked out, 'Well, what are you staring at now, eh? What have you found this time?' but already he heard Isobel saying, 'What are you waiting for, dear. You should be out in the lovely fresh air,' and Robert saying, 'I'm waiting for Aunt Agatha to come down.'

Thomas finished winding the clock, but he did not alter his position, he stared through the glass face at the pendulum and listened.

'Poor Aunt Agatha has a bad headache today, I'm afraid she won't be coming down, dear.'

'Oh,' exclaimed Robert, the sigh swelled into the cavernous hall. 'Could I go for a walk with you, Aunt Isobel?' asked Robert.

'Sorry, dear, I've got to go out and I'll be away most of the day. Perhaps your Uncle Geoffrey will take you with him, he's setting new traps, he might take you on the lake again if you asked him nicely.'

'He doesn't want me at all today, Aunt Isobel,' and she caught the tremble of the voice, the sadness behind it.

'Oh well,' exclaimed Aunt Isobel, and went off upstairs.

Thomas swung round.

'H'm. You're out of luck today, Master Robert.'

'You shut up,' Robert said, he looked fiercely at Thomas, 'I hate you, and I hate here because you brought me here.'

Thomas was astonished at the boldness, the directness, the bright eyes glaring at him.

He patted the boy on the shoulder.

'Poor little boy,' he said, then he drew himself up and said, 'it's a pity you hate me, because perhaps I might have thought of something for you.'

'Oh do, Thomas, think of something we can do together.'

'But not today, Master Robert,' and he marched off in the direction of the kitchen.

'They don't want me, none of them,' Robert told himself, 'they don't like me any more,' and he ran off into the drawing-room. Seeing the piano, the lid up, Agatha had been playing the previous evening, he made a sudden violent rush towards it and sat down on the stool. He began to hammer on the keyboard, he struck thunder out of it which rolled upwards penetrating the house, he clenched his fists and hammered them all the way up the keyboard, and was still hammering when Mrs. Mortimer came in.

'Robert, darling,' she went up to him and caught his hands, 'what on earth is the meaning of this. *What* a terrible noise to make, why you can hear it even down the lane. Come away at once.'

Sullen, he allowed her to take his hand, allowed her to lead him out to the garden. At the end of the lawn they sat down together.

'What is the matter, darling?'

'No one wants me.'

'How silly. Isn't that just silly,' she hugged Robert.

'I don't like here,' he said, he freed himself from her embrace, he looked her fully in the face. 'I don't like here, grandmother.'

'Why don't you like here, darling, why I thought you simply loved going on the lake with Uncle Geoffrey and Aunt Agatha has taken you some very nice walks. Your grandfather of course is different, he is not like the others, and besides, he's very worried at present. Perhaps you had better come with me to the kitchen. You can watch us cooking.'

'I don't want to go into the kitchen.'

At which Mrs. Mortimer's patience rebelled.

'Very well. Then stay where you are,' she said, and immediately got up and left him.

Thomas saw all this as he lay back in the bed.

'Right through the whole of this day that kid's been lost. Didn't know what to do with himself. And now he comes in here, which nobody has ever done before to tell me that he heard noises and did I hear them. Did *I* hear noises. He didn't hear any, he was just a lonely little boy that's all.' He got out of bed and put on his dressing-gown. He went to Robert's room. Opening the door silently he went in. He could see a high heap in the bed. He heard sobbing, as he stood over the bed he watched the clothes rise and fall. 'Poor little devil,' he thought. Gently he put his hand on the boy's head, he leaned over, said softly, 'Master Robert, don't be frightened, it's only me.'

The head emerged from beneath the clothes.

Thomas saw the whiteness of terror, the set misery of the lost.

'I wasn't *really* angry with you, Master Robert,' and, sitting down on the bed, Thomas reached a hand inside the clothes and drew out the boy's hands. 'Smile,' Thomas said, 'smile,' and when he wouldn't he inserted a finger in the boy's mouth, and gently pressing down on the lower lip, said, 'go on, smile. I won't harm. you, why should I? I was angry with you yesterday because you sneaked into the kitchen when I was . . .'

Robert sat up at once, he scrutinized Thomas, the half sleeping eyes, the oily face, the matted black hair.

'I saw what you were doing with Joan but that's nothing because once I saw that in Paddington, too.'

'You see too much, Master Robert, for instance you see too much of one side of me. You think I'm funny, don't you? *I'm* not funny, it's the others who are funny. And though I used to laugh at them, behind my hand as you might say, I don't now. Some things can be funny for a long time. I remember now the way you laughed at me when I first copped eyes on you in that room you lived in in London, and you laughed the other night when I came in to see what you were screaming about. Since you're only a little boy I don't really mind. I watched you all this gone day and every time I saw you I knew you didn't know what to do with the next hour or even the next minute. What you want, Master Robert, is other little boys. . . .'

The boy's hand clutched at Thomas, 'I only want daddy,' he said, 'you know where daddy is.'

He looked earnestly into Thomas's face.

'If I gave you the money, every bit of it that I've saved up from what I got from grandfather and grandmother, and what Aunt Isobel and Aunt Agatha gave me, if I gave you all that,' and suddenly excited, 'I've got it all here in a little red box, if I gave it all to you would you tell me where daddy was took, and would you put me on the train that goes to Paddington, would you, Thomas?' and at once Thomas's arm seemed to hold all the weight of the leaning, urging boy, he could feel it touching him all over, 'would you, Thomas?'

'D'you know what dead is, Master Robert?' Thomas asked as he covered the boy's hand with his own.

'What's dead?'

'It's what happens to people when there isn't any more love anywhere, not anywhere in all the world, you suddenly feel the cold coming and then you're lonely, and then, all of a sudden again you're *real* cold, not like the cold when you put your hand on the wet slate, but like that high up cold in the sky. . . .'

'And then?' demanded Robert — he looked at the hairs in Thomas's nostrils — 'Daddy was cold, it was awful cold, and he didn't say anything and his eyes were tight shut . . . I tried to open them. . . .'

'Did you, *well* . . . this high up cold gets all round

you and inside you at the same time and you can't get warm any more and nobody can warm you ever again and then you go away.'

'Where?' said Robert eagerly, 'where, Thomas?'

'You go to a place that you don't know where you're going to and they don't know who take you, nobody knows, only the cold knows. . . .'

'Is daddy gone to where they took him where they don't know?'

Thomas slowly shook his head. 'I don't know that,' he said, 'here, you get right down into that bed and you go off asleep there's a good little lad.'

'Why is your hair all sticky, and your face, Thomas?'

'My mother used to say, "Put oil on your hair every night and you'll never be bald, and put oil on your skin every night and your face will shine like a winter apple".'

Robert burst out laughing and Thomas said, 'Ssh!' Thomas sat up, he felt relieved, 'Sometimes you're such a *nice* little boy,' he said, leaning forward again. 'Yes, I know that stuff smells but it wouldn't do you a happorth of harm, Master Robert. When you used to ride in that big fat lorry of your father's did he ever take you to see your grannie at Deptford?'

'Oh yes, many a time. I liked there. We used to go there when the lady was out,' said Robert, he folded his arms, he leaned back against the bedpost, he didn't want Thomas to go, he liked Thomas, talking like this, he didn't hate Thomas any more, it was only the others he hated, they didn't want him, they didn't want him all day.

'You mean your mother, I suppose, why'd you call her lady and not your mother?'

'Daddy said all the time she is a lady. I expect – she was my mother till she went away, and now I know I haven't got a mother, have you got a mother, Thomas?'

Whispering, Thomas said, 'Ssh! Don't talk so loud. Yes, I've got a mother, she lives in a little white cottage under a mountain. . . .'

'And do you go to see her, Thomas?'

'Sometimes. If I climb that high hill back of this house, climb right to the tip of it so you think your head will touch the sky, I can stand there, and I can see right across the country, almost to the very mountain under which she lives. One bright sunny day I went up there on my afternoon off and I think I could see the smoke climbing up out of the chimney pot. . . .'

'Um . . . fancy seeing all that way, Thomas.'

'Isn't it wonderful, Master Robert? If I tell you something you promise you won't tell anybody?'

Robert pressed two fingers against his mouth, he looked at Thomas and shook his head.

'Well, I think your grandfather is going to write to where your mother is, he may even have written already, because the other day when I was passing the drawing-room I heard him saying something about it to your grandmother. Now that *would* be nice, Master Robert. She'll be wearing that blue gown I told you about, as blue as the sky, and one fine morning she'll be standing at the foot of your bed, this very bed, little boy,' and Thomas tapped on the bedpost, 'just think of that, and when you open your eyes. . . .'

'Thomas?'

'What?'

'I like you, *now*, Thomas, like this, *now*,' Robert said, he gave a wide open smile to the man on the bed.

'And I like you, too, and I'll like you a lot better if you get off to sleep like a good little lad.'

'Did *they*, the people, always live here?' asked Robert, and Thomas said, 'Did *who* always live here?' and in a loud voice the boy replied, '*Them*.'

'Sssh, ssh! Not so loud, little boy. You'll wake the house up.'

'Uncle Arthur *is* awake, Thomas, I heard him going downstairs, that's what the noise was, that's why I came to your room, at first I was frightened because Uncle Geoffrey said Uncle Arthur hates little boys, I heard him walk up and down his room, I was listening all the time, I was sitting in my tunnel when I first heard him. At night he comes out, Thomas, I *know*.'

'Just fancy that. Fancy you hearing it. You should have been fast asleep like other little boys. Yes, he does sometimes go out at night, I think he likes the night air, and he may like talking to the owls, there's lots of them about here, I hate owls, do you?'

'I don't know, I haven't seen one, Thomas, but my daddy said they have big soft eyes, and when they fly he said you can't hear them flying they're so soft when they fly.'

'Sometimes of course,' said Thomas, his voice falling lower and lower in his throat, 'sometimes he doesn't go out. That's when he's frightened I think, he's been frightened often, I think he's frightened of the devil, *really*. . . .'

'What's that, Thomas?'

Thomas made to get up, but immediately the boy clutched at him, 'Don't go, Thomas, please.'

'But you must go to sleep, if somebody wakes up and finds me here there'll be the dickens of a row, and then I might be asked to go away and you wouldn't see me any more, and I wouldn't see you, Master Robert. . . .'

'What's the devil?' asked Robert, whilst Thomas

watched the wide open, shining eyes, felt the powerful clutch of two tiny hands, 'what's the devil?'

'It's something with horns, Master Robert, but if you go asleep now and don't come into my room any more without knocking, which isn't what proper people do, Master Robert, anyway I suppose except up at Paddington, then I'll tell you about the man with the horns tomorrow. There.'

He pressed the boy back on to the pillow, he tucked him in. 'How sad a little boy can be, sadder than anything I know. I'm sure he would have been happier at Deptford, I'm almost certain,' and he stared into the eyes of the waiting child, he could see him waiting, he could feel him waiting, 'how it strains at you, strains, this sadness of a lost little boy.'

'Tomorrow,' he said.

'Now,' Robert said, his fingers gripped Thomas's chin, 'now, Thomas,' and when he smiled, Thomas knew he could not go.

'Ssh,' said Thomas, and they both were motionless, listening.

'Did you hear something?'

'Nothing,' Thomas said, 'it's nothing, sometimes when a house is fast asleep, and you stay still and hold your own breath and listen hard, you sometimes do hear something, even breathing. . . .'

'I didn't hear anything,' whispered Robert, he looked confidingly at Thomas, 'I won't tell anybody anything, is it a man with horns, or is it a woman?'

Suddenly to stop himself from laughing Thomas buried his head in the clothes.

'I know,' Robert said, 'Uncle Geoffrey's got devils on his wall, I've seen them.'

'Oh,' said Thomas, his mouth brushed the boy's ear, 'you know I sometimes think, Master Robert, that your Uncle Arthur is frightened of the devil.'

'Is he?' Robert sat up again.

'If the devil gets into his room he goes out, I once heard him in the middle of the night downstairs, I thought it was rats got into the house but it wasn't, it was only your uncle nibbling in the pantry. He does that, too, very often. I've seen him eat nothing at all at dinner, says he has indigestion and they're sorry for him, and then after a little while he excuses himself and goes up to his room. Then in the middle of the night he'll go down and nibble his dinner in the pantry.'

'Have you ever been in Uncle Arthur's room, Thomas?'

'Twice in two years, Master Robert. It's just like your room in Paddington was, 'cept that there are hundreds and hundreds of books there. He smokes all the time and he reads and reads and reads. Sometimes he does nothing at all except lean on his chair with his head in his hands, that's when he's thinking about something hard, really hard, like his hands on his forehead were trying to press it out of him. . . .'

'What does he think?'

'How would I know that,' replied Thomas; he turned his head suddenly and looked at the clock, 'jawch, it's gone twelve o'clock, it's gone half past twelve, Master Robert. I must be going now, at once.'

'He hasn't got any money, has he?' asked Robert, he leaned on Thomas, he looked up at Thomas, 'has he?'

'What! Now how do you know that?'

'Because he didn't give me any like the others, and, Thomas, you haven't said yet what about if I gave you all the money I've collected if I gave you all that would you take me away from here and put me on the train to Paddington?'

Thomas, momentarily contemplative, paused, his eye fastened on the heavy curtains, he watched a dragon's downward movement, he said abruptly, 'I wouldn't do that, no, I wouldn't do that.'

'Why?'

'I just wouldn't, Master Robert, d'you know what I've been thinking?'

'What?'

'It would be rather funny if one night the devil appeared at Uncle Arthur's window, he wouldn't half get a fright. . . .'

'You mean the man with the horns looking at Uncle Arthur lying in bed?'

'Well, he mightn't be in bed at all, he might be dressed, he might be walking up and down in his room, because sometimes he thinks he's on a ship, and the others don't like that, the walking gets on their nerves, especially in the night time. . . .'

'I know,' cried Robert, 'I know,' and quickly Thomas covered his mouth.

'Ssh!' he said, 'ssh! What do you know?'

'The devils on Uncle Geoffrey's wall. . . .'

Thomas grinned, the lines on his face sharpened, the boy could see one tiny rivulet of oil shining from nose to chin, he was no longer worried by the smell.

Thomas leaned down, 'Good night, Master Robert,' he said, 'it's nearly one o'clock in the morning.'

Quietly, with complete satisfaction, with complete assurance, Robert said, 'Good night, Thomas.'

He watched the door close on Thomas, the room was in utter darkness, Thomas had blown out the night-light on his way out, but Robert did not seem to care, and as the door closed his head disappeared under the bedclothes.

VIII

'I LIKE you,' Robert said, he held on hard to Agatha's hand. They reached the end of the lane and began to climb.

'Do you, darling,' she said, and turned and looked down at him.

It touched her deeply, it had come so quietly, as though the boy had been holding it in readiness, and most of all, it seemed to Agatha, it had come right out of those bright, frank eyes, so blind with trust in this moment.

'Yes,' Robert said. 'You're nice,' and Agatha would never know how much love had gone into it.

'If I thought a week ago I should be doing this,' she looked at Robert. 'Not so fast, dear,' she said, slackening her step as the path steepened. She had often walked this way with her sister; it had, too, been Arthur's favourite walk when down on his rare visits from Cambridge. She had walked with Gabriel up this hill, before his manner of life had changed, before the indulgence in isolation. How many times up and down this path? Scores and scores of times. Yet this morning it was like an adventure into entirely new territory, a new kind of day, a beginning. She held tightly to the boy's hand, who returned it with even tighter grasp.

'It's a long way to the top, dear, I don't know really whether I should be doing this,' she paused, conscious of her pounding pulse, she turned and looked back towards the house.

'Will I be here a long time, Aunt Agatha?' His hand slipped out of her own, he looked up at her.

'How high you are,' he said, and she liked his smile.

'Am I?' she asked.

'Yes, this house is full of high people, except Mr. Thomas. . . .'

'Thomas, dear,' she corrected, 'shall we go on again,' and he said. 'Oh, yes, let's, Aunt Agatha,' and he caught her hand again, they climbed higher. Already she could feel the strain of this too sudden, too incautious climb. But it was an adventure all the same, away from the pattern of yesterday, knitting in her bedroom, the walk through the village in the afternoon, the ritual of writing to Miss Seddon and posting the letter, the same chat with the postmaster, the sexton, the blacksmith, the about turn, up the long drive, so cruel on her feet. She visualized the wooden bench hidden behind that clump of bushes, that jungle of bramble, and she longed to sit down and rest.

'How high up it is,' shouted Robert, 'how higher is it yet, Aunt Agatha?'

'One teeny bit more and then we're there,' she said, her breath coming short. 'Then we'll sit down and look back down the hill. You can see such a lot if you look from this height.'

There it was. It seemed to rise in front of her as though by magic, and when finally she sat down she did not speak, but remained motionless, recovering her breath. She was pleased with the child because he did not ask her a lot of stupid questions, he sat as quiet as a mouse, holding her hand. She felt the peace of isolation, of complete separation from down there.

'I can see Uncle Geoffrey on the lawn, he's gathering sticks.'

'What eyes you have,' said Agatha. 'Can you see the lake, dear, there. The water is shining, just through those trees, look.'

She watched him. He put his hands to his eyes like a practised mariner, he shouted, 'I can see it, just over there.'

'And the boat, too?'

Agatha looked down at the gates, the long drive beyond, it was extraordinary that Gabriel never did anything about that drive, he didn't seem to realize, he didn't even seem to care that she had to walk up and down it most days of the week. Celia was just as indifferent about it. It looked so untidy, it completely dwarfed the stateliness of that belt of trees. 'It must have looked beautiful in grandfather's time,' she thought.

She looked further and could just glimpse the white gate, hanging hingeless, the paint blistered and stained. Surely Thomas, who was a very handy man, could do something about it. She looked further still until she saw the stone pile of the house itself. How drab and lost and resigned it looked this morning. She could see her bedroom window from here, the lawn, and that shut window to the right of the side door which was Arthur's. She had been thinking a lot about Arthur these past two days. It did seem most odd to say of a man, at the ripe age of forty-eight, that he was futureless, finished. Yet that was the impression he gave. Islanded in a tiny piece of territory of his own fashioning.

'No income at all. No inclination to find one, to do anything for himself except mope in his room.' Two long years now. How patient they had been with him, and they had done their best. Arthur seemed anchored for ever. He wouldn't emigrate, he wouldn't venture into the world, a thorough coward she thought, and he wouldn't be a missionary. She thought this cowardice filched away the sadness of his fall. Why couldn't he be a man, instead of living like that on his eldest brother, taking advantage of his soft-heartedness, his horror of having 'scenes', of having to explain?

'How lucky I am,' she thought. 'I have at least a small but assured income. I can hold my own, Geoffrey can, so can Isobel. It's been most trying for everybody.'

She had a sudden vision of Arthur at dinner the previous evening, staring so brazenly and at the same time so stupidly at the boy. 'Such a complete lack of understanding, he understands nothing except his own misery. It's awful.'

Two laughing eyes were looking at her now. 'Shall we go down now, auntie?'

Agatha got up, she was rather glad, she felt now that the effort had been too much, but she remembered Robert's 'I like you,' it had sustained.

'Very well.'

'I want to go to the lake, I want to go in the boat,' Robert said, he was full of a nervous excitement, at any moment she expected him to race away from her, and she held tight to his hand.

'You must ask your Uncle Geoffrey about that, dear,' and then she held him to her and said, 'I hope you are going to be happy here, Robert,' and Robert said. 'I hope so, too.'

'I wonder where his mother is now, I wonder if he knows,' she thought.

'Robert, dear?'

'Yes, Aunt Agatha.'

'Where is your mother?'

'Gone away with Uncle Christopher. He always used to bring me a big box of chocolates. . . .'

'Imagine that. And did you love mummy very much, dear?'

'I think I did, but I know I liked daddy lots more. I want daddy, I do want to go back to him. . . .'

'Oh God,' she thought, 'what have I done now?'

'Mr. Thomas knows. Hasn't he got a lot of teeth,' Robert said, 'he puts oil on his hair at night, I saw it.'

'Imagine that,' said Agatha, 'he must have looked funny, we must get back now, dear. I'm sure you'd like a glass of milk. . . .'

'And *cake*,' said Robert.

'And cake, dear,' Agatha said, starting off down the hill towards the grey stone pile and the mist, the knitting, hot cocoa in her room, and Isobel reading *The Times*.

'It is a big house, isn't it, Aunt Agatha. We used to live in a big house, right at the top of it. I used to open the window at night to see all the lights. Each time daddy got angry with me and slammed the window down. He didn't like the air coming in, he said.'

'Oh!'

'He didn't like any windows open he said, because of his chest.'

'I see – what did daddy do?'

'He drove lorries, big high ones, sometimes I went with him, it was nice. Once I went right down to the North it was right through the country you could see the lights on the trees and rabbits and moths flying about, he said if you wish hard enough you'll see a lion any minute, but I never did though I wished and wished. That time we stopped at Clara's and we had hot pies and tea and pickles and cake, lots of cake.'

'Where was mummy?' asked Agatha.

'Over the water.'

'Just think of that, careful, dear, careful, it's very slippy here,' and when they reached the lane Agatha stopped again.

'You're red, Aunt Agatha,' Robert shouted, but she did not answer and did not look at him. After a while she recovered her breath and they went on. The boy's hand gripped the hem of her short green coat.

'My bed that I sleep in now isn't as warm as daddy's bed,' he said. 'I always slept with daddy, we had big Indian blankets that he got from the army stores down our street. Once we went to the Zoo.'

She listened intently. 'It will all come out,' she thought. 'Here we are, at last.'.

Robert sang 'here we are again,' and ran on in front of her, he pulled on the gate, 'We used to sing that on the lorry. . . .'

'Sing what, dear?'

' "Here we are again", and he let me take hold of the wheel. Once he gave me two whole shillings to stay home from school and tell me what she did.'

'What who did, your mother?' Agatha returned from the great distance to which she had wandered, she had been thinking of Arthur again, she repeated, 'Who, your mother?'

'Yes,' piped Robert, and with greater shrillness, 'Once she gave me five shillings to tell her what daddy said.'

'You must be very rich then,' and Robert, dancing away up the drive cried back, 'I bought a train with the money and lots and lots of lines.'

'That was nice,' Agatha said, but he hadn't heard her, he had forgotten her, he was already half way up, he suddenly flung himself at the railings and clung there, swinging his legs, waiting for her to come up.

From behind a tree Geoffrey came as a surprise; he did not notice the boy, he hurried down to meet his sister, took her arm.

'You shouldn't have done it, Agatha, old dear,' he said, 'it's far too much for you, far too much.'

She waved her hand at him. 'I quite enjoyed it. That child has been telling me things, they quite surprised me. For one thing the mother gave him money for spying, and the father seems to have done just the same thing.'

'Spying?'

'On each other. The boy seems hardly to have been at home, he can have had very little schooling, seems to have spent most of his time travelling about with Dolphin, even at night, once all night. . . .'

'How extraordinary. D'you know Gabriel's been trying to persuade Arthur to go away. I thought it rather sudden, considering he's just let him lie in comfort for two years. . . .'

'Pity he ever returned after that Hastings affair, it's left a stain on the place, I suppose it's a question of money. . . .'

'I haven't any,' announced Geoffrey.

'Neither have I,' replied his sister, they passed through the hingeless, rotting, white gate, 'every time I see that gate it makes me feel positively ill, you'd think Gabriel would have something done about it. Oh he is neglectful of practical things. . . .'

'No, afraid he'd have to try and touch Celia herself, yet I have a feeling he's here for good, he'll never go. I don't mind what he does personally so long as he changes his manners, is more civil for one thing, especially to Gabriel, who, after all, is the one who's keeping him. He's really abominable at times.'

'I do agree with you,' Agatha said, and then they had reached the house.

IX

'W E are going to have a visitor,' announced Mr.
Mortimer as soon as his wife returned from
the bathroom.

'A visitor?'

She stood in the middle of the room, her dressing-gown draped about her, a net over her hair, she smelt strongly of eau-de-cologne. Then she crossed to the mirror. She could see her husband seated on the bed, in dressing-gown and slippers.

'Aren't you bathing?' she asked. 'Do hurry along, you know what late breakfast means for me by now, or you ought to. Do hurry, Gabriel.'

'You should read this,' he said. 'I think you had better read it now. . . .'

She turned on him. 'I can't read anything now,' she said, then saw him rise, taking the letter from his pocket.

'All the same you had better read it at once,' Gabriel said.

'Give it to me. Get along now, for heaven's sake. Just *look* at the time,' and sat down to read. She read quickly. She said at once, 'What are you going to do?'

'I don't know, I don't really know, I never expected this. . . .'

'But it's come,' Mrs. Mortimer replied, at which remark Mr. Mortimer walked from the room.

The moment the door closed she threw down the letter on the bed and returned to the dressing-table mirror. With deliberate calm she proceeded with her toilet, she thought of what they would have for lunch, on such matters she had to think well ahead.

She was dressed and ready to go down when Mr. Mortimer returned. He started to dress. She flung quick glances at her reflection in the mirror, she watched him dress, she patted back rebellious tufts of hair.

'But you *must* know what you are going to do, Gabriel, a matter like this is serious. She will be here tomorrow afternoon, you have to make up your mind.'

'That's the trouble,' he said, 'it's difficult, you must see that, I can see that woman's point of view.'

'You wrote to Elizabeth last week I gather. She must know what has happened by this time. That Daphne Crowe would have telegraphed her, wherever she was.'

'I did write, I put the letter in my pocket. This morning I found it, I'm afraid I forgot about it completely, still I'll get it off today.'

'*Fancy* forgetting a thing like that, Gabriel. You take these things so casually. Won't you ever realize that there are things in life which are very important? It's useless sending that letter off now. You must telegraph her, get the address, then telegraph your daughter, tell her to return here at once. It's the only thing. Do you understand. At once?'

As they went downstairs, he said, 'It's not *your* child, dear. You're safe. You don't have to make the decision.'

'Tut, tut,' she said, she felt suddenly angry with him. 'What cowardice', she thought.

She brooded on this matter, the morning incident fresh in her mind. She was sitting alone in the little study, to which Robert had now been confined for his meals. It lay just behind the drawing-room. Until the coming of the boy it had hardly ever been used. The clue to its isolation lay in its ever open door. It never occurred to anybody to shut it, people passed it by with scarcely a glance. At this moment she was very conscious of the boy, he was everywhere in this room, he was in the atmosphere, there were traces of him all around her, even to the crumbs from last night's supper, she could see them under the table, Joan had not yet cleaned it out. Though Robert was vivid in her mind there were no connections with Deptford. Deptford was far away, the letter had fallen into a void; she had quite forgotten about it. She was thinking of yesterday. Yesterday afternoon. She had occasion to go into the drawing-room, she couldn't exactly remember why; she had found Robert stretched out on the carpet.

'Hello, dear. What on earth are you doing there?' she asked. 'You'll catch cold. Get up at once. Can't you feel that awful draught?'

'Nothing,' Robert replied. His chin rested on his clasped hands, he lay facing the window.

'What are you looking at?' and her gaze extended beyond him to the garden. 'What have you seen?'

The boy did not answer, he raised his head and looked at her.

'No,' he seemed to be saying, 'I'm looking at you.'

She stood there looking down at him. Such a fierce, intense longing she had never seen before, not on any child's face, on anybody's face. It saddened her. She felt unable to speak. This longing seemed to rise up and touch her, gripped her.

'What is the matter, darling?'

'Nothing,' Robert said, yet she knew it meant everything.

'Behind that look,' she told herself, 'is the terrible will power of a child,' and she was on the verge of repeating herself, and realized the meaninglessness of asking again. 'What is the matter, Robert?' – it seemed the silliest question now. The intensity of the boy's look never wavered. 'You can't answer that with words,' she thought, 'how stupid he must think I am.'

'But you simply *must* get up, Robert dear, you can't lie there like that. You'll get a terrible cold.'

'Yes,' Robert said, not moving.

'Then get up at once,' Mrs. Mortimer said. She knelt down and caught his hands, she pulled, somehow she was conscious of that will power, he resisted her efforts, the expression on his face never changed. She gave a sudden fierce tug and he was on his feet, he had broken free of her and had run from the room. She caught a last glimpse of him running down the garden.

'How *dull* it must be for him,' she thought, 'if only there were another boy his age. Of course there are in the village, but Gabriel is dead against that. One must find a school for him,' and then, with the speed of light the Deptford letter had risen from the depths of her mind. 'Oh dear! I forgot all about this woman coming down. Yes, he's right, she has a point of view. What a mix up it all is. And all through that young woman. How right I was, I never liked her. Gabriel's so blind.'

She suddenly laughed, it surprised her, and then she knew why. Her mind had travelled back years, she saw herself the wife of a very busy, very active doctor. She saw herself widowed, alone. It was the proposal in the Underground station that had made her laugh. The whole scene lay vividly before her. She even remembered the time. Half past nine in the morning. And she had accepted Gabriel, and she had never regretted it. She had a dread of loneliness, the loneliness of a town, of a flat, and she had reached a critical period in her life, the danger signals were all about. Once one had married one had learned something.

'Something happens inside you and you cannot be alone any more.' And with Gabriel she had accepted the responsibility of running a house, a house hidden away in the country, running it and its occupants. 'I've never been sorry,' she told herself. 'I've never regretted it.' 'We're nonentities, my dear,' Gabriel had warned her, 'but I think you'll find us all right nevertheless.'

When she first arrived at the house it had seemed to her like a monastery. A violent change-over, the calm sea after many turbulent waters.

'If it had been anybody but Gabriel I should never have done it.'

The curious dug-in quality of their tin-pot lives at Greys had at first disgusted her, had ended by charming her.

She saw how their lives centred round Gabriel, they could never be very far away. Even Geoffrey and Agatha, who had travelled about the world, had in the end returned to stable. It seemed a pity that Isobel had never married, it seemed a pity that Geoffrey never broke clear of the monotonous rhythm of his life, but they would answer that they were quite happy, they were quite content. The crusading spirit was carefully wired off, it had no place in this great, rambling, damp house, whose life touched only the bare fringes of the outer world. How fortunate for Agatha and Geoffrey and Isobel that they had their little bit of money, how very fortunate that Gabriel had his. 'Arthur is the thorn here. How any man can go on like that, simply living on his brother's charity, is quite beyond me. And Gabriel's far too nice ever to do anything drastic about it.' Yet she saw something of menace in this very kindness. One day there would be a showdown, it had to come. To live like a recluse for two years, just because you had overstepped the accepted moral bounds. . . .

'In the end *I* shall have to tell him to go. Just as I shall inevitably have to make the decision about this child. I know that at the last minute Gabriel will hedge, and finally back out. This family are quite incapable of making any decisions, as for making them for other people they loathe it.'

She could hear footsteps passing up and down outside. She thought, 'I wonder if that's Geoffrey, perhaps it's Gabriel.'

She could never be alone for very long. Somebody or other was always after her, wanting something, wanting advice, even on the most trivial things. But she was determined not to be interrupted. There must be some occasions when she called her soul her own.

'Perhaps I myself was a little hasty, having that child brought here. We are indeed living by the skin of our teeth.' That was a most predominant factor in Mrs. Mortimer's life, the other was Thomas. She did not like him, she had never liked him. But somehow or other her husband could never manage without the man. She often wondered about their curious relationship. Time and again she had begged Gabriel to get rid of him. But always he fought for Thomas, and not even the warning, 'we simply can't afford him,' could make the slightest difference. It was the one instance of the rock in Gabriel, it never showed elsewhere. He fought for Thomas's retention, and Thomas remained.

'Perhaps I should have got somebody else to go to town that day, but the effort – no, it couldn't have been done.' She was quite certain in her mind that none of them would have made a move. It was Thomas or nothing.

'To have accused me like that, when he knew perfectly well he would never have made the effort himself, far less the others. But I'm here now to make up my mind, I've simply got to. I wonder what sort of person this Mrs. Dolphin is?'

She knew Deptford, she knew it very well, she had the advantage there. To the others it was a part of London, and Gabriel had once passed through it in a car.

The sudden commotion outside brought her to her feet. She could hear her husband talking in a loud voice, it struck her he was angry about something. And then she heard Robert crying. She came out quickly, confronting them both in the corridor. Gabriel was quite white with rage, he had a tight grip on the boy's arm, down whose face tears were streaming, he kept rubbing at his mouth.

'What on earth is the matter?' she demanded, 'do leave go of that child.' But Mr. Mortimer, ignoring his wife, went on with his questioning.

'What have you done with it? You were in that room yesterday afternoon, I know, Thomas saw you there. I myself heard you pounding on that piano, although you were told not to touch it. Now what have you done with that music?'

'Music,' exclaimed Mrs. Mortimer, she hurried to her husband's side and whispered fiercely in his ear, 'Do you know that both Thomas and Joan are watching you from the kitchen doorway? This is disgraceful.'

She caught Robert's hand, 'The drawing-room is the place for this, not the kitchen corridor,' and as she pulled at Robert, Mr. Mortimer pulled the other way.

He did not once look at his wife, but kept his eyes fixed on Robert.

'You have to tell me what you have done with it. Do you hear? For believe me, my child, if you don't then I'll have Thomas pack your things and you can go back tomorrow. Do you understand me?'

He shook the boy violently.

Mrs. Mortimer had never seen her husband so excited, it surprised her, it shocked her.

'Please . . . Gabriel. . . .'

'I tell you he knows where it is all right,' Mr. Mortimer barked, 'he knows quite well what he has done with it, he's stubborn,' he never took his eyes off the boy. 'Just as he knows that on Thursdays Agatha and I have an evening of music. He knows also that I look forward to this, I'm certain he does, and his aunt does, too, he heard us talking about it yesterday, I saw him. Agatha is very upset about this, we both are, we were so looking forward to this evening, and now she wants to run through those Brahms things, they can't be found anywhere. You know, Celia, how we look forward to these Thursdays, but this horrible child, and he *is* a horrible child, won't tell me what he has done with it,' his free hand suddenly grasped Robert's other arm, and this time he shook the boy so violently that Mrs. Mortimer protested, and, still conscious of the watchful eyes of Thomas and the maid, said in a low voice, 'Gabriel, go to your room and leave this to me. Leave go of the child, can't you see you are hurting him?' and at that moment Mr. Mortimer raised his head and looked at his wife.

It frightened her, this was a side to Gabriel she had never seen before.

'I won't be careful,' he said, and turned his attention to Robert; their faces were level with each other. The boy had stopped crying. He stared back at his grandfather, and he maintained a stubborn silence.

'Robert, dear,' said Mrs. Mortimer.

'I don't know,' replied Robert; she suddenly noticed the tiny clenched fists gripping his shorts.

'But if you *do* know, dear. Your grandfather is very angry with you. What did you do with the music? Where did you put it? Surely, if you think hard .... you'll tell your grandfather at once. Poor Aunt Agatha won't be able to play. I'm sure you wouldn't do anything naughty like that. Come now, Robert,' she put a hand on his head, ruffling his hair, 'haven't you a handkerchief, do wipe your face, dear, it's filthy. I'll have to ask Joan to take you to the bathroom. . . .'

'No,' shouted Robert, 'I won't.'

'You see, my dear,' said Gabriel, but at that moment Mrs. Mortimer was looking the other way. She caught Thomas and Joan, she drenched them with a look, their heads vanished at once.

'Do control yourself, Gabriel,' she went on, then dragged Robert free of his grandfather, pulled him into the room after her, 'you are a very rude child, Robert. To do a thing like that to your grandfather, and poor Aunt Agatha, she has been so kind to you,' then a final glance at her husband. 'Please, dear, for God's sake go away, I'll look after this matter. Such a fuss about nothing.'

She could not have made a greater mistake, for suddenly she was retreating before the oncoming Gabriel, he advanced boldly into the room, she retreated to the far corner of it and sat down, she held fast to the boy.

'Nothing. I like that. And that beastly boy knows perfectly well what he's done with the music. Fuss.

I should say so. We have always had these Thursday evenings in the drawing-room and I hope shall go on having them. He's hidden it, if he hasn't torn it up, the little savage. It was there yesterday, I myself saw it, Agatha and I went through the bureau . . . those Brahms things, dear,' he suddenly lowered his voice, though she saw his hands still trembling from the excitement.

'What Brahms things?' For a moment Gabriel thought he detected a slight note of disgust in her voice, she paused for a moment, 'Couldn't she have played something else; you know she can't play Brahms at all, and certainly not those things you're looking for, the Intermezzi, and *has* it to be Brahms, dear?' she said. The acid tone in her voice was not lost on Gabriel now.

'Oh dear,' he thought, 'now she's upset, too, *all* through this child. He should never have left Paddington, I can see that now, I don't care if he does go tomorrow.'

He fixed his eye on Celia.

'I'm rather afraid it has to be Brahms, my dear, that's all, and I think Agatha plays him very nicely, you never had an ear for music, my dear, you're completely tone deaf, you know you are, besides why all this fuss, anyway?'

'But it's you who's making the fuss, Gabriel,' calmly.

'I look forward so much to these evenings, Agatha too. . . .'

'You're repeating yourself, dear.'

'Agatha loves playing to me, as for your remark about her playing, it's rather cheap, don't you think? I'm thoroughly upset about this. It has never happened before, it's only happened now because of that child. Spoiled, thoroughly spoiled. Must be taken notice of, *must* push his way in everywhere. He's become a perfect nuisance to poor Geoffrey. The way you tolerate this sort of thing.' He turned quickly and stamped out of the room, he left the door gaping wide behind him.

Mrs. Mortimer quietly got up and went to the door and closed it. She returned to her chair, by which Robert was still standing. He refused to look at his grandmother. She sat down, he suddenly felt himself pulled sharply, he was standing in front of her, he heard her say coldly, '*Now*, explain yourself.'

Agatha was still in the drawing-room, plodding laboriously through the music piles. When Gabriel went in he was immediately struck by the chaos of it all; there was music everywhere, on the floor, scattered over the top of the piano, every drawer in the music bureau was standing wide open and from each one music protruded, the piano stool was littered with it. It had depressed Agatha, seeing so much of it, she seemed to realize at last how much of it was beyond her. She was bent over the music stool, steadily searching. Gabriel, standing beside her, felt suddenly sad. He noticed two things about his sister: the violent trembling of her hands, as she picked up book after book of music, the forlorn look she wore. He had never seen Agatha look quite like this, he kept staring at her profile.

'Poor Agatha,' he thought, 'it is a beastly shame,' he was certain that the boy had found the music and hidden it somewhere. He had been caught in that room on two other occasions, once by Geoffrey, once by Thomas. 'It seems as if the little devil was bent on disappointing us both.'

'I suppose you know already,' he sat down on the stool and looked up at Agatha, 'I mean about this person calling tomorrow.'

'I did hear something about a visitor coming,' replied Agatha. She went on with her search, but when she began to retrace her way through the pile already gone through, Gabriel became so irritated that he cried out, 'Please, please, dear, give it up, let's give the whole thing up,' but she ignored him, and continued.

After a while he said gently, 'Do you think we could have something else, dear, for instance,' he paused, 'you know you play Mozart quite well, perhaps that D minor thing. . . .'

'The Sonata?' not moving, not looking at him.

'That's it, Agatha, do let's have that, it's better than nothing, though I would still have preferred the Brahms. . . .'

'For heaven's sake, don't go on about Brahms,' she said brusquely, 'I wanted that and nothing else, I'm sick of all the other stuff,' she waved her hand over the scattered music, it looked like a wilderness to her.

'It's you who's *really* disappointed,' Gabriel said, and she was touched by his remark.

'Well, we'll have the Mozart,' she said, and Gabriel immediately said, 'and that boy hasn't beaten us after all.'

He helped her to put the music away.

'Yes, this child's grandmother is coming here, that man Dolphin's mother, dear, she wrote me a letter, rather an odd letter I must say, she's coming to collect Robert apparently, take him back, she says. . . .'

'What?' exclaimed Agatha.

'But I thought you knew, didn't you know, dear?'

'Nó! I didn't know.' Her expression suddenly changed.

'You seem very surprised, Agatha,' he interrupted her. 'But as far as I'm concerned, well, he may go, perhaps it was a mistake, mistaken charity, how dangerous a thing feeling is, so tumultuous and wayward, it throws one off one's balance, it's thrown us all off ours. Things used to be so different, the place was quiet, there was order about the house . . . I don't know . . . Why, he's even made himself a nuisance in the kitchen of all places. Thomas mentioned it to me this morning, hangs around there, why heaven knows, he says he spies on them, on Joan and he I mean. . . .'

It made Agatha laugh, 'How absurd,' she said, and went on laughing, and though Gabriel thought it slightly out of place, he was at the same time relieved to hear it, it helped to lighten the atmosphere.

'What on earth would he be spying on in the kitchen? And is Celia going to allow the boy to return then?'

'That I can't say,' replied Gabriel, he bit on his finger nail, 'I'm having nothing to do with it at all, I'm leaving everything to Celia to decide. . . .'

'That is not unusual, dear, is it, you always do? You've lost whatever independence you ever had, it seems a great pity to me, we are all being run by Celia, more or less. You have her to thank for the absence of your daughter.'

'I don't want to hear anything about that, Agatha dear, and please . . . you see I don't want any quarrelling, of any kind, I hate it, always have. . . .'

'But you have written to Elizabeth, you've telegraphed her.'

'I don't know where she is, I've had two letters returned marked address unknown, one from Rome, another from Salerno. I don't know *where* that girl is. I wish to God she would come back and see to her child.

The more I think about it, the more awful it seems, what does this mother think a child is, in God's name. But all the same, he has been a little beast this last two days.'

'Perhaps the child is unhappy,' said Agatha.

'Tut! tut!' Gabriel flung a hand in the air, 'unhappy? Why he gets almost everything he wants, plenty to eat, plenty of room to play about. Everybody has done their best for him, I'm sure you have, my dear. He's upset us no end, but on the whole we've been nice to him.'

'He wants another child, Gabriel, another boy, anybody can see that, this house is full of grown-ups, old people, he can never be otherwise than out of place.'

Looking thoughtful, Gabriel said, hesitatingly, 'Well, there's something in that, I suppose, the boy should be at school, the sooner the better. . . .'

'There *are* other boys,' Agatha reminded him.

'Where?'

The word struck Agatha like a pistol shot.

'There are some boys in the village, dear. Mr. Potts's little boy, for instance. He's nice, and intelligent, too.'

Gabriel got up, he walked over to the window and stood looking out.

'You think like Celia, but I cannot agree, I'm afraid. I don't want him mixing up with the village boys. Let his mother come back and look after him, that is the solution.'

'She may *never* come back,' replied Agatha.

'Oh, I don't know . . . but I've worries enough as it is,' he was full of regret the moment he said it, how on earth had it slipped out like that? 'I don't want to discuss this matter any more, definitely.'

He returned to the stool and sat down again. He

lifted the piano lid, struck a clumsy chord which reverberated through the house. 'About this evening, Agatha. Do play that D minor thing, I would like that particular one.'

'I'm not good enough for that, Gabriel, you can skip things in Brahms, but never in Mozart. Can you think of something else?' She caught his arm, 'We both enjoy these evenings together, we always have, I love playing to you. It distracts the others of course, but does that matter very much, think of something else,' she repeated.

He sat silent.

'Tell me something,' Agatha said, she leaned forward, he turned and faced her.

'Tell you what?' and Agatha's expression seemed to say, 'Something serious, that I want to know.'

'For instance,' she went on, 'I've often wondered what there is between Thomas and yourself. You seem so very close together. . . .'

'That can often happen, you remember Bellowes?'

'Of course I do.'

'Well. . . .'

'But sometimes I've noticed Thomas being actually rude to you, the others may have noticed, I don't know, but I have, rude to the point of impudence. It wasn't always like that, he clings to you like a leach. . . .'

His smile was disarming, he said slowly, 'And so would you, dear, if you were Thomas. He hasn't had a penny from me in three long years. . . .'

'Gabriel. . . .'

'It's perfectly true, my dear,' he said.

'Does Celia know?'

'I think not.'

'Can't you pay him?'

'No.'

'How awful, Gabriel, and you've kept this hidden all the time. . . .'

'For the peace of the household, yes. Thomas isn't a bad chap. He's never *actually* been rude to me, true he's done some things I haven't liked, but I've overlooked them, especially in a man like Thomas who has a natural malice. . . .'

'What did he say?'

'Say? Well he said, I'll give you his very words, "Well, sir, I'll wait, I quite understand." There are not many servants like that, Agatha, you must agree. And he's very efficient, I can leave anything to Thomas, anything at all, he turns up trumps every time.'

'When can you pay him?'

'That I don't know, either.'

'Arthur knows about this?'

'How did you know?'

'Just guessed, that's all. What a horrible business. It has quite upset me, Gabriel, really it has. I don't know whether I can . . .' her voice broke suddenly, 'Oh, Gabriel,' she exclaimed passionately, then she got up and left him. He saw by her white face the profound shock she had experienced.

'Damn,' he thought, 'what on earth made it slip out like that?'

'Now, Robert. Stand up. I want you to tell me everything, and it must be the truth.'

Mrs. Mortimer sat on a high chair by the window. Robert stood before her, facing the light. Looking at him now, she liked his eyes; in them she seemed to catch many glimpses of the young woman she could never like, his mother. She wondered whether she would return. This child was so terribly alone. She now held his hand, she looked straight at him, and repeated, 'you must tell me everything, dear.'

He stared up at her, he did not speak. She bit her lip with rage, she could not forget the altercation in the corridor, the watching servants. She imagined her husband had suddenly lost his head.

'Are you going to speak?' she asked; she shook him. 'What have you done with the piece of music belonging to your Aunt Agatha?'

'I tore it up,' he said. For a moment he thought his grandmother was going to strike him, but he did not flinch.

'You tore it up. Why did you do a thing like that?'

'I didn't want them to play it,' Robert said, and lowered his eyes, but only for a fraction of a second.

'Why not?'

'They wouldn't play with me,' Robert said. She could see his fingers pulling at his shorts, and it irritated her, 'Stop that,' she said, 'stop it.'

'Play, who wouldn't play?' she asked.

'They wouldn't,' the boy endeavoured to free himself from his grandmother's grasp, but she said, 'Keep still,' and held tighter to him, 'keep still, do you hear.'

There was a short silence.

She wondered if Thomas was listening outside the door.

'What a dreadful thing to have done,' she continued. 'Your Aunt Agatha has always been so kind to you. Kinder than anybody indeed, she understands you.'

'How on earth did he know the music she was going to play?' she was asking herself.

'Yes, how did you know that?' she demanded, and at that moment drew back a little, conscious of the intensity of the boy's look.

'I heard them talking about it,' Robert said. 'Then

when they went away I went into the drawing-room and looked for it, and I found it. Then I tore it into little pieces.'

'Where is it?'

'Over there,' Robert replied. His expression changed, she saw at once the ruthlessness, the sense of triumph.

'Go and bring it here at once,' she let go of his hand.

She saw him cross the room, take down a tall blue vase; he returned with it.

'Is that it?'

'Yes, that's it,' the boy said, and turned the vase upside down; a shower of paper fragments clouded down to the carpet.

'Robert,' her voice rose suddenly to a shout, 'Robert.'

Quietly she removed the vase from his hand and put it down on the floor beside her.

'Are you sorry?'

He did not answer her. She put her finger under his chin, she raised his head, looked at him for a moment. She struck him across the face with her open hand. 'Leave the room,' she cried.

Watching him go, she thought, 'How dreadful, I should never have done it, I should never have done a thing like that,' and then she seemed to see in the bold carriage of the head, the almost stubborn lift of the tiny shoulders, a cold and measured indifference. It came as a relief to her. It helped to lessen that blow, she could still hear the sound of it, that sudden fall from grace, 'I lost my temper, and I've never lost it so utterly before.' She sat motionless in the chair, long after the door had closed. She stared down at the littered carpet.

Agatha had gone straight to the morning-room, she

saw Gabriel climbing the stairs. As she reached the door she hesitated, she felt nervous, her hand shook, rattling the knob of the door, and at once Isobel's voice, with its faint echoes of some parade ground, called out, 'Who's that?'

'Only me,' said Agatha, she pushed open the door and peeped in, 'I've only come for my spectacles, I believe I left them in the window there.' She shut the door behind her.

Isobel's upper part was completely lost behind the pages of *The Times*, and the lower half did not escape Agatha's eye. She had never come upon her sister quite like this. It seemed as if fate were determined to hand out one shock after another this morning. She thought, glancing at Isobel, 'This is revolting.' Isobel had one long, muscular leg sprawled out in front of her, the other, knee bent, the foot resting on a nearby chair, revealed a thigh no less muscular than her calf. 'How awful,' Agatha thought, 'so abandoned-looking,' she turned away and crossed to the table. She picked up her spectacle-case, and as she did so she heard the rustle of paper, *The Times* was being lowered, Isobel was looking at her.

'Why, dear, how startled you look. Is anything the matter?' But Agatha made no reply. She stared fixedly at her sister's legs. They fascinated and re-pelled her. She thought there was a lot of male in Isobel after all. She had always thought so.

'You haven't found your aunt then, I gather?' said Agatha. She saw at once that her sister was at her usual game of obituary hunting. 'I've often wondered whether there is an aunt at all, Isobel.'

'But there is, in South Australia, and I should think she is a very old aunt,' and the paper rose again, obliterating the purplish-red face, the mannish air.

'Have you heard about this person coming down tomorrow?'

Agatha waited, then Isobel exclaimed, 'Fancy that. That Gay Lilly is dead, extraordinary . . . what were you saying?'

Agatha repeated.

'Oh yes, rather. I did hear Celia say something about a woman calling here, from Deptford, it'll be fun. So few people call. Visitors from that part of the world are rare. How awful these new hats look, have you seen them?'

'I'm afraid I haven't. Did you hear the commotion out in the corridor a little while ago?'

'Commotion. No. Has something happened?' *The Times* fell to the floor.

'Well no, not exactly,' said Agatha, she went towards the door.

Isobel lurched, then sprang to her feet, she hurried after her sister. 'Agatha, my dear, you do look dreadful. There is something the matter. It's not like you to be like this. Aren't you well, dear?'

'I'm quite all right,' Agatha replied. 'It's nothing. My liver's out of order probably. I must ask Turner to check me up.'

She felt the sudden grasp of Isobel's hand, Isobel's eyes searching her out.

'Do tell,' Isobel said.

But Agatha only said, 'Is Geoffrey about, he promised to fix up those hangers in my wardrobe, and the book rack, too.'

'Ah! That's it. You've had no sleep much lately, you read far too much, Agatha. Those awful books. . . .'

Forcing a smile Agatha replied, 'That's probably what it is,' and left the room.

Isobel returned, to the couch, the fire, the sprawl,

she started on the Personal Column, and immediately
forgot Agatha. Her mind was in fact a complete
blank. She couldn't remember how she had spent
yesterday, and there seemed to be no plans for today.
Suddenly she thought, 'Sunday, Sunday next, it's
Communion Sunday. I mustn't forget that.' She
continued her reading.

But she had been dragged out to an early lunch,
and she hadn't liked it. 'Thursday again,' she said
grumpily, 'imagine it.' How quickly the weeks flew.
In the hall it was something of a rugger scrum. Mr.
and Mrs. Mortimer were there, Isobel and Geoffrey,
whilst Thomas looked dutifully on, ready to help with
coats and scarves, bags and gloves. Outside the car
was waiting, the engine panting, as though with
dread.
'Everybody ready now?' inquired Mrs. Mortimer,
she was almost lost in a squirrel coat and fur cap.
'We're ready,' Mr. Mortimer said, somewhat
huffily. Like Isobel he wasn't in the best of moods,
he hated Thursday afternoons, but it was always nice
to return in the evening, to listen to Agatha playing.
The car would be packed with Mortimers, lurching
down the drive, tossing like a battleship along the
cart-track lane. The adventure in the village, and
after everybody had done their little business, the
village watched the Mortimers pile in again. Today
they were visiting the Polsons, who lived in a craggy
bastion in the high hills. They all secretly hoped that
the car would be equal to the occasion; it had broken
down a number of times. They would have afternoon
tea, look through the windows, sharing the grey sky,
the slate-coloured hills, exchange opinions on a
desperate February.

'Where's Agatha, isn't she coming?'

They piled out to the door, Thomas bringing up the rear.

'No, she *isn't*,' snapped Gabriel, and Isobel snapped back, 'But you are.'

There was a general silence as they got into the car. As Thomas was closing the door, Geoffrey leaned out and asked a question.

'Has Robert turned up yet, Thomas?'

'No, sir. I'm afraid he hasn't.'

Mrs. Mortimer, filled with sudden compassion, could see the red cheek again, the downcast eyes.

'I daresay he's somewhere about the house. I've given Joan instructions what to do, he's probably wandering around somewhere. And Agatha is here. So I don't feel uncomfortable about going, really.'

'He wasn't with you, Geoffrey?' asked Isobel; the roar of the car shut off Geoffrey's reply.

The car had a sudden sinking moment as though it might collapse, then, having negotiated the first gate, its spirit seemed to rise, it tore down the drive like a tank.

'This drive is really getting worse,' announced Celia, and everybody sat up.

'It does want seeing to,' said Geoffrey.

Gabriel, slumped in the back seat, said nothing, he stared at Thomas's broad back: that little secret was out. 'They must all know by now.' That was what you got for endeavouring to keep a house, a family together.

'That Gertrude Polson's home from finishing school,' said Isobel.

'Fancy. I didn't know,' Mrs. Mortimer replied.

'Yes, I saw her yesterday. Extraordinary what a common walk that girl has got,' continued Isobel.

Mrs. Mortimer hugged tighter her coat, she buried her chin in the soft fur. Thomas sat motionless, straight, almost to Guardsman stiffness. He was thinking of this evening, his night off, the two hours at The Gunman, the lone walk back through the cemetery.

There was silence in the car. Isobel and Geoffrey sat facing Celia and Gabriel. They stared dully at each other.

'I hope Agatha's not going to be unwell,' Mr. Mortimer broke the silence, 'a person as cheery and gay as Agatha . . .'

'Perhaps it's just a slight cold, dear,' said Mrs. Mortimer, 'she ought to have a fire in her room oftener than she does,' she hoped Thomas was listening, he had been rather neglectful of late, he wanted sharpening up.

'Worst February I've seen,' Geoffrey said, 'wonder where that kid got to?'

There was no reply. The car came into the village street. It pulled up outside the Post Office.

'I'm not getting out,' said Gabriel, 'nothing I want.'

'Nothing I want either,' added Geoffrey, 'only came out for the run.'

Celia and Isobel got out.

Mr. Mortimer looked at Geoffrey. 'My dear chap,' he said, 'do you never want *anything*?'

He was disappointed, he wanted at least five minutes alone with Thomas.

'*Never*,' Geoffrey replied, 'not in this dump. I just said this minute, you *must* have heard me, I came out merely for the run, a chat with the Polsons.'

'Oh . . .' Mr. Mortimer raised his eyes, he looked somewhat disconsolate, 'well . . . would you mind getting me some stamps, old chap?'

'Celia is getting stamps for everybody, she said so, she always does, anyhow.'

Mr. Mortimer gave it up. He stared gloomily at the floor of the car, the grease spots, the bread crumbs, the wisps of straw, the worn upholstery. He wished his brother was more sensible, more understanding, he might be able to talk to him. Unfortunately he wasn't, he had never grown up.

'I simply can't understand where that boy can have got to,' Mr. Mortimer said. 'My God, I was angry with him this morning, he seemed positively possessed of the devil.'

'When I went to my room after breakfast,' Geoffrey said, 'I found all my trophies scattered about the carpet, everything off the walls, even my medals out of the drawers, thought it might be burglars at first. It took me an hour putting everything back.'

'*I* say! What bad luck. You didn't lose anything I hope . . . little . . .'

'I think there's a lot of Dolphin there, really,' went on Geoffrey, 'a *lot* of Dolphin. When on earth is that kid's mother coming back? I thought you'd written to her ages ago, after all, it's only fair to the child, isn't it?'

'I suppose it is. There is always the possibility that she might not come back at all. She may be very happy where she is, you know how selfish she always was. I disbelieved it at first, but I'm afraid Celia was dead right from the first. . . .'

'But it's *wrong*, a child should have its parents, if not both, then one of them. I expect the poor kid's crazy with loneliness. Sometimes he strikes me as a sad child, I must confess. We've been showing him our silly toys, and he probably hates them. Isn't Celia arranging about a school for him?'

'Schools cost money. . . .'

'We're not as broke as all that.'

'That may be.' Mr. Mortimer kept his eyes fixed on Thomas's back, he thought it moved slightly. 'I think what he did this morning was beastly to say the least. Poor Agatha. That's what has upset her, I'm sure. Tearing up her music like that. A cunning in one so young, don't you think? He must have heard us talking about it the previous evening, then gone in and searched and found it, and torn it to shreds. You can't so easily replace those things today. You never saw such a mess. Celia smacked him. It has quite upset her. She has never struck a child in her life.' After a pause he added, 'It saved me striking him.'

'Did it?'

'Yes. I wish they'd hurry up in that Post Office,' Mr. Mortimer exclaimed irritably. 'Not that I'm looking forward to the Polsons at all. Devilish dull lot I think. At the moment the mother's busy trying to marry Gertrude off, they're terribly broke . . . it's awful, really, don't you think?'

Geoffrey sat up. He said suddenly, 'What's that?' He had been day-dreaming.

'Nothing. I do wish they'd hurry. What can they be buying there?'

'Probably talking, women usually do.'

Gabriel glanced at his watch, 'They've been twenty-five minutes in that poky little shop already.'

'You know I was seized by a desire to go up and drag out the Biblical beast and bring him along.'

'The Biblical beast!' Mr. Mortimer looked astonished, 'you're not referring to Arthur, I hope.'

'Who else? It's time he did something, don't you think? He's been vegetating up there far too long.

We're keeping him, we're all keeping him there. It's absurd. You don't make things better either, by tolerating it.'

Geoffrey felt his knee violently pinched, he came up against his brother's glaring eye.

He exclaimed in a low voice, 'Here they are. At last.'

'Sorry we kept you waiting so long,' Mrs. Mortimer said, as she and Isobel climbed back into the car.

'Not at all,' said Geoffrey, he gave a roar like a bull, 'right, Thomas.'

The car started off on its journey to the hills.

X

ROBERT had walked out of the room, and immediately he had shut the door, he ran. He flashed past the kitchen door so quickly that Joan, bending over the stove, swung round and exclaimed, 'What was that?'

Thomas, imperturbable, quietly cleaning the silver, replied, 'What was what?'

'Something flew past. Sometimes those birds fly in here. They quite frighten me, they're a nuisance.'

Slyly, glancing her way, Thomas focused his attention on the rise and fall of Joan's bosom, he smiled, said nothing, went on with his work.

Robert ran through the kitchen garden; he did not stop running until he had reached the spinney. He flung himself headlong through the undergrowth, into the solid masses of dead leaves. Then he sat down under a big pine and put his hand to his cheek. He had not expected that, it had hurt, he could feel the burning sensation on his cheek. Grandmother had surprised him. He kicked furiously at the dead leaves, he cried bitterly as he stared through the spinney. High above him he could hear pigeons, and somewhere on the spinney's edge he could hear the curious call of a carrion crow. Already he could feel a dampness penetrating the seat of his trousers, he felt that part become suddenly cold. This so annoyed him that he got up and began kicking dead leaves everywhere, over his head, to right and left of him, it became a sheer orgy of kicking, he turned round and round. Only when he had stubbed his toe on the trunk of the tree did he suddenly stop. He used a phrase he had often heard his father use on a night journey when the lorry for some reason suddenly stopped and refused to go any further. Swearing, his father would get out and lift the bonnet to discover the reason.

'Blast me black,' exclaimed Robert. Then he promptly sat down and cried again. He could still feel that sting in his cheek, he kept his hand there. He thought if he looked into a mirror now he would see a great red mark there, where grandmother had struck him. But the moment she did so he had felt happy, because then he was glad he had torn up the music like that. If she hadn't hit him he supposed he would have been sorry at once. Later, he heard a voice calling to him from the garden. Somebody had come out to look for him. He ceased crying at once, he ceased kicking out at all those leaves, he smiled, he stuck his hands into his pockets, he lay on his back, flat against the trunk, and quietly listened to the voice calling: 'Robert! *Rob* – – – ert. Are you there, Master Robert?'

Again he was happy, because this was Thomas, he hadn't recognized the voice, but he knew that only Thomas referred to him as Master Robert.

'Poor Mr. Thomas,' thought Robert, his face brightening to a smile, 'calling, and I know he's calling, I can hear him, and he doesn't know where I am.' He felt so pleased by this that he forgot the burn on his cheek, and not feeling this any more he forgot all about his grandmother. His trousers were already soaking wet, but he didn't care.

'If I catch a big cold, they'll all be sorry.'

Immediately he pressed himself further into the wet foliage. Occasionally a cold drip from the overhanging branches struck his forehead. He liked it, it was cold and nice. He picked up a twig and began chewing on it. He listened intently. But the voice had ceased calling, there was complete silence. He put his hand to his cheek, but it didn't hurt him any more, he began rubbing his eyes with dirty fingers. He wondered what time it was. A flight of rooks passed over, some pigeons scattered, there was a sudden excited twittering in the branches. A brown owl, flying low, floated silently past him, it seemed hardly to disturb the air. But Robert had never seen an owl. Watching it fly past he thought of it as a bird he did not know anything about. After a silence he saw a pair of eyes staring fixedly at him. He gave a shout, the eyes vanished, he glimpsed the tail of the house cat, the black and white cat that always lived in the kitchen. He remembered he had never seen it in any of the other rooms in the house. Then he shut his eyes. He wondered what grandmother would be doing now, what his grandfather was doing, then he cocked his ear and was listening again. He thought he had heard a voice calling his name.

'I wish I knew what time it was. I wish I'd never come here. They don't like me any more. I wish I could shut my eyes tight, then when I opened them I'd see Christopher there, and he'd say, "Why, Bobby, what on earth are you doing here?" ' and then he'd give me a big box of those wonderful chocolates. He could see the box quite clearly, the polished lid with the drummer painted on it, and a purple ribbon right round it. He remembered the words on the lid. Super Delicious.

'I'm hungry,' he said, and stared down at his shoes. They were soaked through. Perhaps he shouldn't have come here after all. Then he remembered Thomas and laughed. That was funny. He knew where they were, and they didn't know where he was. It made him feel happy again, their not knowing. It was worth being hungry, and not minding it. He looked up through the trees at the sky. 'It's always the same, the sky is.'

Where he lived before the sky was full of lights. Everywhere there were lights shining into the sky, and great blue flashes across it as the trains thundered through Paddington.

'I didn't want to come here, and I'm here. I didn't want to leave daddy, and I did.'

When he thought of daddy, he would always remember the hot mugs of tea, the fish and chips, red hot from Zennor's, the grey blankets and the warmth of daddy in the bed with him.

'Robert!'

Robert sat up at once. He was smiling. He felt cold and wet, but he continued to smile.

'Robert . . . *Rob* – – ert. Where are you, darling?'

This was his grandmother. He recognized her fluty voice, the way it trembled when her voice was high.

'Robert, where are you, dear?' she called again.

Robert crouched. He smiled again because it meant that grandmother was worried because she didn't know where he was.

'It might mean she's sorry now she hit me,' thought Robert, he hugged himself with great satisfaction. Even his grandmother didn't know where he was. She would go into the house again, she would tell the others. They would all come out. They would all be sorry for him then.

'They *will* be when I catch this cold,' he picked up some dead leaves and deliberately stuffed them down inside his shirt.

'I'll make them sorry, I'll *make* them.'

'Even Uncle Geoffrey, he'll be sorry, too.'

He laughed into the folds of his jersey, he remembered how his uncle had woken up, how he shouted, 'Get out, get out at once,' he had been angry, it was half past seven in the morning. It was the first time his uncle had shouted at him.

When Uncle Geoffrey had gone down to breakfast he had sneaked up to his room and taken that big sword off his wall. He felt brave as he slashed everywhere with the sword, cutting the photographs off the wall, watching the smiling faces fall to the floor. Then he had turned out all the drawers and scattered everything on the carpet, then he picked up the sword and swept the silver cups off his uncle's desk. Afterwards he had dropped the sword and kicked it under the bed. He had run out, laughing.

'Yes, he'll be sorry, too,' thought Robert.

He sat up, he folded his arms. He was certain that Uncle Geoffrey would soon come out and call him. He might even come and search for him. That would be fun.

But he wished he knew what time it was, and he was feeling hungry again. He might sneak along to the kitchen. No. That wouldn't be any use. Joan would be there. He hated Joan. She bossed him about, and, always when Thomas was there, she was rude to him. He decided he had better stay. He was still happy that they were still looking for him, and he had almost forgotten his soaked behind. Another icy drip fell on his hand. He began rubbing his hair and eyes again. They felt itchy. Suddenly he was staring at his knees, which had turned slightly blue. He rubbed them vigorously with his fingers, it was only his knees that were really cold. He supposed it would soon be time for another call. He grew quite impatient, waiting The cat returned to stare at him; he flung sticks at it, and it vanished through the trees. Then he heard what he had been waiting for. The booming voice in the garden.

'It's him, Uncle Geoffrey.'

Robert sat up, he felt his trousers, they were soaked through, leaves adhered to his hair, his legs, his face. It had seemed less uncomfortable lying back against the tree, he returned to this position and waited.

'Are you anywhere about, little man?' cried Uncle Geoffrey. It sounded to Robert as though his uncle were standing on the lawn. He didn't feel uncomfortable any more. He buried his shoes in the leaves, he listened to his uncle's voice rolling across the lawn and down to the spinney. He had an idea that his uncle, more venturesome than the others, would come down the lawn and go into the spinney. He had already decided what to do. This was better than his grandmother's high voice, and Thomas's Welsh yell. He had made a great mound of leaves, he would get right under this and hide. Uncle Geoffrey would never find him. Hearing the plodding feet coming down the lawn, Robert disappeared under the pile of leaves; he lay quiet, hardly daring to breathe. He heard the steps come right to the spinney, the continuous squash squash of the wet leaves. He hoped his uncle wouldn't slip and fall on top of him. He thought his uncle was now so close that he imagined he heard him breathing. Robert's eyes itched more than ever, he spat leaves out of his mouth. He began to shiver. But he didn't mind, he was sure that very soon they would all be sorry for him, grandmother most of all because she had hit him so hard this morning.

'I'll catch this death of cold,' thought Robert, 'what they call pneumonia.'

He was quite sure that his grandmother would cry.

It filled him with intense delight. Then he heard Geoffrey calling again, he lay rigid, holding his breath. He could feel his uncle very very near. Uncle Geoffrey was talking to himself.

'Damn the boy,' Uncle Geoffrey exclaimed wildly. He kicked his way through the dense wet mass, and for a moment the boy became frightened; he thought his uncle might kick at where he lay.

'*Rob* – – ert. Robert, where are you, come along now, we can't hang around all day in this weather looking for you. Come along, little man.'

Robert hugged himself close and smiled. This was the best game he had ever had. There was a great shout from his uncle.

'Blast!'

Robert heard him go, heard the heavy steps on the gravel, then silence.

'They won't come in here any more,' thought Robert, and slowly he emerged from his hiding place. He went and sat under the tree again. He shivered with the cold. Laughing, he said in a whisper, '*He'll* be sorry as well.' He said this with great conviction. Then, and without realizing it for a moment or two, he was sobbing and feeling miserable. He felt terribly hungry. He remembered the burning feeling on his cheek, and he cried into his cupped hands.

'I don't care. I don't care.'

He cried himself to sleep. Later the sounds of a car woke him. He heard many voices. He listened, then got to his feet and, crawling to the edge of the spinney, lay down. He could look right across the lawn from here, he could see the front door, a piece of the drive. Then he saw the car.

'They must be going out.'

He was filled with intense anger, he scowled at the

car, whilst he lay listening, trying to catch what the voices were saying. They must be in the hall. He watched and scowled until suddenly he saw his grandfather come out and stand by the car. Thomas seemed to appear from nowhere, he saw his grandfather speak to him. He strained his ears. Were they talking about him? Thomas was wearing his chauffeur's uniform, and Robert remembered that always on Thursdays Thomas put this on, then in the evening, he wore his blue suit and that funny bowler hat and he went off to the public house in the village. He could hear every spoken word. He noticed that it had got lighter, and he stared about him. The outlying hills were shrouded in silence and grey softness.

'You're certain you've looked everywhere, Thomas,' he heard his grandfather say, 'everywhere?'

Thomas said, 'Yes, sir, everywhere. I've searched all the likely places.'

'Then where the devil can he have got to? Really, he's becoming a nuisance.' Robert tensed. Grandfather wouldn't be sorry. He saw him get into the car. After a while his grandmother came out, and the boy stared fascinated at the fur coat, the fur cap. Thomas opened the door for her, and as she climbed in he heard her say quite clearly, 'Extraordinary, Thomas, very strange. I wonder where the child can have got to. He's bound to be hungry. But that'll drive him out, I'm sure,' his grandmother gave a curious little laugh, and Robert hated her laughing, 'I do hope . . .' she paused on the running board.

'Nothing'll happen to him, mam,' he heard Thomas reply, and then with much emphasis, 'I shouldn't worry, mam, I've a feeling nothing ever will happen to him,' and Robert exclaimed under his breath, 'blast Thomas black.' That was two who wouldn't care now.

Uncle Geoffrey came rushing out, followed by Aunt Isobel.

'Oh . . . he'll turn up all right,' Uncle Geoffrey said, and Aunt Isobel replied quickly with, 'Yes, I'm sure he will,' paused, and added with a smile, 'like the proverbial bad penny, I'm afraid,' and then she got into the car.

The boy wondered what she meant. Like a bad penny. It worried him, he was furious with himself because he didn't understand what she meant.

Then he heard Aunt Isobel's voice raised, heard her say, 'Fooling around somewhere, poor kid, amazes me how he finds things to amuse himself in this dump.'

Thomas closed the car door. Then he got in. Robert lay breathlessly watching. He saw the car move, there was a little squeak, he wondered if Thomas had run over a mouse. He lay flat on his face, his chin in his cupped hands, he listened to the gradually dying sounds of the car. He heard the big gate clang. He got up, hesitated, he wondered if he *should* sneak up to the kitchen, take something when Joan wasn't looking, it wouldn't be *very* difficult, now that Thomas was gone out. But if she saw him, she'd know. That would spoil everything. He had better remain where he was. They had not searched for him very long. He felt disappointed, he had hoped they would all come. He had wanted that very much, he had imagined them moving across the lawn in a body, all calling, 'Robert, Robert, come along, dear.'

'I'm hungry.' He leaned forlornly against a tree. 'I'll sneak up.'

Agatha was standing in the kitchen talking to Joan. The boy could see them from where he stood, but they would not be able to see him. His aunt was wearing her dressing-gown, and she had a white mop cap on her head. Robert thought she looked very funny with this cap on.

They had their backs turned to him. Joan was leaning lazily on a broom handle, as though she didn't care what was happening to him, or to anybody, anywhere, in the whole world.

'He's just a nuisance,' Joan was saying, 'you only see one side of him.'

'It's very worrying,' Aunt Agatha said.

Robert could see her staring round the kitchen, at the shelves, the pots and pans, the rows of plates and cups and saucers on the green sideboard. For Joan it was a very rare occasion, she could not recall Miss Agatha ever having got so far as the kitchen.

Agatha looked into the bright log fire. 'He's been away so long.'

'Not *very* long, Miss Agatha. Two hours about. That's not long to a child. They haven't any idea about time at all. But it is naughty of him, I agree. Expect he's prowling about somewhere, and if you ask me he's probably enjoying himself, too,' she gave Agatha a wide smile, it seemed full of assurance. 'I've something here for him when he turns up, please don't worry yourself about him, Miss Agatha.'

A question from Miss Agatha rather surprised her. 'Joan! . . . I presume you're quite happy here?'

'Very, Miss Agatha, best place I ever had.'

'What I mean to say is . . . well. . . .'

'Yes, Miss?'

'It's probably silly to ask this, but . . . well, you get your wages regularly?'

'Oh yes, Miss. On the whole mistress is very good. Sometimes it's late, sometimes it's very prompt. But I *do* understand. So does Thomas. We *really* do, Miss.'

Agatha regretted her curiosity. She felt suddenly humiliated. She returned to the boy again.

'Yes, I expect you're right, he'll turn up as soon as he gets really hungry, boys do. He'll come in soon. But I hope he's not sitting out somewhere, in this damp weather.'

'I hope not indeed, Miss,' Joan stood away from the broom, put it away in the corner. She crossed to the stove, began lifting pan lids, peering at the contents of the pans, testing, sniffing, she forgot Miss Agatha. Agatha realized it was time to go. She certainly was not wanted here. Robert watched her go.

'They think I'll be all right, but I won't, I know I won't.'

He decided to go back and sit in the spinney. He hated Joan more than ever.

'Now I'll make them not find me.'

Mrs. Mortimer found Agatha sitting in her room. She was quietly knitting.

'My dear, I'm so sorry about what happened. A dreadful thing for the child to have done. I really lost my temper with him. I've *never* seen Gabriel so upset, never.'

Agatha, without looking up, replied, 'Well, it's done now. There are some things that don't seem to matter very much in the long run. I admit I was very disappointed. It actually shocked me.'

'I'm sure it did, dear, well, never mind. Poor Agatha. I've just written to town to a musical friend of mine asking him to get me that book of music. Those things are very difficult to replace these days, very difficult.'

Agatha, suddenly conscious of scent in the room, looked up. Her sister-in-law had just had a bath. She was sitting on the edge of a chair near the door, she was looking at her with great concern.

'It's early lunch today, Agatha, but you know that. We're going into the village immediately afterwards, there are some things to be got there, especially stamps. It seems extraordinary the number of stamps we have in this house, yet nobody seems to write to anybody, and hardly any mail comes here. There'll be room, I know you like a run in the car. The Polsons have asked us to tea, they want us to meet Gertrude, she's just returned from her finishing school in Switzerland.'

'I met her once, a nice child,' casually Agatha dropped her needles in her lap.

Mrs. Mortimer got up. 'Don't be long, dear,' she said, as she swept to the door.

'I shan't be coming, Celia, please don't wait for me,' said Agatha. Would you tell Joan I'll have lunch up here.'

Mrs. Mortimer paused, her hand on the door knob.

'You're not ill, dear?'

'No, no. A slight headache. And if you don't mind, I'd just rather remain in my room for the afternoon, I feel rather tired today.'

Mrs. Mortimer crossed the room, she sat down, she looked closely at Agatha.

'Really! You *are* all right? I don't want you getting ill. What a nuisance that child running off like that, it seems he has a little temper, too. We've all of us been out, calling everywhere, it is rather odd. Not a sign. Hidden himself somewhere. What a morning it's been, quite upsetting.' She got up, saying, 'I *must* go. So sorry you're not coming with us, still. . . .' She laid a hand on Agatha's shoulder,. 'A disturbing morning for us all. Is there anything I can get you, or send up with Joan?'

'Nothing, dear. Do go. You'll be late. I know you want to get on. I'm quite all right, don't start worrying over me.'

'Very well. Bye-bye,' Mrs. Mortimer said, she watched Agatha take up her knitting. The door closed.

Later Joan came up with lunch. Some time afterwards Agatha heard the car go bumping down the drive.

Thomas had been rushed upstairs to light a fire in Miss Agatha's room. She was seated in front of it now, the light on, Geoffrey's socks in her lap, the needles idle in her hand. She had been hearing the needles click for a long time. Her fingers had moved automatically, she was quite indifferent about those socks. Agatha felt miserable, sad. Such a day. First the rumpus over that music. It had seemed such a fuss at the time. But her brother's almost casual mention of his state of affairs had shocked her. She was worried about the boy. She had only picked at her lunch. When Thomas came in to light the fire, and had exclaimed cheerily, 'Good afternoon, Miss Agatha, I hope you are not ill,' she had been unable to reply. She could only stare stupidly at the man's back as he bent over the hearth. Then she thought, 'I must make some reply. It would seem so rude.'

'I'm quite well, thank you, Thomas.'

The rest had been silence, broken only by the man's heavy breathing as he heaved the big coal scuttle about from one side of the hearth to the other. Finally he had staggered out, the door banging loudly after him. She had heard them calling for Robert. Geoffrey and Celia and Gabriel.

'I wonder where the child is, poor little fellow. Probably hiding somewhere, terrified I expect.' She ought to go out and look for him herself. 'He'll feel so frightened and lost.' She *must* go out and search for him.

Yet somehow it seemed difficult to move. It wasn't the growing cosiness of the room, the feeling of peace and quiet that held her to the chair. It was Gabriel's problem and Gabriel's position that held her pressed down like this. There was no way of dodging this at all. It stared her in the face with all the ruthlessness of cold, hard fact. She seemed to see a great black question-mark dancing about in front of her. How had all this come about? She supposed they were comfortable here, moderately so, but comfortable. Gabriel had his own small income, so had Celia. As for Isobel and Geoffrey, they practically kept themselves.

'They ought to pay Thomas,' she told herself, 'and then get rid of him. It's unfair to everybody.' Indeed it was dreadful. Three years. She found it hard to believe. And why did the man stay here, anyhow? Was there something else between Thomas and her brother? No. She thought it was just her brother's weakness, sheer inability to make up his mind. How weak that showed him to be. He had never been anything but weak. And a peace at any price man into the bargain. 'But,' thought Agatha, 'that's all very well in its way, but unfortunately life is not like that at all. And what was Celia doing about this matter? Did the others know?' She could see these questions whirling round and round that black question-mark, they circled in her mind in wild confusion.

Her little green clock chimed three o'clock. She glanced down at her knitting. She knew she would do no more today; she got up and put it away in her work-

basket, crossed to the window and stood looking out.
'I wonder, yes, I'll call Robert, I'm sure he'll come
now. He's bound to be hungry, poor little chap,' and
she shot up the window. But when she opened her
mouth to call, she found she could not speak. It was
then that she had put on her dressing-gown and gone
down to see the maid in the kitchen.

It was now a quarter to four. She sat looking into
the fire, wondering. They would be back before dark.
They never stayed out much after half past five. Their
return was something much more certain than the
matter of the lost Robert. How *could* he have remained
out all this time? He must surely know they would
be worried about him. And he *must* be feeling
hungry, 'and probably very cold, too. Silly little
boy. . . .'

The problems were still there, nothing had been
solved. Thomas was still owed that three years wages,
the Brahms Intermezzi were hopelessly lost, Robert
was still missing. The whole house seemed suddenly
shut in, trapped by silence, heightened when she
suddenly heard her own laboured breathing.

Life, hitherto so calm, had become suddenly very
complicated, uncertain. For a moment or two she
imagined the car load of Mortimers, Thomas concentrated at the wheel, forcing the aged machine up
towards the hills, through lanes the Romans had
never seen, up cart-tracks, bumping and turning, and
Thomas as usual with his frown, worried in case there
should be a breakdown. She could see the great red
brick house where the Polsons lived. See them all at
tea, facing each other across the sprawling dining-
room table, the big dark room, full of an everlasting
sort of twilight. She had sat there so often herself.
With this scene vivid in her mind she became more

conscious than ever of the growing silence of the afternoon. It seemed to carry forward with it a desolate air. How surprising the echo in this house! She went out into the corridor, past the closed doors. How the damp seeped into the house on these afternoons. Not a sound anywhere. Half way down she hesitated. She wished she could settle herself down. Perhaps she ought to go back and take up that knitting again. There might be something left undone, lying in the work-basket. But when she returned and went through it there was nothing. Yet she took up her needles and some fresh wool. Hardly realizing it she began to knit. The play of the needles induced in her a feeling of somnolence. After a while she saw the futility of it all. She put the things away finally, she could not settle again now. How stupid of her brother to go on like this. There was a rift somewhere, there would be a break, she could see it coming. She exclaimed into the empty room, 'Where on earth is that child?'

That was what unsettled, that was the worry; for the first time she seemed to realize the seriousness of it. Where on earth could he be? He had been out hours now. The long silence of the afternoon, the absence of the child's voice in the house, a sudden feeling of isolation . . . she buttoned up her dressing-gown, threw a scarf over her head and went out to look for Robert. For a moment or two she stood on the edge of the lawn, for an instant she thought, 'He'll see me, he's watching somewhere about.' The light was fading, she felt a tang in the air, it would soon be dark. She stepped on to the lawn, in the centre she stopped. She hoped the party would soon be back. Never had she felt so alone, 'I might have gone with them, I daresay I should have enjoyed the run.'

She found him after searching for over an hour. She found him lying on his back in the spinney. Bending down, she held him closely, fiercely – how cold the boy was – she spoke to him.

'Robert, darling.'

But he remained motionless, eyes closed. She drew back with horror, for a moment she thought, 'My God . . . what has happened?'

She tried to lift the child, held him, then put him down again.

'Oh dear,' exclaimed Agatha.

She tried again. 'How heavy he is,' she raised him up, then fell with him, herself lying across his body. Agatha began to cry. Her fingers on his forehead felt heat, 'Oh God,' she thought, 'Robert darling, Robert dear,' she clutched him, pressed him to her, 'Oh, Robert darling,' held fast to him, to what had become her living dream. This child might be hers, conceived and borne by her. This was her life now, holding on to him, holding on.

'Darling, *do* open your eyes, dear, do speak, this is your Aunt Agatha.' She stared helplessly at the motionless child.

'I must do something.' 'I must get him into the house, he's feverish, he's very ill, I know he is, what a thing to have happened.'

Summoning all her strength, she lifted him up. She knew not how, and she didn't care, but here he was at last, out of that horrible spinney, here, on the lawn. He fell heavily from her useless hands, lay sprawled where he fell.

'I must get help.' It would happen like this. She glimpsed the Polson's table, saw them all seated there, her brothers and sister, her sister-in-law. Monsters of indifference. She staggered to her feet, and ran awkwardly, painfully towards the house. Reaching the kitchen she cried in a weak voice, 'Joan, Joan, come at once, please. Something has happened. Hurry. *Please.*' The girl, hearing the sudden call, dropped what she was doing and ran out into the corridor. She met Agatha, white-faced, distraught, helpless.

'Oh dear, Miss Agatha, are you ill?'

Speechless, Agatha could only point wearily towards the lawn.

'Oh . . .' exclaimed Joan and rushed to where the boy was lying.

Then Agatha was behind her.

'I think he's unconscious, look', said Joan.

'I know. I know. We must get him to bed at once. Do hurry. I couldn't manage him, he's so heavy.'

Joan lifted the boy up. More calmly she said, 'He's very ill, it's a fever.'

Agatha could make no reply. She stood there, bereft, her spirit flapped like the slackened sails of a ship. She knew in this moment that nothing could matter but this child. She watched the girl disappear with him into the house, then slowly followed. But when she reached the stairs she felt too weak to climb them. She suddenly knelt where she stood, even as the girl, white-faced, appeared on the landing. She came quickly down. 'You had better telephone for a doctor, Miss Agatha. Hadn't you better tell Mr. Arthur?'

Agatha looked up. 'Arthur! No, no. I'll do it. Don't worry. Go back to him. I'll telephone for Dr. Turner right away.'

Joan leaned over her, whispered, 'And please come up then, Miss Agatha, *please.*'

'Yes,' her voice shaking, 'of course,' and she saw Joan fly up the stairs. And then she could not move.

Something had happened to her. She could not move one foot or the other. Quietly she prayed. Joan was at her side again.

'You'd better telephone the Polsons as well,' she said, then was gone again, whilst Agatha answered, 'Yes, of course, at once.' It had been a great effort, but she had said it, and now she clung to the stair-rail, endeavouring to rise.

'Poor little boy,' thought Joan, 'now he's gone and done it. What a worry children are. How quiet everything was before he came.' She heard the telephone receiver being lifted, 'Thank God. She's telephoning now.'

She had quickly undressed the boy. She had rubbed him down vigorously with hot towels, she had filled two hot water bottles, buried him in blankets, all in the space of a few minutes. She felt a sudden grudge against the family.

'Why should they be out this afternoon? Just when this happened,' her mind went back to the scenes of the morning. 'Such a commotion there has been to-day, quite lively indeed for this house.'

She stared down at the flushed face of the child, 'How horribly dirty he's got.' She began to comb the black ruffled hair, removing dead leaves. There was no movement from Robert. She called softly to him, again and again, she spoke into his ear, 'Bobby, Bobby.' There was nothing save the laboured breathing of the child for answer.

'Poor little chap. They should never have taken him away. Much better where he was I should think, never happy here, sure he wasn't. Silly things people do. Thomas said it was real bad. Cruel to his real grandmother, poor old woman, it was *her* child by rights, her who is coming down tomorrow.' Yes, she knew all about it. Thomas had told her everything. What a shame it was. No mother, and now no father, no wonder things went wrong. The poor kid didn't really know who he belonged to. Perhaps he never would. She kept wiping perspiration from the child's face. The water was boiling, the towels hot. There was nothing else she could do now except sit here and watch him until Miss Agatha came up. She sat down on the edge of the bed, stared fixedly at the flushed face; she supposed he *must* be unconscious, he lay so still. Her ear was alert for the sound of a telephone ring, for the sound of a car, of voices; she prayed they wouldn't be long now. The light was almost gone, how dark the room had got. She went and put a match to the night-light on the table, then returned to her vigil. As she did so, she paused for a moment, looking at the wardrobe. Its doors were partly open, and through the opening she could see dresses and coats hanging on their hooks. His mother's clothes. Just fancy. What a cruel person she was to go off like that with another man and leave her poor husband to look after the child.

'Cruel,' Thomas had said, 'cruel that one is.'

Agatha had reached the telephone room. Twice the operator at the exchange had inquired for the number she wanted, and was still waiting, but Agatha had put down the receiver. She sat, trembling, feeling her racing pulse. She said quickly, 'Dreadful, dreadful.'

After a while she felt calmer; picking up the receiver again she asked directly to be put through to Dr. Turner's house. She then spoke to the maid. The doctor was out, but he would come directly he returned home. Yes, the maid said, she would see to that. Agatha said, 'Do hurry now, thanks so much.' She

got up, slowly made her way back to the stairs. For a
moment she stood there, then went up. Reaching the
boy's room, she went in, Joan, hearing the door
opening, looked round. She saw Miss Agatha put her
hand to her lips and slowly approach the bed. In a
low voice she said, 'You're a good girl, Joan, and *so*
helpful. He's not spoken?'

Joan shook her head.

Agatha leaned down, and whispered, 'I'll be back in
a few minutes. I have something urgent to do. Please
remain here, do not bother if the telephone rings. Just
sit quietly there and don't budge until I return. You
understand?'

Joan, looking assuringly at the tall, grey-haired
woman, nodded her head. Agatha then went out.
She went straight to her brother's room and knocked.
There was no answer. She knocked louder, but
receiving no reply, would wait no longer. She opened
his door and walked in. Only once before had she
entered Arthur's room. As it was then, so it was now.
The place reeked of stale tobacco smoke, stale air. As
usual the windows were closed. She could see her
brother curled up in his chair. He seemed to be fast
asleep. This did not surprise her, he slept so fitfully.
For almost a minute she stood there, staring down at
him. Then she spoke.

'Arthur!'

The sound of her own voice astonished her. Its
strength had returned, she thought, 'I feel better.
But I had better hurry.'

There was a grunt from the man in the chair. His
very appearance repulsed her, but it also fortified her
resolution. She no longer felt weak and afraid.
'Wake up! I have something to tell you. And there is
something you must do.' Her brother was wearing the

dirty flannel trousers, the old patched tweed coat. His hair was uncombed, he had possibly not shaved for three days. The dirty stubble seemed somehow to accentuate his somewhat bloated appearance. When at last he opened his eyes and yawned, she saw them red-rimmed, with great black circles underneath. The features, for a man of forty-eight, seemed heavily lined. She even noticed his hands. There was nothing about his appearance that in any way lessened the general atmosphere of squalor.

It seemed difficult for her to believe that a man had lived in this room for nigh on two years. She stood back a little, watching him, waiting for him to sit up. But she knew she would not wait much longer. Here was a man completely changed by one single incident in his life, who had lived in this room as any hermit might, who rarely ever left it, except at night, to go on his nocturnal walks, when he was not standing in the pantry eating what he was too proud to accept with the rest of the family. Thinking of this now, Agatha saw the pride wither to dust, the sheer self-deception of it. There must have been with it an inner misery. She suddenly wondered. A brother who was no brother. A man who had slowly inflated the sense of injury to himself, and who never for a single moment realized, or, if he did, was completely indifferent to, the injury he had done to others. A man who was not really a man at all. Idle, self-pitying, living on an elder brother's weakness, taking advantage in every way, living on them all. He seldom spoke to them, he shrank into corners, sometimes would not share the table with them. An utter stranger.

There were times when they completely forgot he existed. He had become 'something up there'. What hurt Agatha most of all was his cringing, cadging money as well as pity. What sort of life was this? No life at all. If it was not stopped now it would go on for ever. Only the thought of Gabriel, his position, that sudden revelation, all the more shocking because so casual, the knowledge of his indebtedness to Thomas, of all people, had spurred her on. She was filled with an iron determination; the silent house, the stricken child held it fast. She would speak now. This thing would be done now. At this moment there were only two people existent, this man slumped in his chair, and herself. Facing him, she leaned forward and tapped him on the shoulder. He opened his eyes, looked up at her. As he did so, he saw her glance towards the ever ready, ever packed suitcase. From the suitcase to the utter chaos of his desk, then, turning again, faced him, her eye taking in the hearthstone, littered with dead matches, torn papers. Always in her nostrils the horrible stale smell, the airless window-tight room. Studying him now she could only think of an animal.

'Arthur.'

How suddenly hard her voice, it startled her, 'Arthur! Get up at once.' He sat up at that. For a moment he seemed unaware who was addressing him. Then he got to his feet. This action of rising to full height seemed to crowd in on Agatha all the squalor and shame that this room held. She faced him squarely. 'Arthur! There is something you have to do at once.'

'Agatha! Why, it's you,' Arthur said, like one emerging from long sleep, 'what is . . .?'

'Your case is always packed and ready,' Agatha heard herself say. 'You have made a number of attempts to leave this house. Today, indeed now, you will finally pack and go. Only today have I come to realize what you have meant here. You have meant nothing. Nothing. You do not belong here, you never have. I have never been so pained in my life, as when this morning, and by the sheerest accident, as Gabriel and I were searching for some lost music, it slipped out accidentally; he has told me of the whole horrible position. You must go away from here at once. In saying that I am speaking for us all. They will never ask you, and certainly the one who is practically keeping you will never do so. You take advantage of that. How you could have even tolerated your position this last two years is quite beyond me. I'll say no more. You had better go and get ready. I'm so determined on this matter that I shall remain here until you are ready.'

'It's difficult . . .' Arthur began to stutter.

'Everything is.'

She sat down in the chair by the desk. Arthur then went out. Agatha looked at the open desk. On it were two great files of letters. Her curiosity aroused, she examined them; she had never seen them before.

It made her smile. One file consisted of letters written over the past two years, from people who sympathized with her brother. 'Heavens!' she thought, 'he has fans.'

The other file consisted of hundreds of letters written by Arthur, not one of which had ever got into an envelope. On the top of the file he had written in block letters: LETTERS OF PROTEST. She thought it pathetic. She could hardly believe it, but she thought she heard the sound of the bathroom tap being run. She was suddenly full of dread. 'Suppose I fail. Suppose he . . . no, the less we talk the better. There is nothing we two can talk about any longer.' She had only to recall Gabriel's face this morning, when he had told her that horrible news. She refused to be surprised when the door opened and her brother came in.

'At least you look better.' She went to the door, and took his overcoat off the hook. 'Here is your overcoat, you will want it. I will go with you as far as the gate.'

He did not answer, he would not look at her. Was this, she asked herself, the sense of shame out at long last. It could hardly be anything else. 'Your bag is rather heavy,' she said. He bent down and took it from her. He stood for a moment staring at the objects on his mantelshelf. Then he saw the ashes lying in the grate. He put down the bag. He went to the grate.

He stood there contemplating.

'What are you looking at?'

'Nothing,' Arthur replied, it was the last word he spoke to her. Then he got up, picked up the bag. From the mantelpiece he removed a tiny green stone horse; he put it in his pocket, he gave a final glance around the room, opened the door and went out.

'Wait,' cried Agatha.

She followed him down the stairs and out of the house. They walked down the drive. Agatha thought that this drive would never end; her feet were aching, but she struggled on, she was determined. This man should go. Better for them all, perhaps the making of him. They reached the gate. They stopped.

'You have often walked down this far, and then for some reason, which nobody but yourself knows, you have turned back. I have often wondered what happens. What you see. But really, Arthur,' she continued, pointing with her finger, 'there is nothing beyond this except the world, other people. You need not be afraid of them, they will have forgotten all about *that*, people have short memories, besides they are too interested in themselves to be thinking of you. Nobody will see you, and nobody will take any notice of you. Here.'

From her pocket she took ten pound notes and crushed them into his hand. For a moment their hands touched, and quite impulsively Agatha squeezed his own, but his remained limp, grasping limply the money she had given him.

'Goodbye, Arthur,' Agatha said. 'Write and let us know how you are getting on.'

As she said this she lowered her head and would not look at him, but turned away and went slowly up the drive. When she had gone about fifty yards, she turned sharply and looked towards the gate. Arthur had gone.

'Thank God! It seems like a miracle, I could never have believed I could do it.'

Her heart suddenly lifted, and, coming in view of the house again, she looked at it with new eyes: that great shadow which had hung over it for so long had vanished. She went in, went upstairs. She stopped to regain her breath. What an hour it had been! Then she went on to the boy's room. The telephone bell rang. Agatha went inside. The girl was still sitting by the child's bed, the boy had not moved, and his eyes were closed. Whispering, Joan said, 'Oh, I'm glad you're back, Miss Agatha, so glad.'

Agatha replied softly, 'I'll stay here now. You had better see who is on the phone.'

As the girl walked to the door, Agatha gently called her back.

'Yes, Miss Agatha?'

'Mr. Arthur won't want tea in his room this evening, you will remember, won't you?'

'Yes, Miss Agatha.'

'Thank you.'

She took the boy's hand, 'Poor little boy,' she said, then she heard the door close.

'Oh God, I do hope Dr. Turner will be here soon. I'm so helpless, I'm so afraid, poor little chap. *Why* did he go out like that? What on earth had Celia done to him? Could it be that even she could not understand a child?'

She lay her head on the pillow, she stroked Robert's cheek, she sang into his ear, 'Robert, Robert darling, it's me, it's Aunt Agatha. Wake up, dear.' She dozed. The sound of a car made her sit up.

'It's them. Thank heaven, they're back.'

Joan came in. She tiptoed across the room.

'It was the doctor, Miss Agatha. He is coming now. The others are back, too. I went to meet them at the door, Miss Agatha. They did look queer.'

'Queer, what do you mean, girl, queer?'

'Well they all looked blue with the cold, Miss Agatha, but it was their eyes, miss. They looked wild-like.'

'You may go,' Agatha said.

'Wild-eyed and looking slightly blue,' Agatha smiled to herself, 'what an extraordinary girl.'

XI

MR. MORTIMER, who had never eaves-
dropped in his life, stood outside the door of
the boy's room, listening. He could hear them
distinctly, they were discussing Robert. He glanced
behind him, just to see that his bedroom door had not
closed of itself; he was ready to scuffle back the
moment he heard footsteps inside the room. He heard
the man's voice and recognized it at once.

'One has to be so careful with children,' Dr. Turner
said.

'Yes, I know,' Mrs. Mortimer replied.

'One has to *understand* them,' continued the doctor.

Gabriel imagined him standing at the foot of the
bed, he thought one hand would be in the air, the
preaching attitude. He knew the Turner manner so
well. And how the voice boomed out; the man was so
infernally healthy. He heard the quiet voice of his
wife, 'Yes, doctor, I know. One must.'

'It was only yesterday, curiously enough, that I
heard you had a child here.'

To Mr. Mortimer it sounded like an accusation, as
though he were saying, 'and why wasn't I informed?'

'As though a child wasn't entitled to be at Greys,'
thought Gabriel.

'What exactly happened?'

Gabriel leaned against the door, he did not intend
to miss a word of it.

'Very little, really. My husband was rather angry
with him this morning. I agreed with my husband,
doctor. The child had deliberately torn up some music
belonging to Miss Agatha. When I questioned him he

infuriated me by his stubborn and, in my opinion, impudent attitude. I hit him.'

'You struck him,' Dr. Turner said.

'I'm afraid I did. I don't very often lose my temper. You'll realize, doctor, that we are . . .'

'May I ask, Mrs. Mortimer, who is the child?'

'My daughter-in-law's.'

'Oh! Is she here then? I understood she was not at Greys now.'

'My God,' thought Gabriel, trembling with rage, 'this is going a bit too far. The very idea. It's an inquisition.' What on earth was his wife doing, going on like that? Dr. Turner had no right to ask such questions. He hoped Celia wasn't losing her common sense.

'She is away at present.'

'I see.'

'I hope I'm not being rude, Doctor,' Mrs. Mortimer was saying, 'but I don't think this matter concerns you. We are a little worried of course, we have never had a sick child here.'

'Naturally. He must feel rather lonely, if I may say so, no other children to play with.'

'He is going to school very soon.'

'Oh.'

'Damn this man,' thought Gabriel, 'must I go in and stop the whole thing?'

'He's not,' he heard his wife saying, 'he's not seriously ill, Doctor?' She added, 'We have sent for Robert's mother.'

'Of course. One would do that. No, I shouldn't say he was seriously ill,' replied Dr. Turner, 'but as I say, children are funny little beggars, you have to be so careful, to understand them. . . .'

Mr. Mortimer put his hand on the doorknob, he

half turned it, he wanted to shout, 'Stop asking such questions,' then hesitated as the voice boomed on.

'Keep him warm. Plenty of milk. No solids. And quiet. No worrying. Not *too* much attention. Up to the age of ten children are like pups and kittens.'

Gabriel waited, there was no reply from his wife. He was relieved. What a question, what a comparison . . . animals! He thought it a perfectly stupid observation to make, quite beside the point.

'Indeed,' said the doctor, 'he should be as right as rain tomorrow. But a very good job he was found when he was, very fortunate indeed, it might have been much worse.' The voice stopped; Gabriel heard a step in the room and prepared to disappear.

'He's a perfectly healthy child in every other way,' Dr. Turner went on, 'when did you plan to send him to school, Mrs. Mortimer?'

'Soon.'

'I gather he's a town child, from London.'

'Yes, he was born in London.'

'Ah! He'll· miss London. Town children rarely settle in the country, unless they're made to. Well. . . .'

Gabriel opened the door and walked in. He had had enough.

'Ah! Good evening, sir, I hope you're well, Mr. Mortimer, tricky little business, this.'

'Yes, very worrying, poor little chap,' Mr. Mortimer replied. He flung a glance at his wife which said, 'Get him out.'

Mrs. Mortimer moved slowly towards the door. 'Well, thank you ever so much for coming along, Doctor. We'll do as you say. I hope he'll be able to get up tomorrow. . . .'

'Perhaps, perhaps towards evening, I'll look in.'

Moving Dr. Turner nearer to the door, Mrs.

195

Mortimer said quickly, 'Thank you, I'll ring, Doctor, I'm sure we'll manage all right. And thanks again.'

Gabriel was pleased with her. How well she was edging out this abominable man, this prying, interfering man – he had never thought much of him as a doctor, though Agatha swore by him. Talked far too much, a nose like a fox, always finding out something, even the Polsons couldn't stand him.

'Good evening, Mr. Mortimer,' he heard Dr. Turner say.

Gabriel was standing at the foot of the bed, looking at the boy.

'Evening,' he replied absentmindedly; he was staring hard at Robert. Robert's eyes were open, they were intently watching his grandfather. Gabriel moved to the head of the bed.

'Well, little man. How are you, dear? What a worry you've been today. Are you getting better? I hope so. The doctor says you'll be as right as rain to-morrow,' he went on and on, like a parrot, he hardly knew why he did it, but he kept repeating himself, fascinated by the child's inquiring eyes. The door suddenly closed. They had gone. He was on the point of seating himself, when the door opened again, and he heard his wife say softly, 'Gabriel.'

He turned. He called, 'Yes, dear?'

She beckoned. He went, and gave the boy a smile as he went out; he felt miserable when Robert ignored it.

They left the room, stood in the corridor looking at each other.

'Nobody's had any tea yet,' Gabriel said.

'Everybody'll have tea presently,' Mrs. Mortimer replied. 'Poor Agatha. I must go to her. What a day it has been for her, poor dear.'

'It was really, wasn't it,' Mr. Mortimer said. 'I say, did you notice the way that Gertrude Polson kept eyeing Geoffrey at tea. Full of meaning. Geoffrey actually blushed. It was rather amusing.'

They had reached their bedroom. Opening the door, Mrs. Mortimer pushed her husband inside.

'I'm not interested in the Polsons at present,' she said coldly, 'you'll hear the bell for tea.'

She shut him in and left. She returned to the boy's room and sat with him.

'What an angel Agatha was, really,' she told herself, 'and just think, that brute sitting up there in his room all the time and never a move from him. He must have heard the commotion. I'm glad he doesn't want any tea. I couldn't bear to look at him after that. I don't want to see him at all this evening.'

Robert lay quietly looking at her.

'How excellent of that girl, how sensible, too. I must give her something special for that. How clean Robert looks, his hair has been cleaned and combed.' She noticed how strongly the dark lashes stood out against the white skin. Suddenly she put her arm behind him and raised him up.

'Robert.'

'I'm sorry I hit you, dear,' Mrs. Mortimer said, 'there,' she kissed him, she wished he would speak.

The small voice piped up. 'Are you, grandmother?'

'Yes, darling, I am. I shan't ever hit you again.'

'You can't . . . really,' Robert said, his voice shaky, 'not tomorrow. Thomas told me. My *real* grandmother is coming tomorrow.'

His eyes never left her and he saw her draw back a little. She felt as though the child had suddenly struck her, and then she heard him say, 'I will go to Paddington on the train. . . .'

'You mustn't talk, darling. Dr. Turner says you must be kept very quiet. If you are a good boy and do as you're told you may be able to get up tomorrow.'

He did not answer her, she watched him close his eyes. In his eyes he could hear the very remote sound of wheels, the train in the tunnel, the wheels of his father's lorry. His fingers clenched on the sheets, he pulled. He knew his grandmother was still sitting there, he could feel her near him, he could smell the scent, he could always smell the scent. Then he heard her get up, walk across the room, the door opened and closed. The sound of the wheels came louder to his ears.

'I thought *we* were funny enough,' Geoffrey said, he laughed heartily, 'but those Polsons beat us by lengths. More tea, Agatha,' he said.

Agatha was thinking how nice Geoffrey really was, he had been waiting on her hand and foot, he couldn't do enough for her. They were together in her room, seated before a now roaring fire.

'What a splendid husband you could have made, you're absolutely wasted.' Geoffrey, who loved praise, said, 'You really think so?' His smile was broad, alive.

'Yes, dear.'

'*What* a day you've had, old dear,' and it made Agatha cringe, she hated 'old dear', but she daren't say anything now.

'You know,' he went on, 'I've a good mind to get the car out tomorrow and take you for a run. How about that? Just the two of us. I tell you what. I'll ring The Kingfisher first thing in the morning, get him to put on a lunch for us, we'll have a look round there and then come back for tea. Used to be some dashed good fishing there before it became so popular.

A fly stands no chance against so many worms. Well?'

Geoffrey slapped his knee, and looked expectantly at his sister.

'It's very nice of you, Geoffrey, but I'm afraid not tomorrow. Any other day, but not tomorrow. Tomorrow I shan't move, one doesn't win battles by leaving the battle-ground.'

'What on earth are you talking about?'

'Who would you think I was talking about? Do try not to be so dense, but perhaps you like being dense.'

'Ah! I see. That kid.'

'That kid,' Agatha said; she looked earnestly at Geoffrey.

'You like him?'

'I love him,' she said.

Geoffrey, taken aback by this, thought, 'By God, I believe she does love that kid.'

'You don't want him to go?'

'I shan't let him go.'

'My word! I say, do have another scone, they're lovely and fresh. Joan does know how to turn a scone beautifully.'

'We don't notice that girl enough,' Agatha said, 'we're lucky to have her. She was a great help this afternoon. I think that eventually she'll marry Thomas.'

Geoffrey roared, he literally rocked in his chair, 'Heavens above! Thomas?'

'I'm certain she will. Did *you* know that Thomas had not been paid for three years?'

'What?'

'It's perfectly true. He hasn't. I got such a shock this morning. I felt . . . I can't tell you how I felt . . . I still feel . . . like a lodger.'

'Agatha. . . .'

'But I do.'

'It *is* a fact?'

'Very brutal one. We've been day-dreaming I'm afraid. I never thought that one so soft-hearted, so gentle, so apparently harmless as Gabriel, could in fact be so cunning. It distresses me.'

'Cunning?'

'Gabriel *is* cunning, we've under-estimated him, dear. Quite. I've often wondered why Thomas and he stuck so close together. And I'm afraid the position won't improve at all. Things won't get any better, can't see how they can. I don't think they ever can . . . now. It's awful, just thinking about it. Yet, there are some things. . . .'

'What things, Agatha?' Geoffrey asked. He helped himself to another scone, a third cup of tea; he liked his tea, he liked all his meals, he got from them an extra relish.

'It's men like Thomas who could eventually push us out of here, all of us. You realize that. I shouldn't laugh about it.'

'I'm not laughing, really I'm not,' protested Geoffrey. 'I'm merely trying to finish off this scone. *Won't* you have another one, Agatha?'

'Thank you, no,' Agatha said.

She sat quiet, she seemed suddenly withdrawn, she was gathering her forces. There seemed so little time, and she loved this child, in some strange way she had loved him long ago, and now had drawn him here. The sound of the Deptford footsteps seemed more ominous, they had rung in her ears from the moment she had read the letter that came from Mrs. Dolphin.

She looked at her brother, thinking, 'I wonder if he would be an ally?' She was glad he had definitely finished his tea. She had never much cared for rituals, and for her brother, tea was one.

'Do the others know about this?' he asked. 'Mind my pipe, dear?'

'No. I'm so glad you've finished that last scone,' she replied.

'I couldn't really say, Celia probably, she has a way of worming things out of Gabriel. I know. Secret as he. is, he isn't quite clever enough to hide anything from her.'

'It's all a mystery to me, anyhow,' Geoffrey said. 'In any case, *why* couldn't he have paid Thomas. We're not that badly off, surely.'

'There are eight people to feed here, dear, nine now, if you count the child.'

'I realize that,' he said, 'which reminds me, I ought to go along and look in on the kid,' he made to rise, but Agatha rose too, and forced him back in his chair.

This action re-kindled a doubt in Geoffrey's mind, 'I say,' he exclaimed, 'I can't understand that blighter Arthur not coming down to help. He must have heard the commotion.'

'There *was* no commotion, the whole thing was over in a few minutes. I found the boy in the spinney as I told you. . . .'

'Funny, I searched the spinney myself.'

'Nevertheless I found him there. Joan came out and helped.'

'*He* never came out at all?'

'No. I didn't want him out. After we had got the child to bed, and I had rung for Dr. Turner, I went in to see Arthur. What a pigsty of a place. Then, when I saw him slouched in the chair, fast asleep, I thought, "what a pig of a man".'

201

'Did you tell him what had happened.'

'I told him nothing. He was most irritable at being wakened up. He had one of those pitying moods again. I knew at once. He didn't want any tea, he as much as said . . .' she paused here, her invention was running thin. Geoffrey interrupted and she was glad.

'I used to make it a habit to bang in on him sometimes, in the afternoons, just for a chat. But I always came away depressed. He just isn't interested in anything or anybody, except himself. I thought, "it's quite possible, in the course of time, to forget he's there altogether." Why the hell doesn't he pull himself together, and *do* something, lazy swine,' he said.

'Well, I certainly shouldn't worry him now. It's possible he may not even come down to dinner.'

'He has his nibbling act when we retire,' replied Geoffrey, 'why doesn't Gabriel go and talk to him, he's head of this house, it's his business.'

'Geoffrey dear, I'm rather tired.'

'Sorry. Of course you are. See you at dinner, I hope.'

He put the things on the tray. 'I think I'll take these down.'

'I shouldn't, just leave them there,' and then he went out.

She was glad he was gone, she wanted so much to be alone, she wanted to think things out.

The moment Geoffrey shut the door, he thought, 'I'll go along and have it out with him,' and he went straight to Gabriel's room. He knocked, entered.

'Who's that?'

'Me.'

'Oh, it's you is it,' Gabriel said gruffly.

He was sitting at his desk. The curtains had not been drawn, he looked out into the darkness. There was a fire burning in the grate.

'You've no light,' Geoffrey said, and moved over to switch it on.

'Leave the light alone.'

'All right.' Geoffrey sat down. He made himself comfortable, he took out his pipe.

'Why are you sitting in the dark, do you always do this?' he stretched his long legs, the chair creaked.

'Did you want something?'

'Nothing in particular. You must be inured to this sort of thing by now. In this house there is no communal life, except at meals. One doesn't get together. We live our lives in our rooms. One time this would have struck me as *very* odd, but now . . . well, I'm used to it, too. This family doesn't communicate. We retire to our rooms and communicate with ourselves, which shows you how much we think of *ourselves*, really.'

'What are you getting at?' Gabriel snapped back at him. 'I say, what are you getting at, old chap.' He got up immediately and went and stood by the mantelpiece. He leaned heavily on it, the while he stared down at his brother.

'I've just been talking to Agatha.'

'What about?'

Geoffrey positively hated the tone of voice, and barked back. '*You.*'

'Me?'

Gabriel, smiling down at him now, said, 'Oh, people often talk about me. I never mind things like that. What a dreadful thing it might be if people couldn't talk, they might go mad,' he said.

'Is it true that you owe Thomas a lot of money?'
Gabriel stiffened. 'How do you know? Who's been talking?'

'Agatha told me. You can't go telling people other things like that, and not expect them to pass it on. I only want to know if it's true.'

'I owe him three years' wages, perhaps more, possibly four, I'm not sure.'

'That's very bad, and I'm sorry to hear it,' replied Geoffrey. 'Can't you pay him? You're not actually broke.'

'I exist like you, most of us do, either by luck or cunning.'

'That's all I wanted. Information. I'm not prying. I sympathize with you in this position you're in. I know the difficulties of keeping up a house like this. Why don't you sit down, Gabriel?'

Without a word Gabriel sat down. After a while he said, 'I've been worried for a long time now.'

'You know Arthur drinks a lot,' said Geoffrey, 'lucky devil.'

'Of course I know.'

'In a secret way. The others know nothing about it. You must have given him the money from time to time then?'

'I was sorry for Arthur, I still am. I think he had a raw deal from the august Bishop.'

'And slowly damning him in the meanwhile, ruining him, by your kindness, entirely misplaced if I may say so. Have you ever had a serious heart to heart talk with him?'

'Once or twice.'

'This news has upset Agatha more than anybody, so far. Do the others know, Celia for instance?'

'She knows now.'

'You told her then. Agatha didn't tell her, you told her.'

Gabriel stuttered, 'Agatha told her.'

'Why don't you get rid of Thomas? I never liked him myself, though that's no reason of course. But I always thought him cheap, sly. The most stupid thing that ever was done was to send him to town last week to collect that child, whom I don't believe you really want here. Do you?'

'I never sent him at all. Celia sent him.'

'Why?'

'She looks on us as hopeless. She often laughs at us, behind our backs.'

Geoffrey sat up. He did not speak. He could feel Gabriel's eyes on him. He bent down and stirred the fire with the poker, then flung it down with a clatter.

'A nice kettle of fish,' he said at length.

'Things will straighten out. I've never doubted it,' remarked Gabriel, 'never. A bit sticky at present, but I hope for the best, we all do, we're together in this.'

'That remark sounds extraordinarily strange, coming from you.'

'All the same, I wish you hadn't come barging in here like this, Geoffrey, I really do. I've worries enough as it is. I've that woman, some relative of Dolphin, his mother, but she may not be, people are extraordinary these days, say the first thing that comes into their heads. She's arriving tomorrow, and the child must get himself ill. *She* has to be seen, interviewed. Oh the fuss, the fuss, and then the stupid boy scares the life out of us. . . .'

'Aren't you being a little selfish, Gabriel?' asked Geoffrey.

'*Me* selfish?'

'Yes.'

'For God's sake . . .' Mr. Mortimer exclaimed.

Geoffrey got up. 'Well, now we know. It's cleared the air. I shall talk to Isobel and Agatha about this. Some way of paying Thomas must be found. Moreover the moment it's done, Thomas will go. You'll be a different person when you've seen his back.'

'That may not be as easy as you think,' replied Gabriel sharply, 'there are holds other than cash.'

Geoffrey banged the door and went out. A moment later Gabriel himself went out. To judge from his sudden change of expression Geoffrey might never have visited him. Mr. Mortimer looked far from worried, rather was his the fresh look of the morning. One would have said he looked optimistic.

Isobel had just finished washing her hair. She sat in front of the fire in her room, head bent, lazily combing. When Mrs. Mortimer came in she did not look up, but said, 'Hello, dear,' then continued her combing. After a while she said, 'How's the boy? What an awful thing to happen, Celia. He must have . . . imagine him lying out there whilst we were driving off to the Polsons, whilst we were having tea. . . .'

'The first thing Gabriel said to me after the doctor left was that nobody in the house had had any tea, and that made me forget we had had it at the Polsons, and we had more. Nobody seems to have remembered that,' she said.

'It's been a confusing kind of day, hasn't it?' said Isobel. 'D'you know I haven't warmed up, even yet. It *was* cold coming back, didn't you think so, dear? Poor Gabriel looked positively starved.'

Mrs. Mortimer stood behind the chair, watching the combing continue. She could see the wide open doors of Isobel's wardrobe. The bed was littered with frocks, coats, hats. Shoes were jumbled together in an untidy heap.

'Are you going out?' Mrs. Mortimer asked, her eye on the bed.

Isobel tossed back her hair. 'Oh no. You know perfectly well, my dear, that I always do this sort of thing the last Thursday in each month. I've been ransacking this past half-hour trying to find something decent to wear. I'm so *sick* of my clothes and I can't variate any longer.'

'You *ought* to have a new frock, Isobel? I quite agree. Can't you manage *something*?'

'At present I'm afraid not. I expect I'll look presentable enough for Sunday.'

'Why of course. I forgot it's your Sunday, dear. I ought to go myself, really.'

'You always say that, but you never go. Agatha and I are the only Christians here,' replied Isobel.

'I know. We ought to try more, I'm afraid, yet we don't,' Mrs. Mortimer said. 'What a day. Poor Agatha looks quite ill. Poor thing. She's with Robert now.'

'Yes, she does rather. What a stupid child he must be. Fancy lying out there in the wet leaves, almost looks to me as though it were deliberately done, just to get us worried about him.'

'Perhaps he should never have come. Perhaps . . . however, tomorrow will see,' said Mrs. Mortimer.

'And yet,' said Isobel, 'somehow there is something about him, I don't know what excatly, but there is something fetching. I only wish he would like me. The effort I've made with that boy. But you're not really going to let him go tomorrow are you, with this Mrs. ——? I can never remember her funny name.'

'Dolphin,' said Mrs. Mortimer, 'and it isn't as funny as all that, surely. Gabriel feels we're not right for him, he says we're autumn people . . . he says. . . .'

'In the end you'll say, dear. You run the place, not him.'

Isobel tossed down her hair again, bent forward in front of the fire and resumed her combing. Mrs. Mortimer noticed Isobel's neck; she thought it like a man's. 'Poor dear, no I don't think she would ever have married.'

'I suppose you heard about Thomas?'

'I did. Geoffrey told me. He mentioned something about us all being lodgers, though I didn't take him seriously, I never do. He probably thought it rather funny, but I can't share his sort of joke. But the moment he'd gone I laughed.'

'Thomas doesn't laugh. I'm furious with Gabriel, furious. Now I understand the secret link between them. Thomas hasn't changed at all, he seems just as loyal as ever.'

'You'd be loyal, too,' Isobel replied, 'if you were owed all that money. It's a lot, over three hundred pounds, Geoffrey said.'

'Don't,' said Mrs. Mortimer, 'I can't bear to think about it. There's a reason for it, somewhere, but I'm too upset and confused in my mind even to think of how to straighten the matter out.'

Isobel tied back her hair. She got up, took Mrs. Mortimer's arm and walked her across to the bed. 'What do you think of this arrangement for Sunday?' she asked, taking up a dove-grey felt hat, then a grey tweed suit, grey gloves, a fox fur.

'A nice ensemble, dear. Still, it's time you had a new frock. Why don't you run to town one morning, *make* yourself go. We none of us get out enough. . . .'

'How is Thomas going to be paid, tell me that?'

'We'll find a way, don't worry. Geoffrey's all for

kicking him out as soon as we've settled with him, but that's crude. He's been with Gabriel a long time now. They understand each other, they like each other.'

'If you can afford it of course,' replied Isobel. She was busy trying on the hat, she stood in front of the mirror, making faces.

'It's very difficult. I expect I shall have to get it all out of Gabriel. I hate it, he's so sensitive.'

'Probably a shade too sensitive. But in spite of that Gabriel has managed to lend Arthur money from time to time. I've never mentioned this before, Celia, but I've a strong suspicion that Arthur is a secret drinker. . . .'

'I don't believe you. . . .'

'It's only an opinion, my dear. I often forget he's there, that he's alive at all. I often wonder how Gabriel sees him, he must see him, I've never actually seen him going to his room. Arthur's a part of the furniture. But *what* a disgrace to the family, I used to hate having to sit opposite him at meals, now thank God one doesn't see so much of him, and he seems to do very well in the pantry after everybody else has gone to bed.'

'You'll be excused that tonight, too,' said Mrs. Mortimer. 'I've often waked up of a morning, and wished to myself that he wasn't there, that he'd gone, an awful thing to say, really, but now since you have told me . . . somehow I still can't believe it – but if it's true, then I begin to dislike him myself.'

'And now,' said Isobel, 'shall we forget him. I've my own little worries to comfort me. Geoffrey will do something drastic, fling him out.'

'*Do* look at the time. I must get along now,' Mrs. Mortimer exclaimed. Thomas was standing in the corridor when she came out. He handed her a telegram.

'This has just come m'm,' he said.

'You needn't wait.'

Thomas went off. Opening the telegram she read:

COMING EARLY TRAIN INSTEAD ARRIVE NINE OCLOCK MORNING DOLPHIN

'Oh God!'

Crumpling the telegram she stuffed it in her pocket and went off to the kitchen. She felt as though she were swimming for life through heavy seas; even the air seemed to rock.

Agatha, who had just given Robert some hot milk, now gently wiped his mouth. She smiled.

'Of course, it's only a story, darling. Yet sometimes stories come true, like wishes, like expecting things to happen and they happen. Well, this little boy, curiously his name was Robert, just like you, was alone right in the middle of this big city. His father drove a train. And one day he came home to his tea, just like your father used to do. This father thought of the light that would be burning in his kitchen, a big red fire burning in the grate, the table flowing with cups and plates, and in a dish something that smelt very nice and made him feel hungry at once. But of course, it wasn't true. Because when he got home he found it was all dark there, there was no light, and no fire, and the things on the table were dead things, because it was just as he left it when he went out. Nothing was shining as he had imagined it to be. And his wife wasn't sitting in front of the fire. But in a back room there was a little boy lying in bed. Whilst he was asleep his mother had put on her hat and coat and gone out. But she had never come back. Though the little boy cried because it was his mother, and he *thought* it was his mother, it wasn't really so, because she had never *been* his mother truly, not even from the very beginning. So it was really a fairy-tale, because this lady had known from the very beginning that he would come to her, she had known him all the time, knew he was somewhere in the world, and that one day she would meet him. And she did. And indeed they were very happy together, ever afterwards.'

The boy opened wide his eyes, 'Is that thinking?' he asked.

Agatha felt something warm inside her, something warm and melting.

'And where are they now, Aunt Agatha?' asked Robert.

'I don't know exactly, dear, but they *are* somewhere, perhaps far away, perhaps very near, but somewhere.'

'If you went to look for them then would you find them?'

'I'm sure I could, I mean we would.'

'We could. What are they like,' Robert suddenly sat up, leaned on his elbow, 'what are they like?'

'Quiet, darling,' said Agatha, 'you mustn't sit up, dear, be quiet. You mustn't talk too much, Doctor Turner said so. You must whisper. If anybody heard us talking, they would come in at once and send me out.'

'Out, you mean away,' Robert said. He clutched Agatha's hand.

She lay down beside him, she stroked his hair, 'I must go soon, dear. When you're better we'll do lots of things, you and I. Lots of things.'

'When?'

'As soon as you're better,' she said.

'When is that?'

'Soon.'

'How soon?'

'Perhaps very soon,' Agatha replied.

'You mean nearly now?'

'Very nearly, dear.'

She pressed her face against the cold sheet, and cried quietly; she was filled with an awesome joy, feeling this child so near, her dream child come true, much travelled, worn, the long-journeyed dream. This sudden, fierce, maternal longing frightened her.

'Are you asleep, Aunt Agatha?'

'No, dear. I'm just by you, how hot your hands are.' She raised his head and looked at him. 'I'm your real mother, darling.'

Robert laughed, it frightened Agatha, she put a hand on his mouth, 'Ssh!' The Deptford footsteps were suddenly very close, she gripped the boy's shoulders, held him tightly.

'What?' Robert said.

He felt her lips pressed against his ear. There was something she wanted to say, desperately, but before she could utter it Robert himself had killed it.

'My *real* granny's coming tomorrow. I know.'

'Is she, dear? Which granny is that?'

'My real one, Thomas said.'

'I somehow believe she is,' said Agatha. 'I expect she's coming to see how you're getting on. You must hurry up and get better, Robert darling.'

'*You* don't smell like granny does,' he said.

'Smell, dear?'

'Scent,' Robert said, and for the first time, saw, heard, Agatha laugh.

'We'll have lots of fun together when you're better. Soon it will be spring time, the leaves and grass will turn beautiful green, there will be lots of flowers.'

'There aren't any lights in this sky here,' he said, 'in Paddington the sky is always full of lights, I used to see the long blue lights fly across it at night time.'

'*Did* you. Just fancy that. But sometimes there are bright lights here, too. You won't have to wait very much longer now.'

Agatha sat up, sensing somebody's approach, she sat quiet, listening. Probably Celia. She looked at the boy, 'Tell me, dear . . .' she paused, filled with a sudden dread against his answer, it might be. . . .

'What?'

'Will you promise me something. . . .'

He tried to sit up again. 'I like you best, you're nice,' he said.

'But I'm your mother, dear, that's why.'

'Not really. Only a fairy-tale one,' Robert replied.

'Well, a fairy-tale one then. Tell me. If your granny who comes from Deptford tomorrow says to you, "Come along now, come home," and then I say to her, "He can't come because he *is* home," what would you say?'

She waited, she smiled. 'I don't know . . . not yet,' she heard him reply.

'Are you sure? Just think.'

He said at once, 'I don't know . . . yet.'

When the gong sounded for dinner Agatha froze in her chair. She had expected it, it had come, and now she hated it. She hadn't won yet . . . time was drawing in.

'There's the bell,' said Robert.

Joan came in to relieve Agatha. Agatha got up and went to her. They whispered to each other.

'Thomas offered to come and sit with him, but mistress said I'd better.'

'Quite right, Joan.'

'Is he better?'

'He will be soon, keep him quiet, I'll have his milk sent up later on.'

'Yes, Miss Agatha.'

Joan took the vacated chair, Agatha went out.

'Oh,' Agatha gasped. She had bumped right into Gabriel, who was standing outside the door, 'What a fright you gave me. What on earth are you doing, Gabriel, standing there like a ghost?'

'I've been waiting here ten minutes, to speak to you, Agatha, I didn't want to go down until I'd seen you.'

He looked at her silently, then said slowly, 'Agatha . . . I hope you're not going to disappoint me tonight, you *will* play that Mozart thing, won't you. You *did* promise.'

'Is that all you can think of . . . *now?*' Agatha said, 'certainly not.'

She swept on past him, left him standing dejectedly by the closed door. He stood listening for a moment or two, then went downstairs. 'Nothing's gone right since he came. I'll be glad when he goes tomorrow.'

Each Thursday he had taken his coffee in the drawing-room, he had sat back comfortably by the fire, listened to Agatha playing for him. Tonight there would be nothing.

He sensed the change in the atmosphere as soon as he entered the dining-room. Though a fire was burning there, it hardly seemed inviting. Isobel sat up in her chair, as stiff as a guardsman, waiting.

'Hello,' she said, as he sat down, 'have you unfrozen? My God. What an afternoon. I simply froze in that car. Celia was lucky with her fur coat. *What* a place those Polsons have. And the airs of Gertrude.

How she fished for Geoffrey! There's such a difference in age.'

Geoffrey was leaning over the sideboard. He seemed to be having a hurried conversation with Mrs. Mortimer, standing beside him. To Gabriel it seemed very strange. What was happening? He looked at Isobel.

'Well, you've melted, anyhow.'

'Where's Agatha?'

'Yes, she is late, isn't she?'

'Don't worry,' Mrs. Mortimer said, speaking over her shoulder, 'she'll be here all right.'

Mr. Mortimer realized what was strange. Thomas wasn't there.

'Where's Thomas?' he asked, then, more loudly, aggressively. 'Are we to have any dinner?'

There was a tense silence. Mrs. Mortimer and Geoffrey began carrying steaming hot dishes to the table.

'We are learning to do without Thomas,' Mrs. Mortimer explained, she smiled at her husband, 'and Thomas in turn is learning to do without us.'

She sat down, immediately began to serve.

Agatha came in.

'I've changed your seat round, dear,' said Mrs. Mortimer, 'our lodger's gone into retreat. Take his chair, it's just by the fire.'

Agatha sat down. She smiled at everybody, began fidgeting with her napkin. Soon they were all eating. Geoffrey kept glancing up, looking from one to another.

'Now,' he said, 'we're all here. And we'd better have this matter settled and done with. I know it's distressing, these things always are. We are quite alone, and everybody can talk freely. Who'll begin?'

'What is this? A company meeting?' inquired Agatha.

Agatha sensed nothing unusual in the atmosphere. Though Thomas was not hovering in the background, she had not missed his presence. Her mind was full of happy, dancing little boys, she was not far from that room, her child there.

'Can't you begin, Gabriel?' asked Geoffrey. 'We must settle this matter, you know.'

Gabriel looked at Agatha, his expression seemed to say, 'can't you change your mind, can't we have that little recital?' Agatha's returned stare was ice-like. He knew then how angry she was. He mused. 'Am I always thinking of myself, am I?'

'Well,' demanded Geoffrey.

'Yes, whatever the beastly mystery is, let's have it out now,' said Isobel.

They looked up the table. Mrs. Mortimer was on the point of replying when she caught Gabriel's eye, and at once her resolution failed her. How distressed he looked, how rather odd, in fact, she had never seen Gabriel look like this before.

'Hadn't we better discuss this later on? I'm sure Gabriel and I can settle this matter between us.'

'That's a sudden change of mind, dear. I thought you said you were going to have this matter settled once and for all, and you said here, this evening.' She turned to Gabriel. 'Just imagine that sort of thing going on here, all this time, and never breathing a word about it to us, it's our business, too, Gabriel, we can't go on like this. There's got to be an end. The truth is, we are just lodgers here. . . .'

'Don't talk nonsense,' he then said very quietly, 'may we go on with dinner?'

'The whole thing is simply this. Thomas is owed a

considerable sum of money, and he must be paid. How will that be done?' said Geoffrey. 'We can't tolerate such a position,' he looked at Agatha, at Isobel, 'now can we?'

'For goodness sake, do get on with your meal,' Mrs. Mortimer said.

Geoffrey looked across at Gabriel. 'Even now, all *you're* thinking about is your own disappointment over your old recital in the drawing-room.'

Mr. Mortimer rose to his feet. 'Thank you for that,' he said, and left the room.

'Now you *have* done it,' Mrs. Mortimer flung down her napkin. '*Really*, Geoffrey, I'm surprised at you. This isn't a public meeting, you know how sensitive Gabriel is. . . .'

'We're just as sensitive as he is, he isn't the only one. If he hadn't been so dashed sensitive all along we mightn't have found ourselves in this intolerable position. Just think of it. Keeping a servant here who hasn't been paid for years. And why does he stay on? I ask you? He's got some hold over Gabriel.'

'Please.'

'But he can find the money for the fellow upstairs,' a jerk of his thumb indicated Arthur's room. 'Being sorry for him, putting up with his moods, lending him money, we know he drinks on the sly. Result – we've got somebody here who's got his knife into a crack, and he'll keep it there. Before we know where we are, why, he'll have us out of here. That girl in the kitchen and he are in league together. They'll get married, you see.'

'This is perfectly disgraceful.' Mrs. Mortimer got up and followed her husband out.

'You see my point of view, Agatha,' Geoffrey said.

'There are no points of view left, dear, we don't have

any these days.' Agatha sat back in her chair. 'I think I can see yours,' she said.

'Well, that's something. That fellow's just peeved because he can't have you tinkling on the piano this evening.'

'Please forgive him, dear, I know he has an awkward way of showing his feelings. I *would* have played to him tonight, I felt sorry saying no, he reminded me of a child, but a somewhat irritating one. When I came away from the boy's room, there he was, waiting for me outside the door.'

'Earlier on he was worried because tea was late, as though the Polsons hadn't given him a good tea already. He is selfish, I fear,' remarked Isobel.

Agatha leaned sideways, whispered to Geoffrey. 'You saw Thomas?'

Geoffrey whispered back. 'Yes, he's owed about three hundred and fifty pounds.'

'Well, then, I say, let Gabriel and Celia settle the thing. Shall we leave it at that?'

'I don't know,' Geoffrey hesitated. 'Thomas won't go, he said he would only go when Gabriel told him to. He actually didn't mind being owed such a lot of money. . . .'

Isobel wiped her mouth. 'I can just see him telling Thomas to go, can't you?'

'How everything has changed in just a week,' said Agatha, 'it's like being tossed into the sea very suddenly, from a boat that was too well constructed, too carefully piloted. If Gabriel had been a really sensible man I'm quite sure Elizabeth would never have run off like that, and that child would not be lost.'

'Reminds me, I must go and see him,' said Geoffrey, as he drew out his pipe. 'I'm smoking,' he said; it was fair warning before the clouds of shag smoke went up. There was a faint knock on the door, Joan came in.

Nobody spoke, but simultaneously they rose, moved to the fire and stood huddled by the mantelpiece, their backs to the girl; they heard her clearing the table. Isobel, Agatha and Geoffrey remained quite still. Viewed by Joan, they looked rather funny; she gave a toss of the head and continued her cleaning up. Finally Isobel sank heavily on to the couch. Geoffrey and Agatha remained standing, as though they had developed a special fondness for a water-colour of the village which Agatha herself had done; they stared at this and listened to the sounds of moving crockery.

The door closed with a definite bang. Joan had gone off.

Agatha then sat down. 'We were very late, she hates being kept waiting.'

'The whole meal was a failure,' Isobel grumbled.

'Everything seems a failure at the moment,' replied Agatha, 'let's talk about something else.'

'What?'

'Ourselves,' said Geoffrey, 'it might be a change, don't you think?'

Suddenly he excused himself and left them.

'No. You can't see the boy at all,' Mrs. Mortimer said. Geoffrey had caught her on the stairs. She frowned at him. 'I'm really vexed with you.'

'Vexed? What about?'

'You know very well what about. You spoiled everybody's dinner bringing that matter up. It's purely a question for Gabriel and myself. I thought you were old enough to understand that one does not discuss matters like that in a public way.'

'What on earth is happening to people in this

house?' he asked. '*Public?*' he exclaimed, 'a family discussion round the dinner-table?'

'The way you blurted everything out, I felt humiliated in front of Gabriel. Sitting there gabbling, and you never know who is listening.'

'Not Thomas. He's out.'

'Other people,' Mrs. Mortimer said, 'other people....'

'You come to his rescue every time, don't you,' whispered Geoffrey fiercely, 'you know what I said is true, then you suddenly turn round and claw me. You know perfectly well we can't afford that man any longer. Have you seen Arthur?' he asked.

'No, I haven't seen him. Agatha saw him this afternoon. He was heavily asleep, those drugs. . . .'

'A drunken stupor you mean.' ·

'That is quite enough, dear, he is your brother whether you like him or not.'

'The whole place is upset this past few days. Nothing seems to go right, it always did before. Is this old woman really coming here?'

'Yes, I'm afraid she is.'

'What will you do?'

'The boy will decide.'

'What does Gabriel think?'

'He doesn't, he can't make a decision about anything, he never could. It's this helplessness of his, this awful lethargy that upsets me. But he's too old to alter now.'

'You'll decide for him,' icily.

'I said the child would decide.'

'And if he stays? What about that? Can you afford to keep him? What about schools?'

'One deals with things as they come,' said Mrs. Mortimer. She frowned again, then said, in her most acid manner, 'Will that be all?' She turned on her heel and left him standing in the corridor. She went in to the boy. He was asleep. She sat down and watched him.

'Poor little thing,' she thought, and smiling, 'the fuss you've caused, the bother, the upset. The whole house turned upside down, and I've found out something into the bargain, something I felt suspicious about for so long. How odd that it should have come out like that, in the most casual way. And to Agatha of all people, for whom life has always seemed so safe. What a shock, poor dear. Oh, I am glad she refused to play for Gabriel, I really am, the very idea. Is that all he can think about, his own pleasures? A child. A child like this child, never grown up, he seems *not* to understand people, not to want to, he dreams his way along.'

Below she heard the telephone ringing. A few seconds later Joan knocked and came in.

The doctor would call in. He was passing that way, he'd be here in a few minutes.

'Thank you, Joan. By the way, you've not had your evening out. I'm so sorry, I'd quite forgotten. But you shall have it. We do appreciate how helpful you were.'

'Thank you, m'm.'

Robert woke. He sat up, he looked about the room, she felt his hand on her arm.

'Hello,' Robert said.

Mrs. Mortimer held him in her arms, 'Are you better, darling?' I'm so glad you've woken up.'

'I think I am.' He leaned against her shoulder. 'What time is it?'

'It's just turned nine o'clock, Robert, did you have a nice sleep?'

'Yes, thank you.'

'Dr. Turner is looking in to see you on his way home. Wouldn't you like some nice warm milk?'

'No, thank you, I had a funny dream.'

'Did you, dear?' she held him tightly.

'Shall I tell you?'

'Not now. In a minute you can. I think you'll be as right as rain tomorrow.'

'Will I?'

'Yes, dear.'

'My *real* grandmother is coming tomorrow, isn't she?'

She looked away from him, she felt she could not look at him now, saying this. After a while, she replied, 'Yes, coming tomorrow, she wants to take you home.'

'Which home, daddy's?' She felt a sudden clutch on her arm.

'No, dear. The other one, the one at Deptford.'

'I know where that is, I used to go there with daddy.'

'Did you, darling?'

Suddenly Dr. Turner was coming up the stairs, bouncing into the room, smiling cheerily, 'Good evening, Mrs. Mortimer,' he said.

'Good evening, Doctor, you'll excuse me, I hear the telephone ringing.'

'Certainly.'

She placed a chair by the bed and hurried downstairs.

'Well, little man,' the doctor said, 'and are you better now? Can you stand up, sonny. Let me see?' Then – 'Just slip that jacket off.'

She heard Robert say, 'Yes, sir.'

'Now. That's right.'

A momentary silence.

'There! Well, there's nothing very much wrong

with you now, if there ever was, fuss some people make, the fuss. Physically, you're a healthy boy.'

'Yes, sir.'

'You're a London boy?'

'Yes, I am.'

'Like London? Better than here, I'm sure. Is your father in London, what does he do?'

'He drives lorries, he's dead.'

'Oh dear. And your mother?'

'I don't know . . .'

'Dear, dear, and which do you really like best, London or the country?'

'I don't know. . . . yet, sir.'

The doctor laughed.

'All right, you can put those on again. Perhaps you can get up in the morning, we'll see. Now tell me . . .' and at that moment Mrs. Mortimer came in.

'Thank you, Doctor, how is he?'

'He's all right, Mrs. Mortimer. Let him have a good night's sleep, plenty of milk, one has to be so careful with children, one has to *understand* them, especially these town children. Seems to have forgotten London altogether, rare thing that. Saw thousands of them during the war, evacuated you know, never really forgot the city. Well, I must be off now.'

He turned quickly from the bed. Mrs. Mortimer followed him out. She looked boldly at him and asked, 'Doctor, do you think we don't understand children?'

Laughing, Dr. Turner replied, 'You may, you may not. I don't think you've ever had children at Greys before. . . .'

'We've started to have them, Dr. Turner. Thank you for calling.'

'Goodbye.'

She watched him hurry down the stairs, then went back into the room.

'He looked at me all over,' Robert said. He bounced on the bed. 'He said I can get up in the morning, could I see Uncle Geoffrey, could I?'

'Yes. He'll bring up your milk, dear. I'm *so* glad you're better. Your grandfather has been very worried about you, very worried indeed.'

'Has he really?' he was smiling up at her, 'and was Uncle Geoffrey worried, too?'

'We were all worried, darling. But now you're better, we're happy. You can perhaps get up in the morning, you can even have breakfast with us.'

'Honest?'

'Honest. Now lie down, dear, we don't want you to catch another cold, do we?'

Shaking his head gravely Robert said, 'No. Was Thomas worried as well?'

She did not answer, but sat quietly looking at him.

'What a shame,' she thought, 'if *only* that girl had had some heart. Imagine her never taking the slightest notice of her father's letters. Well, I hope he's changed his mind about her now. She was never any good, I always thought so. I wonder if this child ever thinks about her.'

'Robert, dear?'

He looked up, he said, '*What?*' She was taken aback by the sudden aggressiveness in his voice.

'You must never answer people in that way, Robert. I was going to ask you something, but I won't now.'

'I *am* sorry, grandmother,' he said.

'Are you really?' She laughed then, the grave expression forced it out of her. 'Do you ever think of your mother, Robert, but you must. You must often remember.'

'You mean the lady what went away with Christopher who gave me the chocolates? No, not now. I've forgotten her. But she wasn't my mother, of course. Aunt Agatha told me just now, she said I imagine it.'

'Aunt Agatha said that?'

'Yes, she said *she's* my real mother, she always was, even before I came here, before I saw her she was, before daddy died, she said it was a long time before that as well. . . .'

Mrs. Mortimer stared at him. She could hardly believe her ears. Why on earth should Agatha say a thing like that? To a child. 'Surely . . .' she thought, 'poor Agatha isn't . . .'

'Aunt Agatha said that?'

'Yes, she said *she's* my *real* mother, I like Aunt Agatha now.'

'Tell me why,' she put an arm round his neck, 'do tell me why.'

'Because she said it.'

'Said what?'

'That she's my real mother, I'm sure she is now. . . .'

'How *extraordinary*,' exclaimed Mrs. Mortimer.

'What's that, grandmother, extraord . . .

'Nothing.'

He looked up at her, 'You said you were sorry you hit me this morning, grandmother.'

'I am. I told you I was, dear.'

'But I never said I was sorry when I tore up that music,' Robert said.

'Didn't you? But I thought you were sorry, Robert.'

Nothing was more ruthlessly honest than the look he gave her.

'Because you don't *really* like me, really,' he said, 'and grandfather doesn't, and Aunt Isobel doesn't, and even Uncle Geoffrey doesn't, really, and that's because you just say the things as words. . . .'

'What on earth are you talking about, dear?'

'It's only daddy I want,' he said. He burst into tears, he leaned heavily against her and shook with bitter sobs; she felt the small body trembling under her.

'My dear, dear child,' she said, 'my dear, dear little boy,' and she held him again very tightly, and it was thus that Geoffrey found them, as, silently opening the door, he peeped in.

Mrs. Mortimer saw him, withdrew a hand, put her finger to her lips, and pointed desperately towards the door. Geoffrey smiled, nodded, and closed the door again.

'You mustn't cry like this, darling,' Mrs. Mortimer said, 'of course Agatha is your mother, of course she is. And now you must have your milk.'

She crossed the room and took the tumbler from the table on which Geoffrey had left it.

'Come along now,' she said. She infused a false cheeriness into her own voice, '*come* along.'

He sat up and she fed him, between his violent sobs. She said gently, 'You mustn't cry, dear.' He sipped noisily at his milk, but stopped suddenly. 'My *real* grandmother is coming tomorrow,' he said.

'Yes, dear, you've already told me that.'

She took away the tumbler. 'Now you must lie down and go to sleep. Tomorrow is a lovely day, yesterdays are best forgotten, and today. . . .'

'Today,' he shouted.

'Come along. I'll tuck you up nice and warm.

He lay back. She felt his eyes on her as she settled and tucked in the sheets. She kissed him. She said, 'You must *never* go into that spinney again, darling, it's very dangerous, good night, God bless. . . .'

'Good night,' he said.

'Granny,' said Mrs. Mortimer.

'Good night, granny.'

'I shall leave your night-light burning.'

But his head had disappeared under the clothes. She went out.

'What a strange child,' she thought, 'and, just think of Agatha talking to him in that way, almost silly, I do hope she's not getting senile, it seems remarkably like it to me.'

She stood in the corridor for a moment, and glanced at her watch. It hardly seemed worth while going down again. How silent the house seemed; she paused at the bedroom door, she heard movements.

'Is that you, Gabriel?'

'Of course it's me,' gruffly.

Going in she saw that he was already retiring.

'You're early, dear.'

'What was there to wait up for? Agatha's gone to bed, too. I never got my Mozart after all.'

'Is Geoffrey below?'

'I expect so. Left him wrangling with Isobel. She's on to her favourite theme. She gets these moods round about Communion Sunday, you must have noticed it. Talking about dresses, about going to town, been talking about going to town for years. Yet she never goes,' he said.

'There's much I want to talk to you about, Gabriel,' she said. She looked down at him for a moment, as if to say, 'get ready for what is coming', then crossed the room to undress. She let down her hair. Through the mirror she watched him. She said, and he noted the coldness in her voice, 'Many things must be settled tonight. Many things.'

'There seems to have been nothing all day but talk. I'm sick of it.'

'That's it, Gabriel, too much talk, and never anything done.'

'Haven't we always been happy, Celia? Haven't we always done the things we wanted to do, haven't we had calm and peace, very few worries? And you must know we have kept the house standing, the family together, there's a lot in that.'

'Your intentions were of the best I'm sure,' she replied, 'but for once we must get beyond intentions, we must settle matters tonight. I want to be able to wake up in the morning and feel they are settled at last. . . .'

'Go on,' he said. His voice never lost its gruffness.

'Elizabeth was perhaps quite right, we don't ever know what is happening beyond the gate. We know only what happens to us. We are living on a tight little island. . . .'

'If you've retired just to talk this stuff, then I might as well get up and go downstairs.'

'You'll remain here, Gabriel. The things that must be settled are Thomas, Arthur and Robert.'

'Perhaps you've some suggestions to make, it would be a great help. You know I've always let you run things here, not because I didn't want to, but because you do it better.'

'But I can't get between Thomas and you for one thing,' she replied, 'but I *shall*, I shall, we can't afford him any longer, you'll have to straighten up, Gabriel, pull yourself together. I'll tell Thomas first thing in the morning. He shall go. . . .'

'I can't get on without that man, you don't understand, dear, why I *love* Thomas, he's . . .'

'You also love yourself. Also Arthur will go. Isobel, Geoffrey and I are going to pay Thomas up, and then he goes. That is already settled. As for the child, that's more difficult, it's your grandchild, not mine. . . .'

'You brought him here,' he growled.

'Because he was your child, because your daughter left *him, and* her husband, who for all you say must at one time have loved her.'

'If *you're* settling matters, why talk to me?'

'Sometimes I wonder why I do.'

'Celia!' Gabriel sat up. 'Celia!'

He was shocked. He stared across at her, 'Celia,' he said again.

But she made no reply, she turned over on her side, switched out the light. 'Good night, Gabriel. Don't forget to switch out your light.'

XII

WHEN she opened the front door, fog came in;
she shut it quickly. 'Ooh,' she said.
'Why you go dragging down there on a day
like this, I don't know. You won't get nothing.'

'We'll see. Poor little 'im, when I think about it,
when I think . . .'

'Suppose his mother's *there*, you'll look funny, not
half you won't.'

'Her can't be in two places at once. When I think
of her marrying like that. He was soft, that's Dolphin
trouble all the time, heart's too big for 'em, that's
what.'

'But if his mother's *there*, and how d'you know she
won't be – well what?'

'Blood's blood. Either side blood's blood. Is that
kettle boiled yet?'

'It is.'

'Then let's have something, then let's have it. Ooh!
It's cold this morning, what a day. You mind him
doesn't go sneaking out 'count of the Health lot,
proper foxes they are. I told them lot down there
when I wrote I was coming, about him being laid up
and being under the Health. . . .'

'They'll laugh at that.'

'Why'd they laugh?'

'Them lot always laughs at what they don't understand. Not like us, we worries.'

'Well, worry some tea out of the pot, there's a
girl.'

Mother and daughter sat down.

'If he hadn't become what he had, and more fool

him for it, it wouldn't never have happened, never, I know.'

'Get your tea.'

'Get yours and shut up.'

'I am shut up.'

'You say I have no rights but I have, what would you know about rights if you had never had none?'

'You fuss.'

'You never loved him, that's what. He was a good son to me till he met her, oh the folly of it him being an officer what was never meant and see what he got for his pains, two rooms in Paddington what I wouldn't be seen dead in. I'll never forget her, never, first time I saw her I could tell the way she looked at me with her quizzy eyes and him the fool I could see him watching and frowning at me case I said the wrong thing, that was at Purley, like he was ashamed of me though I don't know why.'

She stopped suddenly to look at the clock. The daughter looked at it, too.

'You'll have to hurry, though I think you're hurrying for nothing that's what.'

'Well, I never said nothing wrong that time to him or her 'cept to ask him if he couldn't bring her down to see us at Deptford and he says I'll think it over while her says where was that imagine not knowing where Deptford was but he never wanted to come, he didn't care over much at that time he was all tied up strong to her, her to him, bed hugging all the time, that's what she wanted, nothing else. No heart, never had, he worked hard for her and her kiddy from all along the line the bloody fool – oh when I think of it all the waste and poor little 'im – down there and his mother away, miles away, there's love for you – there's love.'

'You'd better go if you are going though I can't see nothing you'll get, nothing.'

'You were always hopeless you were – always.'

She looked at her daughter, 'See he doesn't sneak out of bed that's all else he'll have the Health lot on top of him. Go and get me my coat and me hat.'

This was at Deptford; eight o'clock, and fog coming down.

Mrs. Dolphin waited. Her daughter came back, her look begrudging. 'Here,' she said. She helped Mrs. Dolphin on with her coat. She was grey-haired like her mother, but taller by a foot; between her eyes a frown, grown there, anchored, for ever.

She fixed her mother's hat, the feather had come loose. 'There. You won't change your mind?'

'No I can't change nothing. I'm going down there to give them a piece of my mind and I'll bring him back if it's the last thing I ever do, blood's blood. He was my son's child, him what's cold in his grave these ten days count of her why should I change it. I ask you, why should I? You never saw her you never saw him either so you don't know nothing.'

'You're always clutching, you're like an old hen,' her daughter said.

'How dare you say that to me what's kept you all these years, how dare you?'

'Yes, you clutched me all right didn't you, look at me now,' and the frown darkened, accusing. 'You'll clutch at him, he's none of your business.'

'He's my son's flesh and blood and his mother ran away and left them to rot in that stinking hole in Rupert Street what decent people wouldn't be seen dead in and he worked hard and did his best for her what only laughed because she only ever wanted one thing from him, bed huggin'. Now she's gone off on

232

the same thing with somebody else and my son's dead and poor little him lost, that's what. Well, I'm goin'. And mind what I said about that sly devil upstairs who might sneak out to The Crown when you wasn't looking, and then have the Health lot on top of us.'

She banged the door after her, leaving the daughter standing in front of the fire, a fire of ash and slack that had been burning five years now, which had not gone out, and might never go out. Looking into the fire she thought of her own life, clutched at, held, between Deptford bricks.

Mrs. Dolphin caught a bus and was whisked towards the north. She sat tense in her seat. At any moment she might cry out, she looked so tense. People in the bus stared at her. She sat stiff, upright, she looked neither to right nor left. She paid her fare, sat stonily silent. She changed buses twice; every move was vital, the fingers clutching the stair-rail, the strap, the seat of the bus, the tenseness was still there, sleeping inside the small frame an almost animal-like ferocity. At Paddington she wove her way through crowds; she was not frightened, and she was cautious. She voyaged down platforms, pushed through barriers in frantic search for the right train; when she found it, she boarded it and sat down, having slammed the door with great determination. She then settled herself in her seat and stared out at everybody on the platform.

'They had no right, they hadn't any and never had.'

'Never ever writ and said they were sorry, never.'

'Don't care and me with my cold son on me hands, the devils.'

'Laughed at him behind his back, that's what and then pinched poor little him like sneak thieves. No heart, none at all didn't understand what hearts were.'

The thoughts froze in her mind, were suddenly rock, she clung to them. Three minutes before the train left a guard removed her from her compartment; she had got into a first-class carriage by mistake. She stared at the guard, finally got up and tore past him in silence, leaving him to stare after her, wondering. Inwardly she fumed, for now, with the train on point of departure, she had to search for a compartment that had a seat to spare. The train was crowded. She darted up and down, stood a moment to look in; her expression never altered, she scowled, then turned away, madly rushing to another carriage. With the help of a porter she at last found a seat, in a compartment that was already blue from smoke, where she sat hunched between two men, the one reading his newspaper, the other vacantly staring before him. She looked at them all, she hated them. She hated the whole train; unwillingly she had drawn it into the fiery circle of her thoughts. She could only think of the cold son, the dutiful one, the one who did his best, who against her advice had married 'this toff'. The sadness had crusted, hardened, she felt now only the cold misery of the world without him. She thought of his child; the thoughts held her upright like splints, rigid with tensity. Her hands clutched her coat, she lowered her eyes. She felt cramped by her position, but was suddenly afraid to speak. The tobacco smoke choked her, got into her eyes; somebody laughed at a joke in a cheap magazine; the train suddenly rocked, she was aware of the physical weight of the men each side of her. Some clinkers blew into the compartment, then the train swam into the long dark tunnel.

She hoped it wouldn't be late. It was an early train,

she had decided at the last moment that it must be early. She was seized with the idea of getting back to Deptford before dark. With 'Bobby'. It was all settled. The obstacles had already been overcome. There was a small bed in her room and she had made this up. She had stuffed a paper bag containing her sweet ration under his pillow. Already she was holding the candle over his head, saying good night to him who was the 'living image of his dad', his poor dad who had died of a haemorrhage all of a sudden, and hadn't eaten his supper that evening, she'd seen the cold chips on the floor.

'Poor little 'im,' she said to herself, as the train leaped into the light. She had brought with her a leather shopping bag and inside the bag wrapped in new crinkly brown paper a bright green coat she'd bought for him at Jones's. She would put it on him, she would hold him tight all the way back to Deptford. This was her crusade, this was her pilgrimage of the heart, the tumult of feeling was always there, it swept over obstacles like great waves. Suddenly her head was bobbing in the smoke-filled air, her fingers' clutch on the coat had stilled; the worn fingers crumpled to untidy lumps as she slept behind one extended page of the *Mail*, one long uplifted arm. She slept, she suddenly began to snore.

She rocked with the train, swayed with the telegraph poles, she went on sleeping, she had been up early that morning, half past six. The *Mail* fell, the man glanced –

'The old girl's fast asleep.'

'Yes.'

'Isn't she little?'

'Isn't she.'

Another tunnel, the light overhead burning with a

darkened frenzy. The train flying on, clattering over points, nearing Helton, nearer to 'little him', her grandson – her blood, who was coming back with her, this very day.

'Helton! Helton!'

She sat up as though struck, stared about. Three people had already got out, but she had not heard them go.

'Are you getting out, missus? This train doesn't go no further you know.' A red face outside the window, puppy brown eyes looking amiably in. 'Where you for?'

'Helton.'

'Better get out then,' the porter said. 'I think you'd better get out.' For some reason there was a sudden misgiving in the way he spoke as though he were not quite certain whether the passenger was for Helton or not.

He opened the door. He helped her down, there was a longish drop to the platform. She accepted this help in a begrudging manner, she was suddenly back on the old road again, the road of regrets, and endeavours and iron determination, the hand of her son pushing her forward. She stood a moment on the deserted platform. She seemed confused, uncertain, staring about. The porter looked at her.

'London,' he said to himself, 'that's where she's from.'

'Where you *for*?' he asked.

'Helton.'

'I've already told you, *this* is Helton. Where d'you want to get?'

'Place called Greys,' Mrs. Dolphin said. She took a handkerchief from her pocket, blew her nose vigorously.

'Six miles away. Hadn't you better have a taxi, missus?'

'Don't want no taxi.'

'Aren't no buses here.'

'Don't want no buses. Which way?'

'This way,' he said, 'follow me,' and she followed him to the gate.

Here he pointed, 'Straight road till you get to Saxby's corner then sharp right, once on the top of the hill you turn left. And there you are. It's a fair walk.'

'Hope it doesn't rain,' Mrs. Dolphin said, and walked out through the gate. The porter stood watching her go down the road. 'Funny little cuss.'

The road looked long, endless, her old eyes became dazzled by the white line. 'It would have been very nice to ride in a taxi, but you can't that's all.'

Her small feet were encased in a mannish sort of boots, and the steel rims on the heel struck out on the road. A thought leaped into her head like light. 'I'll see him soon. I'm going to him.' Her heart gave a sudden thump. 'But I wouldn't be doing this now if he hadn't been *just* a bloody fool, God rest him all the same the poor fellow. Must have been mad must have you can't keep them lot on five pounds a week. No, all she wanted off him was what he had best his fine manhood and her took it, too, the dirty bitch airing herself in one of them foreign countries with another like her.'

It began to rain. 'Now why didn't I bring me umbrella why didn't I?' A car tore past her, a lorry, at such moments the road itself swayed before her, rose up like a hill, moving like any sea.

'Oh dear! Now if her'd had the slightest intention of helping me her could have said "You'd better take the umbrella, mum," got her bloody mood today, that fog I expect.'

She stopped. She went on the grass verge. She

237

leaned against a thorn hedge. 'I wish I could have took that taxi but I just couldn't. Fancy me at my age having to do this just because a man has his head turned and forgets his right place and doesn't know that two different kinds never mix and never will. Used to laugh at him because he didn't speak proper at first, lost his head complete, the silly fool, God rest him though.'

She went on, under drizzle, under fast greying skies. 'Oh God! I wonder where this place is? Suppose I've lost me way.'

The thought was like a slither of ice down her neck. She suddenly exclaimed, 'Oh I wish this rain would stop. It *would* rain of course. Never seen nothing like it, funny the way it always rains in the country, in London you never seem to get so wet somehow.'

Seized with panic she began to hurry, after a while she fell into a slower pace, feeling breathless, miserable – feeling suddenly lonely, miles from Deptford, from the fog, the fug in the kitchen. Suddenly she said, 'At last,' and turned the corner, and doing so, jumped, cried out, 'Ooh!' as a big lorry swinging round, tore on to the grass verge, sent sods of earth flying.

'You devil,' she screamed after the flying lorry.

'Now it won't be much further,' she said, 'I wonder if Bobby's expecting me I wonder.' She forgot the rain, her heart lifted, she hurried on. 'Wired them. Told them I was coming. Never wired back. That lot never do. Never answer your letters. No manners at all. Rot them, that's what.'

Wind came from the east, Mrs. Dolphin stood for a moment to listen to a strange sound, the hum of the telegraph wires; she had never been in the country before, all her life was Deptford, the sprawling life in the brick and mortar seas. Trees frightened her, the road got longer. When would she turn again, how long would it be before she reached the house, why did people live in such places, they were frightened of other people perhaps. What a place to live, so lonely, so cold-looking.

The thoughts raced, as her mind's eyes saw the everlasting Deptford fire at which in imagination she now warmed her hands. She wished she had never come on such a day.

'What a day, this awful rain, the places some people choose to live – makes me creep. Horrible.' She stopped: She saw the white of signpost, she read, 'Helton', out of reddened eyes, 'Helton. This way.' She turned, walked on.

Her feet hurt, she longed to stop, 'but you can't, the moment you stop they hurt worse oh am I a fool or not. That's what comes of having too much heart. That's the Dolphin weakness, all heart. Look at him back home there, under the Health lot, what a lot of fools they are, tied up in bed cause of the same weakness. Heart again. Helping a friend. There he was on his back. Oh God when does this God-forsaken road end I'm so sick of this walking.'

'No I'm not. No – I'm doin' my duty by him who was rarest son to me, good hard working man that never did nobody any harm 'cept himself marrying what was nothing less than plain whore if you ask me. I've me rights, he had his, which he never got, but I'll get mine, my son's child, no mother and never had. Somebody had to be human.'

Then suddenly she saw a white gate. She looked beyond to a great stone house. She stood, tired, bewildered, cold, wet, miserable. She hoped it wouldn't be long, that she would be able to catch that two-thirty-five back to London, Bobby in her arms. She leaned against the gate, she said aloud, 'No name on the gate, what a place to live, not even a number. I wonder what they're like. I wonder about little him. Poor child, it seems fair cruel to have took him away like that, my son's blood.'

She pushed against the gate. It creaked, it moved, she found she could push it only a few inches, but squeezed her way through.

'Oh God,' she said, 'another road again – what a place to live in, what a place. I thought I'd finished walking but I haven't.'

She started off up the drive, she could feel the cheap fur of her collar wet against her neck, her face felt cold, she was sure her nose looked red. 'What a sight, but you can't help nothing can you. I couldn't have taken no taxi.'

The house seen through the belt of trees seemed striped but gradually the place came clear, the stout cold stone, the big shining windows. She gave a little laugh.

'He's in there my son's only child, not far away now, I wonder if he's grown, I wonder if he's laughing, poor little beggar, only last week he was breaking his little heart in that horrible place. I was glad I lived in Deptford when I went down them there dirty stairs, God frightening things could happen in that awful house. I wonder if he's grown – lovely curly hair he had, funny it wasn't red like his dad's – ah he was handsome all right, big and strong, no wonder her fell for him they always do that lot they like those sort of men I've heard about their goings on. Queer lot they must be, funny living down here it's like living on an iceberg. Give me me own little place any time and that reminds me I do hope he hasn't gone sneaking out the Health lot are buggers, really.'

She reached a second gate, this was wide open, hung precariously by one rusty hinge, the paint blistered, worn.

'They ought to mend that, that gate'll fall on somebody and break their leg they must be a lazy lot indeed.'

As she passed through she looked down her nose at the battered, slowly rotting timber. She hobbled on up the drive, its surface had gone long ago, and many winter rains had pock-marked its quarter mile. She stopped. She leaned against the tall, bare tree.

'Me feet are singing,' she said, 'singing, I've never walked so far in me life.'

But now she was glad, she knew she was glad, she could feel it inside her, playing like fountains, splashing and tossing. She was glad she had come.

'If I hadn't come it would have been the same as having no heart that's what. Oh I'm glad, *glad*. I'll see him that dear little lad which is all I've got left now of the best son in this world what ruined his life by a bit of vanity, being clever and all, being an officer so he had to meet her and so he got what was coming to him through his swollen head the bloody fool, I can't help it, he *was* and this is what come of it. God rest his soul but I wonder if he saw me walking them horrible roads like a tramp, it makes you feel ashamed.'

She stood, suddenly motionless, staring. She was at the end of the drive; before her was the house. She pushed her cold hands up the sleeves of her coat, she hobbled over the pebbles of new gravel, she reached the door. She saw the bell, gripped it and pulled with great energy. The sound tore through the house. But they had already seen her pass the window, Agatha and Isobel, Geoffrey and Celia and Gabriel. They were at breakfast, they glanced idly up as the small, bent figure passed, they resumed their breakfast. Later they heard the massive throbbing of the pulled bell.

'I think,' said Geoffrey, *sotto voce*, 'that's your old woman,' he gave Mr. Mortimer a nudge.

'What's that?' said Gabriel. Taken aback by the sudden nudge, he looked downwards between the chair and the carpet.

'Your old woman has come,' Geoffrey whispered. He saw Isobel looking at him, he smiled.

'I thought I saw somebody pass the window,' she said, and everybody stopped eating.

'You saw who, dear?' inquired Agatha, who had surprised them all this morning by coming down, a little late, in a bright-coloured frock; she had been extra particular about her hair. 'It's probably the post,' she said. She wondered why everybody had stopped eating, she went on with her breakfast.

'The post hasn't come yet, Miss Agatha,' the voice somewhere behind her said and she knew Thomas was there, in his usual place. He had fussed around them this morning, she thought, like some old hen. Perhaps he had had his money at last, the cheque secure in his pocket.

'Whoever it was,' Isobel chimed in, 'there's no need to hold up breakfast.'

'None at all, dear,' Mrs. Mortimer spoke from the head of the table, the bridge of the swaying ship; there might be a landfall soon, but where?

'I think,' she said, she glanced at Thomas, 'you had better see who it is, Thomas.' Thomas went out.

The moment he did so they all looked down at the small figure seated in a chair beside Geoffrey. Robert sat shining-faced, fully dressed, and wrapped in a blanket. He had not spoken yet, but he had eyed them all, he kept a watch on them. He noticed his grandfather's pained look, his grandmother's air of indifference, Aunt Agatha's warning smile. Once Geoffrey said, 'Come along, little man, you must eat your toast.'

'Yes, sir,' Robert said; he had fallen back suddenly into this habit of sirring his uncle.

'Then get on with it, old chap,' said Geoffrey.

Suddenly Gabriel looked up the table at his brother, 'I say, old man, just slip up and see if that chap wants anything. I suppose it didn't occur to anybody to go and find out. We can't just leave him rotting there. Find out if he's coming down or not. He seems to have gone off his food lately.'

'Arthur won't be coming down,' Agatha said, quietly.

'Won't? You've seen him then. Extraordinary the way one forgets he's there,' Mrs. Mortimer said.

'He won't be coming down any more,' Agatha continued.

'What!' said Isobel. Everybody looked at Agatha.

'Arthur has gone. He went yesterday afternoon while you were away at the Polsons. I had meant to tell you, but what with the happenings of yesterday I quite forgot about it.'

'Gone!' exclaimed Mr. Mortimer.

'Are you sure, old dear?' said Geoffrey.

'Well!' exclaimed Isobel.

For the moment the boy was isolated, forgotten. But he kept watching Agatha.

'I'm sure,' added Agatha, 'that Arthur is now happy, and I know he will be all right.'

'But where's he gone. He had no money . . . this is . . .' Mr. Mortimer spluttered.

243

'I had a long talk with him yesterday,' Agatha said. 'I helped him pack. I went with him as far as the gate. I told him how silly he had been, frightfully silly, I felt so glad he was moving at last, beginning to live again, that I almost pushed him outside the gate. I said to him, "There are only other people out there, and they'll be too interested in themselves to notice you." I gave him some money and we said goodbye. I made him promise to write.'

They looked stupidly at Agatha. The door opened and Thomas came in.

'A Mrs. Dolphin, sir,' Thomas said.

'It's granny,' Robert shouted.

'Ssh, dear! Manners, manners,' Agatha said.

Mr. Mortimer looked at his wife, and Mrs. Mortimer said, 'Show her in.'

'Yes, mam.'

Napkins were folded, cutlery clattered to plates, the door opened, a head peeped round. Gabriel caught sight of a small, weather-beaten face, two bright eyes, a bobbing feather.

Isobel said sharply, 'Don't stand there like that, Thomas,' and Mrs. Mortimer said, 'Yes, come inside Thomas. You can stand over there.'

'Yes, mam,' Thomas said, not wanting to, not expecting this.

Mrs. Dolphin had come fully into view. She leaned against the door post, staring at them all.

'I've come for little him,' she said, like a policeman, a sergeant-major. She suddenly caught sight of the boy — 'Bobby, Bobby me little love. Why there you are. How funny you look with that blanket round you — and how are you, my lad?'

'Won't you sit down,' Agatha asked.

'I don't want no chair, I don't want nothing 'cept

my lawful rights which is little him there, my son's child, his blood what was a good father to him and a good husband once to her what's no mother and never was and never will be no heart never had no heart no feelings at all, poor little soul he had his hard days he had.' She called, 'Bobby! Come to granny, darling.'

Robert piped – 'Hello.'

'But are you sure you won't sit down, Mrs. er ——.'

'Dolphin to you please and I just said I don't want no chair as doesn't want to sit anywhere in this place which has no heart and never had the way he was took right from under my eye not a word no asking and nobody never cared about my poor cold son up there in that place who did his best and was father and mother to him and only lay stiff in his bed count of too hard work too much heart that's what's wrong with all us Dolphins too much heart too much bleeding where were you lot when I had to follow that man to his grave that awful day? I'll not forget it not in a long time. Me and me daughter alone watching him go what was nothing 'cept a fool God rest his soul this day and I cried bitter that there day I cried bitter count of him and poor Bobby there took away without so much as a word and not even a flower to grace his dad's grave which he should never have been in, never, I come to take him home what is home what always was 'is home, no feelin's people haven't none none – Bobby come to granny chucks.'

Gabriel sat hunched, watching, astounded. What a torrent of words, what energy, what indignation!

'My dear Mrs. Dolphin,' he said, 'we are of course all very sorry, very very sorry. We did the best thing at the time, the only thing, he is my daughter's child.'

'Where is her now I ask but gone bed huggin' with

another what's like her and all her lot walked out of that house and left her husband who was good to her and worked hard and sweated hard because he loved her in his silly simple way the big-hearted fool that's what, God rest him and she walked out with another man and left him and left her lawful child. Many's the time I've took the bus all the way from my house and gone and helped him I've put little him to bed and got his dad's supper because her was out with somebody else what could think of nothing but bed huggin' and that's what's cruel I say cruel and you know it and you all know what was never meant to see a sight of him who was too good and hard working too honest for you.'

She paused for breath; she never looked at them, but kept her eyes on the child. Mrs. Mortimer pinched Gabriel's knee under the table but he never moved, he was still astounded, still breathless from listening to the words that rolled off the old woman's tongue.

'I can understand your feelings, my dear,' Mrs. Mortimer said. She smiled graciously at the little woman. They had all taken her in now – the thin coat, the ridiculous feather bobbing on top of the quite-sensible hat, the man style boots, the worn hands, red, gnarled, grasping and releasing the sleeves of the coat. Mrs. Mortimer got up.

'Come, Mrs. — Dolphin, you *must* sit down I'm afraid, you see there's a very bad draught coming through the door. Geoffrey, bring this lady a chair.' For a moment something softened in the old woman, then hardened again. Geoffrey put a chair behind her, said kindly, 'Do sit down.' Mrs. Dolphin sat down. She was silent, she stared down at the pile carpet, the pattern, the maze of colours. The

Mortimers continued with their breakfast. Robert did not eat, he looked at his grandmother. He remembered her. He remembered the smell of camphorated oil when she embraced him and tucked him up in bed; he remembered the hard, cold feel of her hands; he remembered the rides in the bright red buses all the way to Paddington, all the way to Deptford. He broke the painful silence of the room. He cried out, 'Granny!'

The old woman's head jerked upwards as though she had been shot, the feather rocked on the hat 'What, chucks?'

'Daddy's gone to where they took him where they don't know.'

'Yes, ducks.'

And then Mrs. Dolphin wept, cried into the long silent room.

'Thomas said . . .' Robert suddenly brightened up. 'Are you crying, granny?'

Agatha thought, 'Oh dear, how terrible. . . .'

'Hush, dear! Mrs. Dolphin,' Agatha said. 'I'm sure you are a good woman, I've very sure. And I'm sure you came down here with the best intentions in the world, it has been very sad, very sad for us all. I can assure you. You must try not to distress yourself, my dear.'

Geoffrey felt so pleased with his sister that he gave her an encouraging smile.

'You must take a cup of coffee, Mrs. Dolphin.'

'I don't want no coffee as never liked it thank you for your troubling, Missus.'

'Then tea! I know you'll like a hot cup of tea. Geoffrey, I think you might bring Mrs. Dolphin's chair a little nearer the fire.'

'I don't want nothing,' Mrs. Dolphin said, and

raising her head she glared angrily at Geoffrey, who suddenly retreated and took up his position by the sideboard.

'Well then,' Mrs. Mortimer said, 'well . . . ' she couldn't make the words come, they were on her tongue, but her tongue suddenly stuck to the roof of her mouth.

Mrs. Dolphin sat, she cried silently now, inside her, as she looked miserably at Robert; all her feelings poured into that long, distracted look she gave him. Her son's child who had not moved, who had only cried to her – 'Hello.'

'Yes,' Agatha went on. She flung a quick glance at Isobel and Geoffrey, as if to say, 'How *dare* you go on eating so calmly – *now.*' 'Yes, Mrs. Dolphin, it was a sad thing. *Very* sad. It was brave of you to come all this way, and in such fearful weather. You took Hale's car from the station I suppose. It has been a nasty wet morning.'

'I never took nothing from anywhere Mrs., I walked here what is well able to walk I'm not afraid of walking I was only afraid of them cars and lorries on the road and them trees shaking and thinking if my husband was all right and wasn't sneaking out when I was away count of the Health spies what never leave you alone once you're ill.'

'I'm sorry.'

'No need to be sorry for me I'm not asking for anybody's sympathy but blood's blood and little him is my cold son's little lad that's what.'

'I know, it's very difficult,' Agatha said, she kept glancing at the others, she wished they would go – this was her show, her battle, somebody must win, somewhere it must end. But the others stayed, mute yet enthralled by this. It had never happened before, not at Greys.

'We are indeed very grateful to you for coming all this way like this. I . . . we . . .'

'I come for him there what's afraid to look at his granny cause of what's happened while he was here I never saw such a frightened child in all me days never – what's afraid to open his mouth poor little lad.'

Agatha looked at Robert. Robert suddenly said, 'Thomas knows.'

'Thomas knows what?' asked Mr. Mortimer. Not once had he looked at the old woman since her entry into the room. She seemed very strange to him, unique, he wondered what that part of the world was like these lean days – he kept repeating the word Deptford under his breath.

'Thomas said you're funny. He said, "they're all very funny but quite harmless".'

Geoffrey raised his eyebrows. He wanted to smile, but felt he ought not.

'Thomas thinks we're funny?'

'Yes, and he always laughs at you behind your backs. I heard in the kitchen. His mother lives in a place under the mountain, over the hill and he said to Joan in the kitchen – "One day I'll have her here".'

'He did, did he,' Geoffrey looked at Gabriel, frowned. Gabriel lowered his eyes.

'I've had that curious feeling for some time,' said Isobel, 'that I – that we were only really lodgers here.'

'He said his brother in America would come here, and his sister in Somerset. He said you'd all be dead one day. He said you were all ane-chent.'

They had suddenly forgotten Mrs. Dolphin. She

sat so silent in her chair, she sat so curled up, and so small, they hardly heard her breathe; she was quiet as mice are.

'I think,' Mrs. Mortimer announced from the head of the table, 'I think we had best attend to the other matter.'

Immediately everybody looked at the little woman in the chair.

'She's fallen asleep!' exclaimed Geoffrey.

'I was just sitting listening what nonsense it is and what bad manners youse people have but I knew it and me daughter warned me she said to me as I come out in that fog they'll only laugh they'll think you're funny and she's right what you think I am is funny and sittin' in that chair is my son's child, with no father and no mother and I come all the way down that road what's ruined me feet this day and I'm sittin' here and you think it's funny what thinks everything's funny I expect even a cold death.'

Agatha got up. She pulled her chair after her, she sat down by Mrs. Dolphin. She put her thin white hand on top of the hard calloused hand and said, 'Nonsense. Nobody thinks you funny, my dear woman. Only Thomas thinks that we are funny. I shouldn't cry. You must try to understand, my dear, that other people besides yourself have feelings, they are not specially the property of any particular people but are common to all since they are very human. You say you have come to collect your son's child. But may I remind you that he is also somebody else's child. His mother . . .'

'Her what's now in some other country hundreds and hundreds of miles from where her heart should be if she ever had any what ruined my only son what used to laugh at my son because he never talked proper. What used to think that people in Deptford was all funny nor what never cared a damn for her home and her family lawfully married by the law of this land by a Christian man. You let me get down there to him. I'll show you how funny I am.' She got up and walked slowly to the end of the table.

'How are you, poor little lad, you've been ill you wouldn't have been ill if you'd been with me in Deptford that's what.' She flung her arms round Robert, and he stiffened in her grasp; he could no longer catch the scent of that camphorated oil. He tried to force away his head, but the old woman held fast, pressing the head to her. 'Poor tot, and have you been ill, ducky?' The company at table were silent and did not move, but they watched, not without interest, this sudden demonstration of love, as they watched with a sort of fascination the coat, the skirt slowly rise as Mrs. Dolphin bent low over the boy, revealing mud-splashed stockings, the boots with the steel heel caps.

Suddenly Robert had freed himself, he cried out for all in the room to hear. 'Granny, do you think they're funny people?'

They listened.

'Who, ducks?' asked the old woman, and Robert drew back in the chair thinking she would embrace him again.

'Those people up there,' Robert said. His fingers pointed to the table, they each of them felt the finger directed at them.

'What, them ducks? No dear, they're not funny. But now I wish they was.' She stood over him, hoping, longing; she kept her eye steadily on the boy, she was seeing her son again, real, life-size. He was looking at her eyes that seemed to him to have melted, and then she said, 'Bobby, won't you come home with gran, there's a boy?'

Agatha rose to her feet, she had heard those words, they were at once warning and threat. Slowly she went down the room. She put her hand on Mrs. Dolphin's shoulder. 'My dear,' she said, 'you *must* sit down. You must rest yourself. You must have a cup of tea. You must leave Robert for a moment. The child must decide. Isn't that right?' The old woman turned and looked at her, and though she did not speak, Agatha never forgot that look.

'Come,' and taking the old woman's arm, she walked her back to her chair.

'It's cruel that's what, cruel. You've turned him against me what was nearer to me than youse ever got nor ever will you don't want children you don't understand,' her voice suddenly rose, 'when I come out this morning her said to me, they'll laugh, they don't understand them people don't, he's all I've got and now he doesn't know me what warmed him many a time when he was cold and warmed his father's heart which was more than his mother ever did. . . .'

Geoffrey got up, he went quietly out and up to Arthur's room to see, in order to believe. 'Now there's a side to Agatha I never rightly cottoned on to, to have got him out like that, as quietly as a mouse, and then to say she forgot to tell us.' He could only think of an Agatha newly born.

Mr. Mortimer and his wife sat close, they were looking at each other all the time. She knew that her husband, who could never face a crisis, could not now face this, although she knew it was his greatest test.

Isobel's head was turned, she was looking into the fire. She heard a chair creak, Mrs. Dolphin had sat down again, Agatha beside her. The old woman saw none but the child, felt nothing except the ice-like feeling that assailed and struck so swiftly. She could yet feel the pressure of small hands against her breast, as though they were beating her back. The silence had been worse.

'I know,' began Agatha, 'I know how hard it is to be passionately fond of a thing and then to lose it. If I may say so I think it was splendid of you to have come all this way.' 'For nothing,' she thought, 'for nothing, I hope,' she thought again, then for a moment could not speak. 'It is very difficult. But perhaps my brother has something to say. It is his daughter's child.'

'I have nothing to say,' Mr. Mortimer looked down at the little woman in the chair – 'nothing to say,' he said.

Agatha had a sudden urge to go to the table and shake her brother.

There was a ring of the door bell. Thomas immediately left the room.

'Both my husband and myself . . .' began Mrs. Mortimer, but the door opened and Thomas came in with letters. There were two for Geoffrey, a catalogue for Isobel, two letters for Mr. Mortimer. Thomas handed them to him. 'The post, sir.'

Gabriel laid them flat on the table and looked at them. 'Mrs. E. Dolphin, Notturno, Via Corredoni, Florence, Italy, and stamped heavily over it in Italian and English. *Unknown. Return to Sender.* Mrs. E. Dolphin, Luca Hotel, Galleria, Milan, Italy. *Unknown. Unable to trace,*' Gabriel read, Mrs. Mortimer read. Mrs. Mortimer rose to her feet and gave a pull on her husband's sleeve.

'Both my husband and I have thought this over very carefully and we think it is for the boy to decide.'

She moved away, Mr. Mortimer behind her. She

stood for a moment looking down at the bent figure –
'You will be served with tea. Thank you for calling.
Thomas will run you to the station.'

Together they moved towards the door.

'He's my son's child that's what,' Mrs. Dolphin
came to life, 'how could you care for him what
doesn't understand what wouldn't have my son near
your house count of his being my son born in Deptford
which is better than here by a long chalk. I come down
for him and I'm going to have him,' she was out of the
chair, hobbling down to the boy.

'Come,' Mrs. Mortimer said, but Gabriel hung back.

He said, 'My daughter is coming home. She is his
mother.' He went out, Mrs. Mortimer followed, the
door closed, noiselessly, Agatha thought quickly –
'he stays.'

She called down the room, 'Robert! Come here,
dear.'

Robert did not answer. He did not move.

'Bobby, come when the lady calls,' Mrs. Dolphin
said, she was crying again. Agatha went to him, she
removed the blanket, she walked him slowly to his
grandmother. She said, 'Stand there.' Robert stood.
He suddenly looked towards the door. He wanted it to
open, he wanted very much for somebody to come. If
even Thomas would come. But Thomas, too, had
gone. He looked at Mrs. Dolphin. He thought of the
lights in the sky, the tunnels, the rides in the lorry,
the fish and chips, the pictures.

'Now, dear,' said Agatha, 'your grandmother has
come a long way to see you. We're sorry she had to
come when you were ill. Now look at me,' she said,
and the boy looked at her, at her hands, at his grandmother's hands. How different they were.

'I'm looking at you,' he said, gravely, refusing to

smile, afraid that the little woman in the chair might fiercely embrace him again.

'They've left everything to me,' thought Agatha. 'I shall not forget this. I shall never forget it.'

'Do you wish to go with your grandmother, or do you wish to stay with me, dear. Now think, darling,' Agatha said, 'just think.'

For a moment he stood there, perplexed, he looked from one to the other.

'You're not my real mother,' he said to Agatha, 'you're only a fairy-tale one.'

'Your mother is coming home. Didn't you hear your grandfather say so? She is coming home.'

'You mean that lady,' Robert said.

'Your mother,' Agatha said, her head suddenly lowered to avoid the terrible glance from Mrs. Dolphin.

'Bobby,' she said.

'What?' Robert said.

'Come home with me, ducks, you'll be happy with me. Aren't you your dad's brave boy? I've made your little bed, remember the little bed, Bobby, we used to have supper in bed together, d'you remember. And a lovely big fire,' she paused, she looked at the tall woman sitting opposite her, 'Come to granny,' she said, the words choking her. Knowing he would not, she thought of the miles back, the hardened road, the swaying trees, her son in his Deptford grave, her aching feet – she would have loved a cup of tea.

'Come, dear, we are waiting.'

Robert walked over to Agatha, he stood close to her, he pressed his hands in her lap, he did not speak. But he remembered that fierce embrace, the camphorated oil came back, he said loudly, 'Daddy's dead isn't he? Really dead.'

Mrs. Dolphin broke down. Robert said, demandingly, 'Isn't he dead? Isn't he taken to where they don't know?'

'Say, dear,' begged Agatha, 'please say, darling.'

'I like you best,' Robert said, and suddenly flung his arms round her neck. She surprised Robert, she surprised even herself, by crying quietly into the black hair that bunched itself against her face. Then she looked across at the desperate, worn, little woman.

'You could always come and see him,' she said.

The words broke free at last, they came, halting, broken, 'I don't want nothing.' Mrs. Dolphin got up. She shook her coat straight again. She looked at Robert.

'They've hurt you so hard that you've hurt *me* like you'll never understand.' She got up. Agatha got up. Thomas suddenly came in.

'Thomas, this lady's cup of tea.'

'I don't want nothing.'

'Thomas will run you to the station.'

'I said I don't want nothing didn't I say I don't want nothing,' her voice rose to a screech, she bumped against Agatha, 'you've hurt me proper, deep in me you've hurt what understands nothing and never will.'

'Goodbye, granny.'

But there was only the banging door, the astonished look on Thomas's face, the sound of heavy boots on the gravel path, the sudden fierce hold on Robert's arm. 'I haven't finished my breakfast,' Robert said.